Erekos

A.M. Tuomala

Candlemark & Gleam

First trade paperback edition published 2011.

For information, address
Candlemark & Gleam LLC,
104 Morgan Street, Bennington, VT 05201
info@candlemarkandgleam.com

Library of Congress Cataloging-in-Publication Data
In Progress

ISBN: 978-1-936460-03-8

Cover art and design by Rhiannon Wright

Map design by A.M. Tuomala

Book design and composition by Kate Sullivan
Typeface: Calisto MT

Editors: Kate Sullivan and Vivien Weaver

www.candlemarkandgleam.com

For Aleks, who never lost faith.

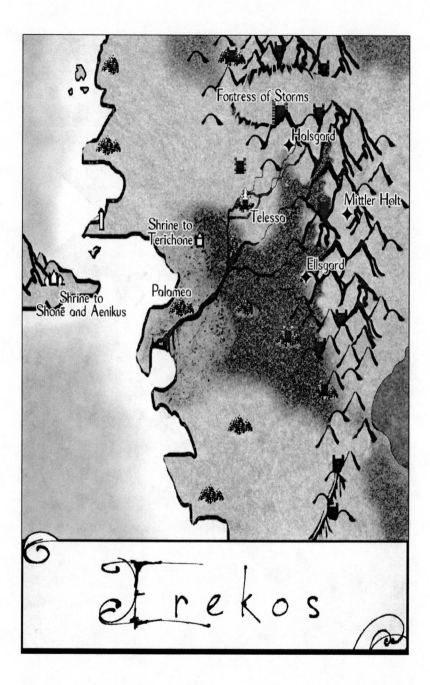

Fortress of Storms

Halsgard

Mittler Holt

Telessa

Shrine to
Terichone

Ellsgard

Shrine to
Shoné and Aenikus

Palamea

Erekos

The long match fit easily through the open slats of the little bronze incense-burner's roof. She whispered a soft prayer to Shonè and Aenikus of the fire and the hearthstone as a thread of fire snaked up the matchstick. The incense caught in the center of the bronze house, and thick, grey smoke began to rise through the rafters until she blew the flame to smoldering.

The winding incense smoke began to fill the cottage. Achane took a deep breath; the spiced smoke almost drowned out the smell of rotten flesh.

Rain stroked the steepled roof of her lodging and, meeting with no rebuff, began to caress it in earnest. The water barrels would be filling at the corners of the roof, but the floats would rescue the house if the rain became a flood. The candles glowed in the darkness of Achane's cottage, while the rain soaked the blinds and dripped to the floor.

"Shonè, give me the strength of the wood," she whispered, dipping her pen into a bottle of ink near her knee.

Sibar.

Heira.

Aekos.

Achane wrote the letters clearly on the papyrus as the incense smoke described the corners of the cottage. It sank into the floats and rose into the rafters to get acquainted with the herbs that hung there; it shied away from the body lying on Achane's floor.

"Aenikus, give me the force of the blacksmith." The pen bent under the pressure of Achane's fingers; the light from three candles shone on the still-wet ink and on the witch's half-shut eyes alike.

Bauke.

Aekos.

Niaa.

"Terìchone, touch my soul with your light—" *the shadows moved in slow circles around Achane, cross-legged on the floor* "—illuminate my soul and make me as buoyant as the wood of your tree—" *no breeze escaped the blinds, and still the herbs moved in the incense smoke* "—and grant me the request that I make of you."

The candles went out.

Erekos.

"Shabane."

Achane closed her eyes in the tarry blackness of her cottage. She barely dared to breathe; long practice had taught her to expect nothing of the gods although she wrote the right letters and spoke the right words. She heard only her own breathing in the room, as well as the slow rustle of the herbs overhead as they swayed in the not-breeze.

There was no reason to suppose that the gods would raise Shabane from death into life when they had refused for so many years to raise her from sickness into health, and yet Achane still listened for her sister's breath on the air. She hardly dared to draw in air herself lest she obscure the sound of Shabane waking; she sat as quietly as she had for five nights before this, waiting for a miracle that had not come.

In the stillness, the floorboards whined at trespass as footsteps tapped it. Red light flared against Achane's eyelids with such suddenness that she opened them without thinking—with hope like the hope that always burns red where death has been.

The corpse's face stared across the candle at her. Shabane's match slowly burned down to her fingers and scorched the flesh to cooked meat, and Shabane did not cry out.

Both sisters, living and dead, stared at the blackened flesh for a long, quiet moment as the wind laughed and beat the roof overhead.

The first night of the rainy season had bruised the flowers. Water and ice had pounded off the last red florets from the snakeblossom vines; they had torn away the remnants of pale, yellow flowers from the alligator palms and shaken their fronds.

The alligator palms had bent in the wind and borne the beating with grace, and they stood now over the other trees to survey the carnage of ripped-up roots and tossed-down vines, the red snakeblossom splashes of blood. The birds flew high; they could not find their homes in the familiar alleyways, and so they circled endlessly without perching. Those forest creatures who had not been uprooted peered warily from their nests with the half-glazed look of survivors.

Soon, though, the alligator palms would drop rough-skinned little dates to the ground below them and feed the hungry. They would collect clean rainwater in their rough bark, where birds could drink freely.

At the end of the rainy season, young backwoods couples just married under the rough auspices of the tempest-god Loukaros would wade out into the swamp to seek out three alligator palms to shape into floats. They would fit the trunks into gaps in the foundations of their marriage houses, where the buoyant wood would turn a low house into a hasty raft in flood season.

Such was the infinite wisdom of Terichone, goddess of the alligator palm, that she provided for all of her children. The hungry, she fed; the thirsty, she gave water; the unmoored, she gave hope of survival. As the sons and daughters of man's race farmed her forests and drained the marshes, and as floods crawled across the newly dry land, Terichone learned new ways to care for her children.

The gods learned.

Man often did not.

Terichone could have followed a red snakeblossom path through the forest, tracing the line of the fallen vine from tree to tree until she reached Achane's cottage. The goddess could have surveyed the damage to the thatch of alligator palm fronds overlying reeds, her hands on her hips, and clucked her tongue at the rust already spotting the pans that hung from the porch roof—payment for a few careless nights of leaving them hanging in the rain.

It was not like her child Achane to forget to bring her pots in after the day's cooking on the hearthstone.

It was not like Achane to leave the hearthstone out of doors when the signs of the land had told her for a week that last night would begin the rainy season.

Shabane's death had hit her harder than sisters' deaths hit most women, who knew that they would lose their sisters one day to marriage or accident or illness and fretted more for their own families. Shabane, though, had always been ill, and her sickness hadn't drawn the girls apart; Achane had always waited by her side with broth or fortifying bean mash or some new remedy that her research had unearthed.

Achane had never married, nor had a family, and the river people knew it as well as did Terichone. The woman had instead become a swamp witch, as did so many unmarried women who wished to live in their own way; she had scorned the black shawl that marked a healer, but not a healer's devotion to curing the ailing and the impoverished, and she had dedicated her days to nursing her sister to a health that her birth had not afforded her.

Of course, Shabane had died in time. All women died, and not even Achane of the tireless love could save her—except that she had.

She had brought her sister's soul back to inhabit the ravaged mortal body, where veins trailed dark tracks across her skin and rot had set into her legs and her delicate mouth and the place between her legs, just as the rot was even now claiming the trees fallen in the storm.

Man, Terìchone knew very well, did not learn.

$$\Longrightarrow \Longleftarrow$$

The sisters used to braid each other's hair when they were young. Shabane would sit on the edge of their shared bed with her older sister leaning back against the pallet, and she would braid Achane's dark, shining hair into countless plaits that threw back the firelight like wet wood. Then Shabane would lift her slender fingers from her older sister's head, smiling a small smile that Achane was too busy standing up to see, and bend her head low so that Achane could make rule-straight rows and looping whorls of braids across Shabane's scalp. They needed no words to communicate their sympathy, and only when they had run out of the cottage to gaze at their reflections in the water barrel did they see how perfectly each had worked.

Shabane's hair had dried like grain husks upon her death, and it reflected poorly from the puddles that broke at her body's every stumbling footstep. Her body followed her sister through the woods with the muteness of one whose tongue had rotted away.

Achane had said nothing to her sister's corpse when it stared at her sightlessly with its burned fingers curled at its decaying breasts. She had only taken a swath of linen from the basket and bound the fingers with slick ointment, just as though her sister's body was still alive and could either feel pain or heal. Through eyes that had rotted out, Shabane's soul had gazed on her sister's cottage and only wished that she could cry.

Achane had insisted on sleeping on the floor and granting Shabane's body the bed, which had only stiffened the swamp witch's back and filled Shabane with guilt as she mimed sleep and stared, ever-waking, at the rafters.

Alive, Shabane had learned by morning, did not mean moving, nor eating, nor nodding at her sister's conversation over the morning tea. Drinking it would only bloat the animated cadaver that Shabane's living soul inhabited.

"If they have hearts in their chests, they *can't* shut us out," said Achane, as she fished the sweetcane gum out of the teapot and put it at the side of her plate. "The priestesses will know how to bring you back to yourself—they *will*, Shabane This isn't the end for us." She caught Shabane's hand in her own and talked on and on about the journey that they would make into the forest, about the goodness of the priestesses of Terichone, about her endless love for her sister, and most of all about how glad she was to have Shabane alive again, even in this state.

Alive did not mean anything at all to do with Shabane's rotting body—not even love.

Now, as Shabane's body staggered into thick-trunked dendrove trees and caught its clumsy feet on the uneven places in the ground, Shabane cast forward with her mind to where Achane walked surely, gracefully as a puma on the driest patches. Her long skirt rode over her knees, tied and pinned in place for freedom of movement, and she carried a burden on one hip, a gift for Terichone's priestesses. When Shabane had been *alive*, she had often watched Achane begin on this pathway into the forest, but her living feet had never trodden the path.

Her dead feet did not know the way.

The snakeblossom vines brushed her unfeeling shoulders like gauze; they hung low after last night's storm. Red, trumpeting florets gaped at her as though she walked naked, although Achane had tied a long-sleeved wrap around her to cover the bare places. She knew that Achane had seen the maggots that sometimes showed themselves in her flesh.

Terichone of the alligator palm was merciful; she had given Shabane this not-life without twisting the knife of the jest by giving her feeling.

The corpse viewed the world through eyes that were not eyes. The soul perceived the world around it with the same senses as the body had once possessed, it was true; impressions sorted themselves into taste and scent, sight and sound, for the soul knew only those forms for understanding the living world. She did not know any longer what her body could or could not do until she tried and failed.

Achane bent under the thick vines as Shabane's body could not; the corpse brushed them out of her way and did not know whether it had been an easy feat or an impossible one.

A stone marker rose from the loose, soft soil, breaching the flesh of the earth. It stood a full handspan taller than Achane, a massive finger of rock carved with a ribbed relief of the Flood Story. At this grey marker, Achane leaned her head against a tree as though nothing else could hold her up. Her hair was falling out of its plaits, but Shabane's fingers were no longer clever enough to braid them right again.

For a long moment that echoed with the cries of homeless birds and uprooted trees, Shabane's body stood still in the mud and watched her sister stroke the smooth, shining bark of the dendrove.

"We should keep moving." Achane lifted her head, and her cheeks were more drawn, her forehead more lined than it had been that morning. "The priestesses will help us."

Shabane's body staggered onward, past the stone and past the dendrove, past a bird's nest long empty of eggs, and ever further from home on the ragged path.

After some time—which seemed no more than the procession of trees encountered and roots stumbled upon, birds screaming and flies impregnating her neck—Achane's shadow fell across the marble threshold of the goddess Terìchone's cottage.

The roof was thatched with alligator-palm fronds, and inside, the incense smoke that Shabane could sense but not smell told her that a bronze house was burning.

$$\ggg\lll$$

The priestesses of Terìchone are seldom slender waifs who grow into tall and ethereal women; they have never worn robes of purest white silk. They know that the most powerful mystic pools come after the rains that rip the world apart, and they lie deep in the forest—not ensconced in marble, where the waters cannot touch the land.

No, a priestess of Terìchone is a firm, comfortable sort of woman with serviceably ruddy arms over which she has always pulled up her sleeves. This sort has reaped the rewards of her hard work in the gardens or with the hogs or out on the boats, and she is often heavy in the solid, maternal way of good cooks. Terìchone's women know a little magic and a lot of good sense, and they often wear the healer's shawl to advertise to the people that, if they cannot work the magic to set bones or heal burns or reattach severed hands, they certainly know someone who does. The priestesses of Terìchone do not flinch at work, or vomit, or death, because they cannot imagine their goddess flinching. They know that their goddess was conceived in the grim determination of two gods to heal a flooded and war-torn world, and that she did not shirk her duty even though she had not chosen it for herself.

They are not the kind of priestesses who chant a water-clock of mystic phrases in long-lost languages for the worship of their goddess. Terìchone prefers work-songs rising from the rice paddy and the spinning wheel.

At dawn, the priestesses of the shrine had burned a censer of incense to the goddess and begun taking stock of the fallen trees that surrounded their cottage with its marble threshold. On another day, they would have been hoeing or weeding or building a new outbuilding to house the sick; today, they diagnosed the ills of the earth and rigged ropes to the tall trees that lay sideways across the land with their roots reaching out to reclaim the earth.

"It may be we can right 'n again, an' may be it c'n grow," the high priestess muttered. She stood with her boots in the mud and her hands on her hips and stared along the length of a fallen daughter of the grove. The branches hadn't been much crushed in the fall, and dirt still clung in heavy clods to the twisted roots. "Hie up, Lytha! Knot 'n up at the next fork!"

Only three priestesses lived at the shrine regularly—
three priestesses, five mules, eighteen goats, numberless
plants, and a floating assortment of women whose men had
done them wrong or young girls who thought that they had
met the goddess of the alligator palm.

And the goddess Terìchone herself, of course.

When Achane and Shabane finally reached the marble
threshold that was the clergy's sole concession to grandeur, they
followed the sound of shaking leaves and groaning wood to
where the mules and the priestesses strained at their ropes like
ships trying to run to the open seas.

When the daughter of the grove stood tall and proud
again at last, the high priestess dropped her own rope and
wiped her dirty brow with her even dirtier hand. "Still must
pack 'n dirt around her," she said to herself, but the other
priestesses were as quick as she was, and soon all three were
patting the roots back down under the all-embracing soil.

Achane found it strangely fitting that she and her sister
had come across the priestesses of Terìchone as they worked to
restore life where it had been cruelly tossed to the ground. She
knelt beside the youngest priestess and lent her hands to the
earth, and there she carefully flattened the ravished dirt.

Shabane was watching her, she knew.

The women stood up as one when the daughter of the
grove had been re-interred, knocking their hands together to
brush off the thin pottery casing of dirt.

Perhaps the high priestess had just caught sight of
Shabane; perhaps she had seen Shabane from the very beginning, and only chose to react now. She stared directly into Shabane's unseeing, hollow eyes, straight through Achane's lined

forehead, and she whispered, "You've raised 'n zombi, child."

The cottage shrine was larger than most of the swamp-cottages in these parts; it held a wooden statue of Terichone with a necklace of alligator palm dates around her firm, thick throat, and the priestesses' shared bed took up a square quarter of the floor. A potbellied stove hunched in one corner of the room, with a kettle atop it; censers kept company with long ropes of roots and herbs that hung from the rafters and brushed the floor. The cottage-shaped censer sacred to Terichone burned at the goddess's unshod feet.

Achane and the high priestess seated themselves before the window, their arms folded on the little table so that they would not be caught reaching to refill their cups of tea to avoid speaking. They met one another's eyes so that they would not have to meet Shabane's body's rotten eyes.

The high priestess broke the silence with her teacup. It struck the weathered wood of the table with a solid, hard thump. "That'n will be trouble to you, Achane. She en't your sister any more than the leaf mould, ner any less; you should have let 'n lie."

"She is *alive!*" Achane snapped, even though all three knew the rot that fragmented Shabane's body. "I brought her back, and she slept in my bed and she followed me here. Shabane's—" Achane closed her eyes briefly so that she could lie more easily to herself. "My sister is alive."

The high priestess smiled the hard flood-survivor's smile; it was a smile that knew that teeth were only bones for chewing up the world. "She moves, I give 'n you, but her eyes see not you ner me ner the goddess in the room. She dun't sleep, I wager, and shan't. This 'n is not alive, but only a body you tied 'n's soul to."

Shabane shifted uneasily, and Achane ignored that the motion had appeared to be a rigor mortis nod. "Priestess," she asked under her breath, from the low, meat-smelling part of her soul that had spent all her life fearing death. "High Priestess, I want to help my sister. I love her so much—"

"If you love 'n, you will let 'n die and get on with your own living," said the high priestess flatly. When Achane raised her chin as though to protest, the priestess raised a hand to still her. "Terichone feeds the hungry," she admitted. Her thick fingers sketched a prayer-shape on the table, collecting spilled tea into traces like writing. "But the goddess knows when the vine has died, and she leaves 'n to feed the land. There en't a thing she can do for a dead 'n but lift it up and dance it around."

Achane clenched her teeth against the curses that she so dearly longed to screech at fate—clenched her teeth until she felt them straining at her gums and her cheeks turned hard and tight. She didn't feel the tic that dragged at the corner of her eyelid. "I want to help her," she whispered.

She had never asked herself whether Shabane wanted to be helped; to ask it now, she knew, might undo her. She had drawn the circles in blood on her papyrus scrolls over the past long days, and she had written Shabane's name in ink made from the bark of the daughters of the grove, and she had burned incense into the long hours of the night until her eyes had swum over the columns of letters. What couldn't heal a

sister could raise her from the dead; what couldn't bring Shabane to life could raise the hope of life in Achane.

The high priestess read all this in the steady throb of
Achane's eyelid.

"Unmake your charms, burn your scrolls, and lay 'n
zombi to rest. Then, you may help your sister," said the high
priestess. "Some things, you can't lay right but by laying 'n
down."

Achane nodded softly as though she understood. The
breeze lifted the hair that had fallen out of her plaits; it tickled
the hanging herbs and waved through the dry hair on Shabane's body's head. It danced the incense smoke around in
lazy curves, as though encircling a woman's body.

Achane drained her cup and stood, tying her skirt up
for the long walk home already, although she had not said goodbye. "Thank you, high priestess. I've brought you and your sisters some food; I hope it will help you to serve Terìchone's will,
and to put the broken world to rights." She lifted her burden
from her hip and passed the satchel into the heavier woman's
hands, kissing the fabric so that she would seem courteous even
though she was roiling like a river in flood.

The high priestess smiled in return, that bone-teeth
smile that reminded Achane of her sister's face across the
candle flame. "Remember what I said."

"I will." Achane had already forgotten.

$$\Rightarrow\Leftarrow$$

The door swung shut behind the sisters departing, its
wood scraping over the marble threshold and resting smooth-

ly against the frame. As she went to help her fellow-priestess-es right the world, the high priestess gave Achane a look of heartfelt sympathy to carry home; she could offer no more. Shabane fell to the ground almost as soon as her bare feet had left the threshold and had to be helped upright again.

From the shade of the righted daughter of the grove, four strangers watched the proceedings with naked interest. They occupied a ramshackle mail carriage, with a young man in the livery of a page-adjutant riding postillion; the driver wore the dress of the swamp-born. Inside the post-chaise sat a man and a woman, the both of them dressed far too finely to be postmasters. The woman was slim and very light-skinned, nearly as light as the almond-eyed, thin-lipped sailors from the motherland; the man who rode at her side could only be her husband, for he was brown as new sugar and bore not the faintest familial resemblance.

The adjutant shuffled his feet as though his boots were uncomfortable—which they were; his eyes shifted back and forth across the dead girl who carefully balanced on feet that she could not feel, as though the sight was uncomfortable—which it was. The driver, in contrast, had seen zombi half a dozen times before. Seldom were the dead so decayed before they rose, and seldom did they walk longer than a day; swamp wizards found it easier to cope with their grief than to live with a zombi's unseeing eyes on them, and swamp witches felt the life that slowly left their own bodies as their magic supported the bodies of the dead. More often than not, witches and wizards chose wisely, and let the dead return to their final rest to save their own lives.

There were already lines across the young witch's

forehead that he suspected had not been there before.

The man in the post-chaise wore a crown; if not on his brow, then in his bearing and in his dark eyes, in which every man became an object. He whispered to his wife with his gaze on the women at the door. "The gods have sent us a boon," he said under his breath, and she nodded her assent.

"Come on, sister," said the witch, putting her slender arm around the corpse as though she did not feel how cold the flesh was. "Let's go home."

The king looked from the shrine, with its wooden frame and rain barrels and floats like any other cottage, to the stumbling corpse with its crusted-blood eyes gaping.

"Hold, witch," said the king, and he swung himself down from the chaise. "I would speak with you."

"So would the wind," the swamp witch answered, drawing closer to the corpse in distaste. She bore such a look of loathing that he would remember it on dark nights for many days to come. "Leave me be—I'm going home."

"Stay as your king commands." The wind shifted, and the horses stamped behind him as the speaking wind whispered to them of the dead.

She shook her head and turned away, leading the corpse by the hand. "You aren't any king of mine, if you stand between a woman and her home."

For a moment like the moment between the stab through the gut and the realization of the wound, the king stood still. His hand clenched at the fabric over the scar in his side, as it always did when he was upset; he had picked at the stitches in the infirmary until the healers had given him a medicine to dull the ache.

He should have died of a gut wound on the battlefields of the north, but Aenikus of the hearthstone had
seen fit to heal him. Shonè had walked thrice around him
in his sleep and blessed his pallet, and he had lived where
many men might have died—he had lived, a few splinters
of shattered iron embedded in his gut for reminders, and
many men had not.

The gods knew that King Milaus had never brooked
defeat, nor suffered himself to be humiliated.

"You and Ilaumeleus, put her on my horse. Bind
her if you must." His words were quiet but absolute, and
they carried.

The adjutant dismounted and the swamp-born man
slithered down from the box, shedding worries of uncomfortable boots and memories of zombi as they went, and took the
swamp witch by the arms.

Milaus watched the capture through a fog over his
vision like the haze of heat rising over the swamp, and so
the witch's struggles appeared as insignificant as the hum of
a blood-fly as it vanished into the night. Ilaumeleus gripped
her dark skin with his olive fingers as the swamp man held
her like a babe in his rough hands, and although she kicked
and flailed and threw her arms around in theirs, they bore
her back and tied her tightly with the leather thongs that had
bound the empty mailbags.

The corpse stared on in what seemed a parody of
horror, but as it ran a staggering sprint toward the carriage,
the uneven ground rose up to meet it and the woman's body
fell facedown in a shallow pool of mud.

The adjutant and the swamp man maneuvered the

witch to sit in the post-chaise while the king himself sat beside her; the queen looked on unseeing, and the party moved on into the forest bestrewn with mist. The high priestess, busy among the fallen trees and flooded gardens, did not know what had befallen Achane in the clearing around the shrine of Terichone, goddess of the alligator palm.

*S*habane's body lay in the still water, pounding at the earth in despair as the marsh bugs came to investigate this thrashing hatching ground. A maggot slipped into the muck, where it wriggled as ineffectually as Shabane's body did.

She couldn't speak to cry for help; her tongue was rotting, and her mouth submerged. She couldn't even lever her unbending body from the ground, and in time, she ceased to struggle.

A crane step-step-stepped past her in its quest for food, pecked at her back, and decided that she was not so tasty as a marble frog or a rat. It croaked in its throat and fluttered its wings, then rose into graceful flight.

Shabane heard the wind dance flirtatiously with the torn trees, who must have shaken their curving limbs at the advance even though they knew that the wind was a troublesome lover. How many times do we love those who hurt us and do not know or care!

The earth became a friend to Shabane in the long hours that her body lay embracing it. Its insects caressed her ears and her fingertips, which comforted her although she could not feel them.

The earth, Shabane knew, loved her all the way through—body and soul. The earth didn't care that she had been diseased in life and broken in death. It wanted to hold her close, as a mother should want to hold her daughter; it wanted to hold her as Shabane's mother had never wanted to hold her for fear of catching her sickness, and she would have wept for the joy of the earth's embrace if she'd had eyes for weeping.

She felt the hoofbeats of the priestesses' mules through the thick mud as it communicated its grasping love of them to her soul.

It must have been seven or eight hours that she had lain dreaming of weeping, because when at last strong, thick hands turned her body over, the sky was dark with clouds outlined by moonlight.

"She's left you, poor 'n that you are. But 'tis better that she do," a priestess murmured. "Soon she'll forget you, as she's right to do, and live proper. Hie, Gamela; let's lay 'n out for to burn. En't family enough to bury—"

Shabane tried to push her body upright, and the priestess backed away in fright.

"Gamela, come help me get 'n up! Achane's left 'n here, still moving!"

Two pairs of hands descended from the sky to grasp Shabane and pull her out of the earth's tender arms, and soon the body stood upright to gaze in grief at the world that only the soul could see. The swamp was dark and dancing with wind, and the priestesses stood in their practical work clothes with their sleeves rolled up and their faces folded in concern.

She tried to thank them, but her mouth only moved slightly and soundlessly.

The priestess Gamela studied her for a long while with shrewd eyes, then said, "The high priestess knows lip-speech. She'll understand what the zombi is saying." The other priestess nodded, then beckoned to Shabane.

"Come, child. The high priestess will see 'n meaning where we can't."

Braced between Terìchone's servants, Shabane stumbled up and over the marble threshold again.

The high priestess sat at the table by the window, sewing a quilt together out of scraps of shirts and sack-cloth by lantern-light. She must have passed Shabane's body in the darkness, and not seen it or let it be—the corpse hadn't family enough for burial, and perhaps the priestess had chosen to let her feed the birds and rats and flies instead. Terìchone's priestess seemed somehow older now, without the daylight to highlight her strength and intimidating eyes; she peered at the needle's path as though she were trying to divine a future course in the stitches.

"She has something to say to us, Priestess," said Gamela quietly, "but she can't speak."

The high priestess looked up from her needlework. Her gaze was as intent as Achane's upon a scroll of charms; she read Shabane with the same slow deliberation.

"Speak—slowly, so that I can read 'n lips."

Shabane opened her mouth, her empty eyes fixed on

the high priestess's.

Help me.

Please, help me. I am dead, and Achane won't believe that I'm gone; she has been stolen from me by the king and his men, and I fear he'll hurt her because she raised me.

I wish she hadn't raised me. She's only brought grief on us both.

Help me.

The priestesses took their seats around the table with the high priestess, and the lantern threw shadows of herbs and censers across the room. In the silence, it seemed even the statue of Terìchone leaned forward to watch the high priestess as she passed judgment.

She smiled then, compassion drawing grooves at the corners of her mouth, and she did not look like Achane any longer. "We'll help you. Terìchone loves all creatures, especially those 'n who have been separated from the earth." She turned toward Gamela, who nodded already in anticipation of the order.

"Take you one of our mules; give 'n medicine so that 'n can't tell he carries one of the dead on his back. Follow the king with her," she gestured to Shabane's body, "and bring Achane back."

Gamela nodded once more, and her eyes were haunted with shadows. "I will, High Priestess."

The swamp was not the same from the inside of a carriage.

Achane sat calmly in the post-chaise, aware already that she would run less easily than the local and the boy, and therefore biding her time. She had tried to appeal to the king's better nature; she had tried to bite and kick; she had thrown herself from the chaise so many times that she felt bruises across both of her shoulders and along her sides.

He had listened like stone, and held her still with one hand as the other held the chaise door, and lifted her over and over again from the ground to place her back on the bench. After an hour of this, even the horses had ceased to regard her antics with any wonder.

Now, Achane merely watched the wooded swamplands to which she was accustomed slip away, and awaited her chance to do the same.

The snakeblossom vines vanished first. Their long, thin trails of red blossoms gave out when the deciduous trees thinned; without their gaudy necklaces, the dendrove trees assumed an ethereal stance in the mist—less like the long-armed dancers she knew, and more like the priests of Loukaros of the storms. The daughters of the grove departed next, waving their goodbyes at the dendroves and the alligator palms as they waded in the warm, golden grasses.

Achane watched the way the soft earth of the postroad sucked at the horses' hooves and felt how it mired the chaise's wheels. When a wheel became caught in a rut, the adjutant climbed down from the horse, stepping from tussock to tussock as though anxious at the prospect of dirtying his boots. In Achane's narrowed, black eyes, this mincing walk seemed especially cruel—she would have stepped down to the wet earth and danced in it if she'd been allowed; she would have traced a circle with her feet and drawn the letters for shelter with her toes to make a safe place in the ring where the king could not touch her. She would have rested there, cross-legged in the heart of her circle, until even the king could sit outside no longer.

They did not let her step down from the chaise, and they did not let her sketch a spell in the earth, and the boy walked awkwardly across the sodden grass and mounted again as soon as he was able.

The queen looked over the soft swamp world without the expression of disgust that her adjutant bore and that her husband tried to hide. She was a cold creature who wore her reserve like a mask of marble, but Achane had heard that she had once been able to joke with fishmongers and sail a skiff and make the rice farmers look up as she rode through the paddies, her horse's hooves throwing up spray like drops of glass. She had heard these stories from the fishmongers and river-men and rice farmers themselves after she had healed their kin, and yet now their tales seemed somehow too bright to be true—the sorts of legends put about by serfs and tenant-farmers when their landlords were unbearable. Achane suspected, as she looked on the silent woman's face, that such stories were easier to tell than stories of an icy woman with neither interest in the world nor the faculty to express it.

The queen, Achane had learned, did not speak. Her eyes remained fixed on the far-ahead, just as the king's mind rested solely on the moment in which he lived (and perhaps the past behind it). The queen wore a murky moss-agate jewel on her brow, and she dressed all in green and grey so that she almost vanished into the mist and the marshes.

Achane suspected that the queen did not speak because no speech was required—her will was writ large in her
cold eyes.

Soon, the party came to a road of sorts; here, the
earth had been raised over a long line of wooden planks that
stretched to the seashore. Over time, the floods had washed
away some of the planks and laid others bare; the water had
rotted some and rarefied others to a starkness of grain. It was
a dim road; it was the road that the dead walked to get to the
other side.

"We'll stop at the way-station of Aenikus and
Shonè," the local man called over his shoulder. He touched
his beard as though it were new to him. "The priests built it
only months ago, and it's quite fine for the weary pilgrim.
And they'll want the mail, anyway."

"This damned road needed a way-station," muttered
the king, but he said no more, and Achane tucked the words
away in her mind.

From listening to the adjutant gossiping with the
swamp-man, she had learned that the king's brief devotions
at Terìchone's shrine were only one of many stops at many
shrines in his long pilgrimage to the temple of Aenikus and
Shonè. Although she'd never made a pilgrimage herself,
Achane had heard that the god and goddess of fire and stone
made their home across the waters, on the island whose tip
touched the horizon when one stood on the delta and looked
out to the west; she had heard that the temple had been rebuilt
a dozen times after flowing fire and stone had destroyed it.

Perhaps Aenikus and Shonè did not want their children so close to their hearth. Perhaps they resented the grown-

up children who insisted on returning to the hearth gods' house, begging for sweets and pets and victories. Perhaps they only wished to keep their eyes on the country across the sea, from which so much grief and joy had come.

"I only pray that they'll listen to my requests, and bless our cause," said the king, to the swamp man or to himself. "Terìchone has answered; Loukaros would answer—but the cost of his blessing makes me wary of asking."

The queen looked up as the post-chaise rattled its way across the gapped planks; her moss-agate was the same grey-brown as her eyes. Her eyes said what she did not need to say: *You will bend your knee to the god of the hurricane one day, and I will be there to watch the storm sweep over us.*

In the queen's too-old eyes, Achane suddenly understood what she had known only dimly and distantly before—they were at war.

here is a world beyond the swamp. Far away from where Achane lies uneasily in a roadside way-station in the marshes, waiting for her guards to sleep so that she can escape, far away from the hasty campfire of the zombi and the priestess, the people of the mountains peer up at the clouds and try to divine the future.

The mountain people have always known the way that a heel feels when it grinds against their backs and drives them into the ground. In a land far beyond even the mountains, they had grumbled at the government's taxes and the government's conscription and sometimes just at the food, and in small groups, they had set out across the plains for a Promised Land that no one had promised to them.

When the escapees of Weigenland had come at last to the bare feet of the mountains, legend said that they had almost turned around and gone back to the taxes and the conscription and the food...and then someone had seen green in the mountains.

This person, whose face had been forgotten and whose name was not remembered, had seen the tip of a tree on the Erekoi side, its bright leaves peering over the mountains to greet the refugees.

On the far side, where the winds drove the rain against the mountains, the trees grew thick and hungry around the shoulders of the peaks, and the Weigers had known that this green land would be their home. They crossed into the mountains, neither returning to the plains nor descending to valleys of the west, and built their homes in caverns and in cottages where the wind raked their skin raw and brought them the scent of wild goats and sheep. The goatherders had smiled at the scent, and followed the rank odor to the place where the creatures grazed.

In time, the goats and the sheep and the people of the mountains had grown together, and although man had his meat when a goat passed out of its prime, or his wool when the coats of the sheep grew thick, the herds in turn learned the comfort of barns and the safety of shelters.

In time, as the war wore on to the north and the mines exposed the bones of the mountains, the king of the western lands had seen the smoke drifting over the mountains from the cookfires of the borderlanders. Just as the green wisp had drawn the Weigers over, the grey wisp drew the soldiers of Erekos, land of the swamp and the forest, to take the enemy-held border.

Erlen had thought to avoid the war between Erekos and Weigenland when he had crossed the plains three months ago, with his empty books in his satchel and his pack full of drawing supplies, his one reference text and a pen reinforced with a metal core and nib. He had come to complete his Great Work for the university, a fat tome on the ways and habits of the borderlanders, and to learn and explain how their magics differed from the magic of Weigenland—for a human quickly learns the ways of the land on which he or she dwells, and magic is one of those ways. He hadn't known then that the borderlands were engaged in a war of their own.

He had taken the university scholarship in his younger days because he wanted the safety from conscription that it had afforded, but every book had shouted of military victory or defeat and every professor had an opinion on the war with the Erekoi. The natural philosophers had abandoned pressing questions on the nature of the air or the substance of fire, and instead they sought the secrets of Erekoi cannons and steam engines.

Even Erlen's scholarship itself had its military purpose; pacifist professors who wrung their hands at the war and the loss of intelligent young men from the semi-educated class eventually got around to wringing their pockets to rescue a few impoverished students from the army's clutches. When Erlen found himself drawn into the borderland raids on hastily erected Erekoi fortresses in the mountains, it had hardly seemed unusual; every subject of study for the most promising upper-level students seemed geared toward ongoing war, and so even a cultural study such as his became everything but a strategic textbook.

His instructors had not said that the Weigers wanted to learn borderlander magic and customs so that they could reclaim the mountains where their escaped citizens dwelt;

Erlen had not asked.

Now, though, as he lay quiet on a goatskin blanket and stared into a fire of fragrant evergreen boughs, he was older. He had fought the Erekoi in their strongholds and in the forests, and he had worked the magic of the borderlands.

He knew the taste of the raw wind and the springs that fed the great rivers, and he knew the taste of his own blood.

He knew, as no university student in Weigenland did, the taste of fear.

As he rested in the central hall of a border holt, sharing his blanket with a borderlander man and waited for the night to claim his eyes, though, Erlen knew that he would sleep more soundly tonight than he ever had in his dormitory bed. The fire still crackled in the center of the floor, rising in a sudden wave when a log shifted, and it filled him with a languid warmth to lie near it.

He glanced over to where the fire illuminated the pages on pages of writing that he had scrawled carefully in the pale, creamy leaves of his tome: *A History of the Borderlands-Erekoi War.*

By Erlen Eppeim and Jeiger Staag.

The scholar-soldier-mage closed his eyes against the world and the laws by which it was governed, then looked across the floor to where Jeiger lay next to him, snoring gently in the firelight, and wondered if this was what it meant to have reached a promised land.

Morning in the holt began with a knock on every door

to rouse the sleepers and the lying-awake-in-bed and the early-morning fornicators; in the moments when all three shared a pang of resentment that they had to relinquish the comfort of their pallets, they became united by one spirit as no battle has ever united men.

Jeiger liked the mornings when he could sit around the communal hearth and cook his breakfast without the knock to rouse him; he had risen with the dawn since his childhood, when his legendary father had carried him up over the peaks to watch the sun rise over the plains. As he had grown older, he had begun walking himself, small feet feeling for the sure places in the stone and sometimes finding the slippery stretches of broken rocks instead; each time, his father had reached down a hand to steady his son.

The first day that he had walked up to the brow of the mountains without his father's hands to guide him, he had been five summers old, and this was his most cherished memory.

He had taken Erlen over the mountains to watch the sunrise a moon-cycle ago, after they had escaped from Erekoi soldiers, and in the early moments when the birds began to murmur to each other in the forests behind them, Erlen had taken his hand as though he, too, understood how sacred the sunrise was.

Erlen had followed him into the forest to hunt the deer who had never heard that theirs was a gentle race; he'd followed Jeiger to search out the best trees for building a new smithy and then taken a hand in bringing the building to its feet; Erlen had led Jeiger on raids against the Erekoi with all the fervor of the newly-converted, and his passion had made the borderlanders—had made Jeiger himself—believe again.

Jeiger had never been to Weigenland, but still he had considered returning to the disowned motherland when the skirmishes had begun to acquire the numbing regularity of war. Then, like a blessing, a piece of Weigenland had come over the plains to the borderlands and loved them freshly and fully, the way Jeiger, who had been born in the mountains, could not.

The knocker finished the rounds and walked down to the common area; the despised waker was a young woman who wore her hair bunned up like breakfast behind her head. She went to the cookpot that she had set up last night, yawning and tugging her sleeves up over her elbows; her face reflected the firelight from the communal hearth.

"I can't see how you wake before dawn," the woman muttered into her cast-iron pot. "I can hardly keep my eyes open when it's my turn to knock on the doors."

"Drink a cup of water before bed and you'll *have* to wake up early," Jeiger answered; he tipped the morning's potato into the stewpot with the water that Erlen had brought from the spring, and then cast about his person for some more flavorful addition to the pot. His hand brushed the pouch where he kept his smoked meat, but he knew that hunting had been slim since the war had begun.

The worms of the water soon ate holes in any deer meat that he tossed into the stream to keep it cool; the worms of the bin soon nibbled at the potatoes and rutabagas that they had neglected during the long growing season; the worms of hunger soon gnawed at the breast of any person who devoted himself to destroying men's lives rather than preserving them. A man had to save his arrows for other men, or else he would die as surely as by starvation. In the annals of the war, this was the record that the borderlanders bore in the forefronts of their minds.

Erlen returned to the common room with onions in one hand and mushrooms fresh-grown from last night's rain in the other, though, and the worm of discontent ceased its gnawing entirely. His pale face was blotched with patches of scarlet from the morning chill, but he smiled as he dropped the vegetables at Jeiger's feet. "I'd like to sketch two of these varieties of mushroom before we cook them—if they *can* be cooked, of course—and add them to the record. They grow in—"

"—circles," Jeiger finished, reaching out to accept the gifts of the earth. "As we work our spells."

"And you never see just one," added Erlen. "Just as borderlander magic can't be worked alone. Just as no one here truly lives alone."

The knocker, Marla, smiled as the truant risers began to file into the common area in thick, woolen trousers that fought off the morning's chill. Most of them were keen-eyed by now, in the first moments of daylight, and they laughed with one another as they set up their cooking tripods and their stewpots in twos and threes. Some had already been to the potato bins or the rutabaga bins; others had picked through the apple barrels for the least wizened fruits, which they sliced into the pot more for the substance than for the taste.

As the first smells of potato and onion soup began to scent the air, Marla asked, "How was the sunrise?"

Although Erlen answered her, his eyes were far away and fixed on the eastern plains. His look might have been marked with regret; it might only have been unfocused. "More beautiful every morning."

There came a low cry of alarm from the watchtower, and Jeiger's head went up like a hunting dog's at the sound. Against the clatter of cooking utensils on cast-iron stewpots came the slow, steady pound of the Erekoi cannons.

Gamela awoke with the dawn, as did all priestesses of Terichone who haggled with night for as many working hours as they could afford, and the corpse was standing over her.

She knew that the corpse had a name, but didn't know what that name was; her eyes shamed her as they fixed on the muck across the front of the corpse's wrap gown or the hole beneath her collarbone where a fly had made its nest. She had wiped the mud from the corpse's eyeless face last night, but it hadn't reduced the horror of that visage.

Like many who worked a little swamp magic to heal the sick in exchange for subsistence, Gamela had tried her hand at raising the dead once. She, too, had caught her own blood in an ink-bottle and drawn shapes on parchment to focus her spirit; she, too, had written the name of the dead over and over again until the letters ceased to have any meaning and her wrist ached from holding the reed pen, until she had engraved the name on her mind: *Nereus*. Nereus, who had been her dearest love and husband until the red death had stilled his hands and closed his eyes. Every man or woman or child who tries to raise the dead imagines that this time, the dead will greet them laughing and alive.

Every man or woman or child who has brought the dead up from the ground's embrace knows despair when that dear one's body stares sightlessly around the room that the soul once knew so well.

Gamela was older now, and she knew why it was folly; she looked on this nameless corpse's face, and although it revolted her, she felt nothing but compassion. The priestess ate a few dried fruits for her breakfast and drank water from the pool in a cupped leaf, and she thanked Terichone for the restful night.

As she saddled the mule again and fed him his morning grain, Gamela caught the corpse staring into the depths of a puddle on the ground.

She could only wonder what the soul saw there.

"Come," said the priestess to fill the just-noticed silence of the little birds who are too polite to sing in the presence of death. "We must get you in the saddle if we want to catch the king's horses."

The corpse had explained to the high priestess with her too-far-gone mouth that the king and the queen both rode on a mail cart, with two men attending. By Gamela's judgment, such a party could not have made it past the way-station of Shonè and Aenikus even if their prisoner had chosen to cooperate—which Gamela did not believe for an instant. Achane had not let her sister's body go back to the warm earth's arms when her resurrection had been less joyful than expected; she wouldn't have waited quietly in captivity while her sister's body lay facedown in the muck.

They had time, even though their mule was slow and swayed from the medicines that made it easy in the scent of a dead body.

Gamela lifted the corpse by one ankle so that she could swing an insect-ridden leg over the mule's back; Gamela made a note to tease out the maggots and flesh-beetles when next they stopped so that the corpse's muscles would not be eaten away entirely. She still wore the healer's shawl on occasion in her work for Terichone, and she still knew the magic and the herbcraft of preserving both the living and the dead.

When the corpse's flesh was gone, she would no longer be able to move—but her soul would still lie trapped in her body.

She did not dwell on such things. Instead, Gamela heaved herself into the saddle behind the corpse and put her arms around the once-lovely woman's body so that it would not fall off the mule.

She swallowed a tablet like the ones she had given to the mule in its grain, and slowly, the scent of death became one with the aroma of trodden snakeblossom vines and the scent of sulfur that signaled the far-away sea.

The page-adjutant's name was Ilaumeleus, and he was terrified of serpents.

Yesterday, he had stepped on the tail of a ratsnake

that lay camouflaged against the brown wood of the road; the ratsnake had started, wriggled fiercely under the boy's boot, and elicited a terrible scream from the youth's thin throat far out of proportion to the danger of the snake itself. When finally Ilaumeleus had ceased his shrieking and leaping, the stunned little ratsnake had snuggled itself into a hole no wider than a finger between two slats of the road.

Achane supposed that she could use this knowledge, if she could summon venomous serpents and if Ilaumeleus had been the king rather than the king's adjutant. As it was, she had merely drawn waving lines like a serpent's sinuous curves in her mind and then cast them out across the floor to ensure that Ilaumeleus did not sleep easily. Today, the boy sat astride one of the carthorses with his head hanging and dark circles under his eyes, and he had not noticed the three ratsnakes that had vacated the roadway after he passed.

Except for the loyal alligator palms, the forest had abandoned the roadway; even the palms appeared only seldom, peering out from the rapidly dissipating mist at the three men and two women who entered their domain.

In the distance, Achane could see rice farmers bending in their fields; she knew these lands well enough, although not from a post-chaise nor from the wooden roadway, and she knew some of these farmers by name. Some of them had walked the long, almost invisible path to her cottage when the priestesses of Terìchone could not help them, and she had come with her satchel of medicines to their bedsides. Had she been closer, she could have called out for them to help her, and they would have come hustling with their great rice-baskets on their backs to find out who had troubled their swamp-witch.

They weren't close enough; she didn't speak. The king remained silent, with one hand absent and sexless on Achane's arm and the other firm on the carriage door; on Achane's other side, the queen held her lips together tightly, as though to keep them safe from the air outside. Even the swamp man only hummed a slow, mournful chantey that had survived from the days of settlement, so many hundreds of years ago.

> *Hey-oh, mother long gone;*
> *Haven't seen the bottle since the ship left land;*
> *Haven't heard my lady since she passed away;*
> *Haven't seen the shoreline, and I shan't today.*

Haven't seen the shoreline, and I shan't today, but in the distance, Achane could see a lighthouse silhouetted against the grey sky. She closed her eyes against the sight; her eyes were tired from staring straight ahead and almightily tired of the disappointment of what they saw.

For what might have been hours, Achane let the world pass by at the uneven pace of the shuddering chaise, in the darkness of her closed eyes. Each heartbeat cried out *Shabane* at her, and each thump of the carriage wheels was her sister falling over and over into the puddle and beating at the earth to rise.

When the swamp witch opened her eyes again, the lighthouse pointed accusation at the unforgiving sky, and Achane wanted to scream.

She closed her eyes against temptation and bid herself wait. The opportunity had not come in the way-station of Shonè and Aenikus; perhaps it would come before they reached that forbidding finger that supposedly shed light on the sea.

For most of the night, Achane had lain awake on a pallet next to the queen, awaiting her chance to escape; she had felt the chill purpose radiating from the woman during every second of her wakefulness, though, and Achane had not dared roll over in bed to see if the queen's moss-agate eyes were open. She had rested still in her bonds until the night had finally gifted her with what felt like a few moments of dear, beautiful sleep.

The imaginary snakes had shaken their coils across the floor, and every stifled gasp from the men's sleeping quarters had been a small victory, hollow as a yawn.

Her eyes opened and traced the roadway beneath the chaise.

A stone's throw ahead, the witch caught a flicker like a speck of metal on the roadway; she knew it for a ratsnake's eye.

Come to me, she wrote on the fabric of the world and the flesh behind her eyes—*come to me, and perhaps we can help one another.*

The ratsnake lifted its head slowly, lazily from the road as the vibrations of hoofbeats warned it of danger; it undulated its thin body and sought out a place that would be safe.

Had it been a snake given over to deep cogitation, it would have wondered that the burrow that it called home in all but the flood season should feel less safe than the strap that hung down from the chaise's door—or indeed, that the cool, dark depths of a young woman's belt pouch should feel more like home. But the ratsnake merely followed the impulses that it knew and curled up with meat that smelled dead and of fire; although the earth shook in a way that was uncomfortable, the snake soon fell asleep.

Achane looked from Ilaumeleus to the king; the first had his eyes fixed on the long, flat plains of the rice-fields, and the second focused too firmly on the shape of the light-house to be bothered with one small snake curled in one small pouch on one small person. The charm had not been noticed, and yet it held.

She did not name the snake. Names were for friends.

Allies in dangerous times had already transcended names.

very time he entered a battle, Erlen faced a wild, horror-struck moment in which he couldn't remember the correct defensive position for a formal duel. Fencing Master Klaver's voice rang in his ears, shouting across the practice room for "Meester Eppeim to please recall that he ees not beeg street brawler!" as a younger Erlen, who had not been raised in a noble house but in a back-alley apartment, took the only defensive position he knew—the spread-legged crouch.

And every time that the flash of sunlight on the first cannonade made him fling his shield up over his head and chest, he remembered that real battles didn't have duels, and in a seething clash of leather armor and whirling flails, the street brawler is king.

This was his forested mountain. He knew it from its feet that dipped into the river to its bald, proud brow, and the Erekoi soldiers who fired up at him from below did not know that the trees under which they stood were full of sharp-eyed men.

As the first cannonballs cracked the trees and made the bracken shudder, Erlen shouted a defiance that he had never been able to express at university and threw himself down the slope in the company of two dozen borderlanders. The Erekoi cannoneers bent to swab the barrels and reload—

—and became wider targets for the borderlanders who fired down at them. Arrows fell like hail, if hail was two cubits long and had a barbed tip; they fell like rain, if rain bit deep into thighs and skulls and arms and brought men to the ground.

Arrows fell like arrows, and as the second volley struck deep into the heart of the kneeling Erekoi cannoneers, Erlen's forces hit them in a wave that bowled the standing men over and trampled the fallen men underfoot. If war is anything of water, it is the ocean in a full gale; it drowns those men foolish enough to try to steer it.

Erlen felt the knife enter his shoulder as his own short sword took a man beneath the ribcage. He twisted his wrist and yanked out the blade, clutching the look of shock on his victim's face as tightly as he clutched his freely bleeding wound.

The next man fell under a well-aimed arrow that rustled the hair by Erlen's ear; he watched the shaft slice into the Erekoi man's forehead and knew that the archers had taken to the ground, so he put his back to a tree only long enough to sight an Erekoi soldier and drive his sword into the mouth of the snarling puma emblazoned on back of the man's uniform.

He thought he heard the Erekoi commander sounding the call to retreat and save the cannons, but he couldn't hear the shouts of battle for the din of the screaming.

As he whirled to take down the man behind him, Erlen recognized Jeiger in time to stay his hand and press his back hard against the other man's for safety.

There was no one to defend against—the borderlanders had claimed the morning.

In the sudden silence of too many men who have just realized that they no longer need to be shouting, three archers loped off into the still trees to follow the trails that the cannons' wheels had left in the leaf-mould. Erlen breathed deeply for a long and shuddering moment, but then he began to walk among the fallen.

Even before he had fought alongside the borderlanders, Erlen had healed the wounded, comrades and enemies alike. He had always earned top marks in magical medicine, practicing in the public hospitals attached to the Husmann's palace; it took a different species of charity to attend to the Erekoi, though, and one that he found harder to bear.

Here, two Erekoi clutching each others' wrists in death; the devotion of their comradeship pulled at his heart, and he looked up at Jeiger to remind himself that his fellow fighter was still living.

There, a borderlander gasping against a tree, her fusebox still clenched in her hands; her dyed-red hair was matted with blood that might have been anyone's, but the blood across her front was her own. Even as Erlen began to sketch a healing sigil on the woman's skin with his pen and ink, he watched her last breath pass her lips, and he moved to the next.

This, a borderlander man who cried out for the wound in his stomach—when Erlen finished the character for "binding," he screamed as his flesh began to knit together all at once. For good measure, Erlen drew the characters for "containment" and "cleanness" as well in wet, black ink beneath the man's ribs, and the sigils flashed silver behind his eyes even though the marks themselves did not change.

He, a borderman waving off the bandages and shouting for Erlen, who began to notice the pain in his sliced arm at the same time that he lifted it to embrace the old warrior. Erlen gently drew the sign for healing on his own flesh and felt the wounds close immediately, and then he saw to the old borderman's wounds.

That, an Erekoi youth whose dark face seemed neither male nor female; Erlen called over two of his fellows and drew the signs that would heal the Erekoi's shattered arm. The rictus grin of agony melted away, and the Erekoi whispered, "Thank you," even though two borderlanders now held the youth captive.

A fine line existed between the soldier and the murderer, and the act of healing the wounded and helping to bury the dead put up a stone fence along the boundary. As Erlen wrote his sigils on injured flesh, he remembered dead men lying in city gutters with their throats cut and their neighbors refusing to look down at the bodies over which they stepped. Those murdered men didn't enjoy the rough mercies of the borderlanders, who closed the staring eyes of their enemies and allowed comrades to say prayers over the bodies of their friends.

When at last the dead had been readied for burial and

the wounded readied for whatever they were fit to face, Erlen finally had a chance to catch Jeiger on his way back to the holt.

"I'm glad you saw to yourself," the borderman said before anything else, looking at the bloodstains on Erlen's shirt with a glance so pointed that it could have opened the other man's flesh anew.

"I'm glad they didn't hurt you," Erlen answered, and clasped Jeiger's hand firmly.

The feeling of emptiness told him before Jeiger's wince could speak it.

Erlen held up the borderman's right hand, which had lost its smallest finger, and he traced the healing sigil awkwardly carved into the flesh of the palm by Jeiger's illiterate fingers.

Jeiger smiled with just his lips, although the wound clearly pained him. "I thought I might try your way; we don't have magic for this."

The two of them said no more, but only walked back up to the holt.

he king and his party reached the lighthouse at nearly noon, when the grey building's shadow no longer lay stretched across the delta like some massive, dark, lounging beast. Instead, it huddled at the base of the tower against the fresh sea breeze that smelled of salt and spoiling eggs and sulfur and life; the lighthouse, though, provided no comfort to the king.

Milaus knew, rationally, that the ferry could not be expected to wait for him on this shore when its travels compassed all of the strait between here and the Isle of Fire and Stone, and yet the delay felt like a cold, ill omen that at first rested on his shoulders like a burden, but then sank into the pit of his stomach, where it remained. After he had dealt with the lighthouse-keeper to see about shutting away the post-chaise and stabling the horses, there was nothing to do but sit on the padded benches of the lighthouse's bottom floor and await the ferry.

It was a chill time of year for pilgrims; most men and women were seeking the shrine of Loukaros of the tempests to ask forgiveness on the land. That shrine stood far to the north in the mountains, with a tall fortress grown up around it and Milaus's brother at the fortress's head to greet the first pilgrims to the chapel. In the swamplands, the king had heard, the first rain of the year had been particularly fierce, and several houses near the river had risen up on their floats and drifted to the very limits of their tethers before the rains had abated again. Frantic house-holders had poled at the ground to guide their homes back to their foundations and rest the floats back safely in their normal gaps. The lighthouse-keeper had whispered conversationally as he brought the horses around to the stables that the bottom of the lighthouse and the stables had been underwater this morning, but praise the sea—it forgave quickly.

Some houses had been so weighed down and off-balance from the iron stove or the furniture that they had wallowed in the floodwaters instead of rising up over them; such was Loukaros's chastisement for modern living.

King Milaus knew, as he considered this first rain of the year, that taxes would hold little promise in spring. Little had been entirely destroyed, it was true; a few landholders had lost their houses, but swamp-folk quickly rebuilt. It was also true, unfortunately, that little had been left entirely undamaged.

He felt a pang of regret for taking the swamp witch from her people in their time of need, but the war meant that the Erekoi's necessity had to be subsumed into *Erekos's* necessity.

If the queen consented, he would lower taxes for the coming year. It was the least his people deserved.

The benches, true to the lighthouse-keeper's word, were still damp; while the swamp man sank down onto a padded bench with no heed for the water that squeezed out between the warp and the weft and at every seam, Ilaumeleus had taken one look at the little puddle on the flagstones and backed himself against a wall that bore a net like a tapestry.

The swamp witch sat with her unbound legs crossed underneath her and fixed her bound hands under her chin; she faced the door, peering ever outward at the impossible escape there. Milaus felt another pang of regret, for although he was ruthless in battle, he was not cruel.

Perhaps she had dearly loved the person whose corpse had come falling to regain her.

She would have to love her country more, then.

Milaus sat beside his queen on a bare, wooden bench as time-carved as the road had been, and in the subtly direct way that she had, she took his hand. There was no emotion in it, really, although he had once hoped that she would love him, when he had been young and she had been beautiful— touch was a duty that she bore ill with her husband. He ran his fingers across the rings that he had given her on their wedding day; this, the malachite chip set in silver; that, the golden band inscribed with sigils for long life and many children; the last, a moss-agate in iron. It was her favorite of them all, and she wore it on her index finger where it caught the light with her every gesture.

She had given him a hoop of pure iron in return, and he wore it on a chain next to his heart.

He met her eyes, so penetratingly grey and brown, and did not think it strange that he called her "the queen" in his mind instead of "Carisica." Carisica was a name for a courtier or even a courtesan; it spoke of caresses and frivolity, with its four syllables of frippery. The queen had no patience for either.

Some women became more convivial upon their marriages, hosting balls and extravagant dinners to combat the sudden loneliness of being bound to one man rather than sought by dozens; some women instead became shrewish, and where once they had showed pliant smiles and easy laughter, they soon became jealous of their husbands' every privilege and fought for petty scraps of control. The queen, though, had been neither such woman—when marriage had scooped her away from the heady social life of the coastal nobility and the glorious freedom of young and powerful women who live far from war, she had closed in on herself and left Milaus on the outside. She had drawn shut like a mussel in the seas and nursed whatever sorrows she felt until they had grown hard and bright as pearl, and she had learned to speak with her eyes rather than betray her thoughts in her words or her smooth, perfect face.

In time, the uneasy grey waves outside allowed a black speck safe passage; the speck grew larger as it traversed the waters. Ilaumeleus bolted upright in his haste for the ferry; the swamp man leaned back and knew that he would not be needed for a day; although Milaus rose, his queen remained patiently seated. The ferry was yet a long way off, and even with an engine to power it, it would take a long time to reach the shore.

Milaus remembered two nights ago—the flood

night—in the passenger steamboat traversing the swamp-river. The rising waters had wrecked the ship and his curricle and forced him to continue his pilgrimage in a borrowed mail carriage, because even the king does not escape the storm without feeling the finger of Loukaros on his forehead and the eyes of Loukaros on his shelter.

When the steamboat pulled into the bedraggled harbor, the king and queen went down to greet it. They had walked only three paces down the stone road to the dock when an exodus spilled bodies across the shore like blind ants who have just had their sheltering stone lifted and do not know which way to run.

Some of these pressing, anonymous bodies were priests and priestesses of Shonè and Aenikus.

"King Milaus!" cried the man who was the head priest, stumbling up the road to the presence of majesty. "I'm sorry that we must meet this way, but you must understand our circumstances."

"Circumstances?"

"The storm," answered the head priest; his eyes were weary and sunken in a sea of rheum. "Surely you know."

Milaus again felt the dread that had gripped him when the ferry hadn't been at the lighthouse; it clenched at his ribs as though it sought to snap them. "Have the gods rained fire and stone on the shrine again?"

"No," the priest replied. "Loukaros has washed it away."

Shabane's body couldn't feel the world—it couldn't study the texture of bark with its fingertips or sense the ground under its bare feet except when a foot stopped moving; it couldn't tell if the air was cold or warm, and only the motion of the wrap and the hair that her body wore told her whether or not the breeze blew through the marshlands. Her body couldn't feel the priestess's arms around it, holding it in place on the mule's back.

As the pale larvae burrowed deeper inside her flesh, though, Shabane discovered that the sensations she had considered lost were returning—in the form of that last insistent guest and bitterest remaining friend, pain.

When a strip of flesh on Shabane's body's neck peeled away and revealed a mass of maggots, the priestess Gamela reined in the mule and helped the corpse down from the saddle.

"This will feel strange," she said, in a way that seemed intended for comfort. "You'll be all right—don't be afraid." Shabane had heard those words in her youth a hundred times as her father had taken her to healers up and down the river, searching for a cure for the coughing sickness; she'd heard them from her sister with every new decanter of crushed berries or spell full of old-fashioned words and burning incense. To hear it when her health had become a foregone conclusion seemed the height of irony—as though Shabane cared any longer what happened to her body.

Gamela gathered up wet, sturdy branches and made a pair of rough frames of them on a solid patch of ground. The bark rubbed off on her hands and stained the rope, but as soon as the frames had been constructed, Gamela went back into the forest.

Shabane watched her return with her arms full of long, straight branches, which she put together into a travois and tied with the remainder of her rope; it seemed impossible that a person should have thought to bring so much rope into the forest. The priestess finally smeared the travois with wet, soft mud and then fixed it over the frames she had built. The entire framework stood to the hem of Gamela's long shirt, like a large and dirty wooden bed.

"I'll help you lie down here, but you have to trust me," said Gamela, and because Shabane did not care how her body was used, she let the priestess undress it and rest it on the makeshift cot.

Underneath her body, where Shabane could not see the motions of the priestess's hands and arms, small sounds arose like rasping and clacking. For a time, the priestess stood and went away; when she returned, she knelt immediately and rasped and clacked at the ground again.

Although Shabane could not feel its heat or smell the sweet, herbal smoke, she could hear the fire crackling below her as if she were a holiday pig on the roaster.

She could not close her sightless eyes against the shaking of the gentle trees overhead, so instead she watched them dance with their elegant hands bent into awkward poses and their arms garlanded with birds. The trees, Shabane thought, would be friends as dear as the earth if only she could join them; she could be still for all her unconscious afterlife, and they would stand tall and wave as her substance melted into the earth.

Deep in her flesh, Shabane felt the voracious worms pause in their feeding and all at once expand their bodies in the little holes that they had made. She had never known a lover's touch, but she thought that it might feel like it did when the worms thrust through the cavities in her muscles—there was a sumptuous pain to their motions that had nothing to do with anything but hunger.

In a moment, Shabane heard soft sizzling sounds like crisp, frying bacon as the fat hit the skillet; the feeling of the worms left her shoulder first, and then her legs, and then her eyes and mouth as the worms followed their cousins to the warmth that they could feel but she could not. They chased the aroma of burning stimweed that Shabane couldn't smell, and they cooked open under the latticework of wet, muddy wood slowly baking like clay. At length, even the lacy-winged flies that had taken up residence in her nostrils gave up and fluttered out to dive into the flames.

Shabane's body lay, purified at last, on its first real deathbed, and she was grateful for the moment of rest.

In time, Gamela tossed something onto the fire that made it crackle and hiss and then die, and she helped Shabane's body down from the lattice with hands more sure now that they did not expect to encounter infestation. She slipped the wrap over Shabane's stiff arms, one sleeve and then the next, and cinched it closed beneath the ribs.

"Come on, then," Gamela said as she dismantled the wooden framework and coiled her rope again. She held her hands cupped to lift Shabane's body back onto the mule, smiling as though her smile meant something.

As the priestess hefted herself up behind the corpse and put her arms back around its slender waist, Shabane spared a brief moment of grief that she had lost the sense of pain inside her. It had been all she had left—all but the sister whom they even now rode to find.

he swamp man drove the post-chaise behind finely dressed, handsome, young Ilaumeleus— he thrust his broad hand into his pocket and hummed his sea-tune, fixing his eyes on the trees. He knew that he was ever apart from King Milaus and the queen in his stature, for they were the sort of people who ride carriages through the marshes, while he could never be more than their driver. Even the witch, whose origins were as humble as his, could raise the dead and heal the sick with a word. To all of them, he knew, he counted for nothing.

The swamp man's name was Keiros; his mother once told him that "Keiros" meant "falcon" in the language that the people of Erekos spoke before they had crossed the sea.

As the chaise rattled through the forest, he thought about the family that he had not had a chance to see since the king plucked him from among the wrecked steamboat's passengers to be a guide. The king had most likely chosen him on account of his particular darkness of skin, which must have indicated familiarity with the swamp roads to a person who didn't *live* in the forest and therefore didn't know that most swamp people stayed put.

Keiros wondered whether his house had been washed away. He tried to envision the cottage lying canted across its foundations, its occupants too few to steer it back onto the stonework without him beside them. He could only imagine the potbellied stove toppling, over and over again; in his mind, it screeched trails in the dark floorboards as the slope of the floor made it slide to the tilted wall. He imagined it catching on his wife's favorite rug every time and then tipping over, spilling out the charcoal and ash that his youngest was always forgetting to clean out.

If he hadn't gone to the capital to look for work, he would've been home in time to face the flood beside his wife and children. Even now, the blacksmith's position he'd found brought him no joy; although the wages were good, he could see already that living would be poor for a long time.

If the flood had washed his house away, though, living would be poorer.

He hummed *Hey-oh, mother long gone* without allowing himself to wonder whether his wife and children were all right. The thought was more than he could bear, so he didn't think it. He dwelt on the way it would feel to wrap his wife in his arms again and kiss her forehead, and the way his children's eyes would light up when they saw the small parcel of sweetmeats that he had bought for them in the capital, and the way that he had always felt a great bursting love for his family that he had never been able to talk about with anyone else.

As they picked their way through the swamp, Keiros heard a bird cry that he had never heard before and wondered if it was his mother's falcon.

Hey-oh, mother long gone.

The rice fields would be utterly flooded by now, and the water might be brackish from the great sea-waves; Keiros didn't like to think about the ruination of his fields, and so he didn't. The yams might be drowned as well, but his wife would've been wise enough to salvage those she could as soon as the rain and flooding went down again. Some men from the temple had supposed that the flooding had only hit badly near the river, based on bad first rains from other years, but Keiros didn't dare suppose that his house and his family had been spared just because they lived far from the water.

He kept picturing the stove sliding across the floor like the blacksmith's job that he didn't particularly want, tripped up in the rug of his love for his family. It might have been a sign from Aenikus, this vision, for the hearthstone and the stove and the forge were all of them Aenikus's domain; while Shonè kept the outside of the house, tending the gardens and bringing in the firewood, the work of the home and the shop belonged to her husband.

Aenikus knew, a blacksmith belonged at his family's hearth.

Keiros saw the familiar footpath next to the tall daughter of the grove with its bark carved with his family's names, and he said aloud, "This is my place."

The king, in the way of kings, thought that Keiros was talking to *him*. "You don't intend to leave us in this damned swamp!"

Keiros only smiled to himself when he answered. "Yes, I think I do, King Milaus. You can lodge here tonight, if we've a house to go back to, and then you can pay my neighbor to take you back to the river—if there is a river to go back to."

Without waiting to hear if he had been given permission to return home, Keiros hopped down from the box and took to his feet on the winding path through the trees and left the others behind. While the king stood gaping after his driver, Keiros followed the winding path of river-smoothed stones. His heart pounded against his ribs, and whether it was from fear or from love or from the fear that love engendered, he couldn't say.

At the path's end, he stood staring, spellbound, at his miraculously upright house and unflooded rice fields, and his wife caught him close and his children came running from the yam garden.

For the king's party, at that moment, an old merchant doctor came rambling down the footpath, selling Special Tonic and a way back to the river road—but for Keiros, at that moment, they counted for nothing.

*A*chane had been nine years old when she had watched her father haggling with a traveling doctor in the clearing by the river. Her father's fishing boat had rested on the water, rocking gently in the lapping of the waves, and the doctor had watched it conspicuously as they spoke together, to hint that there were surely more productive uses of the fisherman's time than trying to convince a doctor to heal an incurable illness.

"I could give you a remedy, but it would do nothing but put money in my pocket," the little doctor had said, spreading his hands. Achane had watched him from the shelter of the trees with her fingers twisted in a length of hanging moss that had fallen from the branches overhead, and she had willed herself unnoticeable as the doctor hitched up his satchel and used his every movement to convey that he had somewhere better to be. "The girl has the coughing sickness, and every man or woman you talk to—every witch or wizard, priest or doctor,

charlatan or genuine artifact!—will tell you that there's nothing
to be done. Anyone who says elsewise already has an eye on
your pocket, and wants a hand in it as well."

It had been quiet in the cottage since Father had
started taking Shabane to see doctors. Mother had grimaced
and avoided looking at the bed on the floor where the children slept, and where Shabane spent her days; she had started
sweeping the floors religiously and organizing their herbs into
ropes of exactly equal lengths from the rafters, scouring their
pots daily and insisting that her two healthy children bathe
in the river twice a day to keep them from catching whatever
Shabane had caught by accident of birth. Mother had only
spoken to shout at her husband for his obsession with his sick
daughter, or else to tell her children to clean up whatever they
had abandoned for a moment (for she could no longer bear
the sight of mess) or to give them some chore to do to keep
them from being in the house with their sister. Soon, there
were lots of chores for their house.

Aerus hadn't understood because he was only three
years old, so Achane had watched over him while they were
at chores or else let her mother cosset him on the porch. He
had big, dark eyes that almost broke Achane's heart, they
were so dear; he had known how to get their mother to sit
still and stroke his hair and stare off into the distance, and
when he did that, Achane had sneaked into the house with
Shabane and they had read stories to one another in whispers.
Shabane had at times gone away to see new healers, and she
had sometimes returned bursting with energy and sometimes
so drained that their father had carried her in. On good days,
Achane had braided her sister's hair and put flowers in it and

said that she was a princess. On bad days, Achane had only stood staring and not listening to her mother as she broke her silence to shout at her father.

It had hurt to hear her screaming at him on this morning. Her mother had held a rope of peppers in one hand and yams in the other, and she had shouted and smashed a dried pepper to little flakes on the floor by the time she was done shouting. Achane had just watched Shabane either lie asleep or pretend to be asleep, and then she had run away into the woods to pick herbs and pretend that she was a healer and that she could make her sister well. At nine years of age, Achane knew in her marrow that she was the big sister, and it was her job to make sure her brother and sister never wanted for anything—even when her head hurt so much from her parents' fighting that she had to get away for a while.

She had been nine years old and had thought that she could change the whole world with just herself, and so she hadn't really listened to the traveling doctor who, unlike most of his brethren, avowed his own incompetence. Achane had been far more like her father than her mother, even then; she had wanted to hope that the world didn't tear up people's lives and then not clean them up again.

With her basket of herbs and windfall nuts and rescued wild berries, Achane had retreated from the clearing by the river and back to the porch of the cottage, where her mother mended clothing with her mouth as straight and thin as her seams and where Aerus looked for his older sister with wide, black eyes.

A witch's greatest enemy is her local doctor. Some may say that this is because the first uses the magic of the earth to guide a man or woman to health, and she despises the scientist whose chemicals would force health where the earth is unwilling; some may say that there is a deep rivalry between the two because witches are often women and doctors are often men.

As every swamp witch or wizard will tell you, though, it's hard to make a living where someone else has already set up shop.

The traveling doctor knew Achane from the area's sickbeds, where they had on occasion hovered over the same body and worked the same art, one hired by one branch of the family and the other in the other branch's pay; needless to say, he tactfully ignored the leather straps that bound her hands and instead kept up a light and easy dialogue with his royal benefactors. The dialogue was made easier in that the king and queen did not reply; with practiced speeches, the doctor offered them hundreds of tonics and brews, and yet they only had ears for his talk of the river.

The floodwaters had gone back down, he said, as they were wont to do after the first shock; it helped that there hadn't been a second rain for a few days to add water to the pot, so to speak. That meant that a few steamboats were up and running, taking carpenters and joiners and flotillas of priests to the places that needed new houses, and they were doing a roaring trade even if it meant their schedules had been tossed off like a bad drink, if you pardon my saying.

"Good," Milaus answered; in Achane's pouch, the ratsnake woke and began to probe at a world that did not taste like marshes. Achane mentally traced a lovely, arcing line for a dangling spider to take toward her pouch, and the spider obliged and fed itself to the snake.

She wondered where Shabane was now, and if she was alone and staggering through the forest—perhaps she was lying face-down in a stream as the little fishes pecked at her skin and tore her slowly to shreds.

Achane knew little about zombi but how to bring a man or a woman back from death; she hadn't thought that she'd need to know. She had never imagined that she, too, would be unable to succeed at restoring true life where every other had failed. She hadn't thought that Shabane would return with the spirit seemingly absent from her body.

The snakeblossom vines dipped down over the road and caressed the sides of the post-chaise; the queen paid no mind to the flowers that courted her like giddy lovers at a festival. Far overhead, the daughters of the grove dropped their last, tenacious maiden blossoms and grew fecund with thick-hulled nuts.

The first sunlight in days broke through the clouds as the traveling doctor laughed at his own joke, and for a moment, even the horses faltered and looked up as they stepped into a broad pool of light.

Someone had lit a fire here that had left ashes strewn across the wet earth, along with a pile of wood now slowly drying in the reborn sunlight. It was nothing more than a refugee campsite for those moving on after the flood, perhaps, but Achane smelled a lingering aroma of stimweed on the air that told her another witch had been here. A woman or man who had needed to drive worms out of some fruit or rescue an infested piece of meat had stopped at this place and purified the flesh of life.

Something about this sunlight-ringed clearing gave Achane a feeling of hope, even when the horses shook themselves and trotted onward down the footpath and the doctor laughed into the light.

*I*n the lighthouse full of refugees, a priestess of Terìchone could not help but lend her hands. As she stirred a pot of stew for the hungry and ladled it out into the rolled-up leaves of an alligator palm, Gamela asked the lost people of Aenikus and Shonè whether they had seen the king and his retinue.

No. A tall young woman who carried a baby and a carved pilgrimage staff reached out to receive the blessing of sustenance with her one free hand, and as she sipped the precious elixir of pork broth, she asked if the shrine of Terìchone had survived the flood.

"Untouched, by the goddess's grace," answered Gamela, "and open to those who need shelter." The woman muttered her thanks for the broth and said some fleeting and oft-repeated thing about getting back to her family. She watched her infant girl with the kind of over-predatory care of a mother who has tried every known means to bring her

child back to health; Gamela only hoped that Aenikus and
ShonÈ had not disappointed her. Too many faithless people
blamed the gods for for their faithlessness already.

No, I've not seen 'n king, said a man in a cap. He
smiled at Gamela, though—a bordered smile missing its
front two teeth on the top. His coastal accent, which reminded her so much of the high priestess, marked him a part of
the sailor's world.

In a dark corner of the lighthouse, the corpse sat
wrapped in a saddle blanket to conceal her ragged flesh, her
head buried in a scarf. Gamela had washed off her dirty face
and then deliberately caked it with thin mud to make it appear more alive; she had rubbed a few handfuls of morticians'
salve on the corpse's skin so that the faint aroma of dendrove
bark would block the smell of decay.

No one paid any mind to another refugee who clearly
was not family.

No king has passed this way. One of Aenikus's priestesses came to stand beside Gamela and helped her dole out
broth; her hands moved in the graceful manner of one used to
giving benedictions and slowly swinging censers.

"Wait—a king *has* come this way," said another cler-
ic, whose more attractive garb and work- and worry-sunken
eyes marked him head priest. "He didn't advertise it, but I
know him well. King Milaus came to receive a blessing for
his war at the shrine of Aenikus and Shonè, but the shrine
has been washed away." He had the tone of one who had
voiced this particular tragedy so many times that the wound
had grown numb.

"Do you know where the king has gone?" asked

Gamela. "Has he gone to the shrine of Terìchone instead?"

"No," answered the head priest, wiping wrinkled fingers across his rheum-laced eyes as though to brush the black circles away. "He was tracing the pilgrimage route, though, and had a swamp man with him—he may have come from there. But if he's traveled on to any god's shrine, it would be Loukaros of the hurricane's. He wanted a blessing for his war, and your Terìchone has no love for the battlefield."

"She despises it—as do we."

A child who carried himself with the grave dignity of the terribly young addressing the very old put his alligator palm-leaf cup into the head priest's hands, where dark, hot broth slowly filled it to brimming. The child bowed before he took his cup back, as though Aenikus himself had granted the boon, and when he held the sturdy, folded leaf in his hands, he blew on it like a man trying to start the world's first fire.

Gamela darted a glance at the corpse, seated with her legs thrust out before her, and sought her words in her mind's deepest pockets. "Did the king return to the capital, or did he go to the seat of Loukaros?" If it were the latter, she might have a long journey before her—the Fortress of Storms stood at the edge of the Great Bowl, far to the north.

The priest shook his head, as did the priestess. "Only the gods know. Did you want to receive an audience with him?"

"No," Gamela answered quietly. All around her, the evening drew closer in, and no matter where the king was going, many miles remained before her and the corpse with which she traveled. "Only with a woman who travels with him."

For a second that flickered in the light of the cook-fire, the priest held his breath. It came out in a low, whistling rush through his gapped and weathered teeth, and the steam swirled over the cookpot as Gamela's ladle scraped the bottom.

Another hungry hand accepted the offering she placed in the leaf of the alligator palm.

"Don't speak with the queen," the head priest whispered.

His rheumy eyes held a trace of a stony gleam in the firelight and the radiance of the setting sun; Gamela suddenly perceived death in his withered face as surely as she did in the face of her traveling companion. She looked away to the priestess on her other side, whose lips had drawn in to a hard, flat line rimmed with whiteness.

"The queen discourses with the gods—and they answer her," said the priestess; she drew in a sharp breath and turned back to Aenikus's work at their makeshift hearth.

Gamela had been raised to believe that every person "discoursed with the gods" daily, because every action touched the divine. For the gods to answer, though—

Gamela looked into the smoke and steam that rose against the sunset. She whispered a prayer for the distance between her and the king, between her and Achane of the cottage in the swamp, between all of the people here in this lighthouse and their homes.

Terichone might have looked up from the sodden debris of the delta, nodded at the small figure who bent over the pot and the ladle, and begun walking back toward the river. The goddess knows the blights on the land as well as the means by which the land may be delivered, and she hears the cries of the flooded and the lost without a priestess to remind her. She could have followed the long wooden road back to the place that loved her and helped to drain the river-ridden lands; she could have stepped onto the steamboat beside King Milaus and elbowed him in the crowd.

The alligator palms waved gently over the rice fields, in greeting or farewell.

chane had never ridden a steamboat before. Although the call of the infirm and the ailing pulled her farther from home than most of the swamp people ever traveled, she had never been pulled up the river to the capital.

The king and queen left their borrowed post-chaise at an office in a dock-town, pressing coins into the postmaster's hands for the loan; they seemed strangely human without the carriage to divorce them from the earth, and perhaps it was the shock of this transformation that shut up Achane's mouth and made her follow them with her hands still tied— this time, with a scarf instead of a mail bag's thongs. It felt no less like bondage.

When the townsfolk jostled past in the lamplit streets on their way to this errand or that task, they didn't meet Achane's eyes or express apology, as though refusing to acknowledge their transgression eliminated it from memory.

Ilaumeleus the king's adjutant shuffled through the comparative press at the head of the group, trying to keep up with the doctor's pitch for foot-pain lotion that he did not really want or need. The young retainer's livery seemed too bright against the dull cotton clothes of the swamp folk; he moved without their habitual hunch, and that marked him an outsider.

The king and queen, though, seemed unaccountably one with their people as they walked the bracken-washed, cobblestoned streets to the recently flooded docks; they tried not to look at the houses that had docked imperfectly back onto their foundations, just as the people did, and they didn't meet anyone's eyes as they went.

River towns knew the ways of the flood, and their houses had the shapes of boats on foundations like the props that held a ship just being built; when next the river rose into the streets, the householders who hadn't managed to fit themselves just right in their little domicile docks would have a chance to try again. Even so, when she saw four lonely pillars rising from the twilight at the corners of an uninhabited foundation, Achane felt her heart wrench a little more for the families that had propped up their houses against a few convenient trees. The men and women of the town moved like boats as well, with the same feeling of a current driving them.

At last, the doctor broke away to see a forlorn-looking couple about his Bottled Curative Elixir, and Ilaumeleus alone led the party to the docks on feet that longed for the relief of even spurious foot-cream. Achane did not waste her ire on a hateful, momentary look backwards at the backwoods quack. Perhaps his remedies would provide some comfort in this uneasy place, and if so, she wished him the best of it.

At the waterlogged docks, where the river still rolled higher against the pylons than was customary, a tired steamboat captain looked up at the king's party and smiled weakly. "Hullo, your majesty," he called, without either tipping his cap or bowing to reduce his dignity further. "Heard you got caught in the wreck of the *Tarancha* a few days ago—I'm glad to see you well out of it."

"As am I, Captain," answered Milaus. "I'd like passage for four back to the capital, if your prow is turned that way."

The captain laughed; Achane had no idea why. "My prow is turned that way, but my coal isn't. We've not enough fuel to get us back unless we use the sails, and the wind's half-dead of late. Go on, your majesty—when will we be getting our coal mines back?"

The king laughed as well, for as inscrutable a reason. "When we win back the borderlands, then perhaps we'll get our coal mines as well. We have a new plan, though," and he glanced at Achane in a way that gave her boiling chills, "which may yet turn the tide."

"Only hope there'll be no more deaths than usual on account of it," said the captain. He had thin whiskers and a weak chin, and it made him look like an elderly rodent. "A land can't fight the gods' floods as well as fight other lands, even be they the Weigers in the borderlands and not the proper Weiger army. Loukaros love you for trying, though."

Achane looked up the gangplank at the crowded deck, full of people whose faces gleamed with old sweat in the lamplight like the faces of those people in the dock-town, but with less sense of purpose. In those temporarily arrested faces, she read a lonely impatience that reminded her of her own unmoving need upon Shabane's death; she thought with a start like a cough that her face must have worn such a mask as she'd prepared the spells to raise her sister's corpse.

When the king tried to place coins into the captain's hands to pay for passage, the captain only smiled and shook his head, saying, "We set out in an hour, wind or none, or else we'll miss the landing time for the capital. Bring us coal for steam power again, and we'll be square."

It was the first time that Achane had imagined any good in the king.

The four of them walked slowly up the gangplank to join the shuffling, half-dead crowd that awaited the journey; below, the quartermaster must have been measuring the meager coal reserves and wondering if new fuel might come down the river to aid them.

Achane felt a shoulder jostle hers in the slowly moving press, but she had already grown used to the nameless face and the unconsidered apology. The people of the steamboat jostled kings and swamp women alike—she didn't look up so that she didn't have to acknowledge that another human had ignored her.

The goddess Terichone paused by the ship's ladder to take in the lowered brows of the king and the swamp witch, but since they didn't look up to meet her eyes, they didn't know that they had been touched by the divine.

The sky grew greyer overhead with every slow mile

that Achane and the king's company traversed toward the capital. The steamboat moved more slowly and surely than the crawling clouds, its great paddlewheel churning at the high waters of the river.

Steamboats came into being in bits and pieces, each part assembled separately: For every ship that a trading family commissioned, there were carpenters hired to put together the wheel and shipbuilders along the river hired to piece together the boat and raise the masts and sails and rigging, and five or six blacksmiths all laboring into the forge-lit blackness of night to create the internal machinery. Later, the pieces would be assembled in dry-dock, each boat a separate creature and each one unique. As a child, Achane had watched them ploughing the river water—the tall one is from Palamea, her father had told her, and that narrow one is from Antaea, all the way to the south. She had lain on her belly on the floor of her parents› cottage, a map spread out before her, and traced the shipping routes with her fingertips.

The trees slid past in near silence but for the slap of the paddle and the creak of the rigging; people were speaking, but their words were just the watery rustle of river-talk. Achane leaned over the railing to watch the steady progression of the dendrove trees.

"May I know where you're taking me?" she asked. The king didn't hear; he was looking over the wake that the steamboat dragged behind its paddlewheel.

"May I know where you are taking me?" asked Achane again, this time turning to present herself with her bound hands before her. Still, he didn't answer her.

The ratsnake grew restive in Achane's pouch as the

smell of rancid meat and rotting fruits rose from the deep parts of the boat's belly. There would be mice down there, gnawing at the ribs of the steamboat just as the insects had eaten away at Shabane.

Sensing the witch's loosened grip on her spell, the ratsnake unwound itself from her pouch and dropped to the deck with a small, barely heard thump. *Stay*, she thought; she would find a use for the ratsnake yet.

The king turned around at the low sound where Achane's voice had not moved him, and she asked for a third and final time, "Your majesty, may I know where you're taking me?" She clasped her tied hands so that her fingers interlocked, the better to clench her hands to quiet herself when he exercised his presumed authority.

"We're taking you to the capital," he answered. She heard the pejorative *witch* in his words even if he didn't say it. *Witch, you who think you can remake the world and answer back to the gods.* "If you cooperate with us, you'll remain there; if you choose not to cooperate, we'll take you to a fortress in the mountains."

"Where your men mine the coal." Achane watched his hand clutch at the fabric of his well-tailored jacket, an unconscious stroke across the embroidery at his waist that reiterated itself into a slow and almost deliberate clawing. She didn't care at all that her words had been meant as an insult; he probably thought she'd meant to praise him.

"Yes."

"With what do you expect me to cooperate?" asked the witch.

The king watched his captive as he gripped the fabric

at the front of his jacket, half-judging and half-irate. Achane watched him in return with her hands clenching each other tightly, and she thought that, had she been untied, she would have leapt into the river and escaped that way to freedom. The king's eyes flickered between her and the water as though he were considering that possibility as well; then his gaze fell on the hard slats of the paddlewheel and the streaming wake behind it, and Achane knew in an instant that such an escape wouldn't have been an option even had she been free.

A wake shapes itself of the air displaced into the rushing river and the water hurrying to fill the place where a boat had been; ahead, though, the unploughed river reflected the grey of the sky, and behind, the wake evened out to the same smoothness. There might have been a lesson in this, had either of them wished to see it.

King Milaus took his hand from his jacket and clasped his own wrist in an unconscious mimicry of Achane's hands. "I'll be clear with you, to make this as quick as possible," he said against the steady groan of the boards by the wheel.

"Be as quick and as clear as you have to be."

"We're engaged in a war—a war not just with the Weigers in the north but also with those Weigers in the borderlands. They've changed the war, after hundreds of years, and we need to change to answer them. This much, you must know already."

"I do," said Achane, although she hadn't known about the borderlands until this morning. "For the coal."

"For the protection of our borders from the Weigers, who would come through the mountains if they could, to strike our cities—the damned Wigs have already been making assaults on our fortresses, probably coordinated by the Weiger generals to the north. I don't have to tell you what could happen if we can't hold them in the mountains," he answered, as though he had said it a thousand times before. "And for our coal and ore as well, but primarily as a military defense measure."

Silence was her answer, and silence his reply to it.

Eventually, perhaps for no other reason than to bring a swift end to the conversation, King Milaus continued, "To fight a war, we must have an army, and the borderland Weigers know the area better than we do—they fight more fiercely than the Weigers we've faced in the past, as well, even when we've sent the cannoneers after them. We've learned this at no small cost to our men," he added like an apology. In his eyes, tugged down by the weight of government, Achane read a kind of horror that she had never known before. "I don't want to lose any more of our soldiers' lives than I have to in this conflict."

"There are plenty of healers in our land," Achane replied to his booted feet. "I don't see why you need *me*—"

"I don't want a healer, or even three dozen healers, although they'll help." Around them, the trees flowed sedately past and the speech of the other passengers was river-talk, smooth and meaningless. The queen looked up from a scroll of meditations and met Achane's wide eyes.

"I want you," said the king, "to make me an army of zombi to fight in our soldiers' stead. I want you to help me to destroy the damned Wigs once and for all, so that none of our young men and women have to die."

The hand burning so that the fingers smelled like

charred meat; the blank and empty eyes across the candle's little point of light and the chill of her flesh that made her feel alone even with her sister beside her.

An army—a shuffling army of blank-faced sons and daughters and brothers and sisters, all of them moving to war with swords in their awkward hands to fight for the people who had raised them, falling and lying hamstrung or hacked to pieces and collecting flies on the ground as their souls lingered within the mutilated bodies—

Achane heaved over the side of the boat and clutched at her stomach with her bound hands; she couldn't wipe the vomit from the hair that Shabane had plaited.

The king kept talking, but a rush like the river filled Achane's ears before the world went dark.

*S*habane didn't mind the scarf that cordoned off the scope of her vision and shadowed her ruined eyes, nor did she mind the saddle blanket over her body's arms. The lengths of cloth were meant to cover the disgusting realities of her body as the wrap that she wore could not, and she knew that most people would view her unhealing wounds with horror. In her own life, Shabane had been unable to attend funerals without closing her eyes against the sight of the dearly departed.

Then, though, there had been the little boy at the lighthouse who had tried to share his soup with her.

"You look like my mother," he had told her, and did not care that she couldn't thank him. After a moment of standing in her presence, he had grown restive and wandered back to a man who might have been his father—or perhaps any other relative at all, or even a caring stranger, in such a time of displacement—and stood there in easy communion with her across the distance and the silence.

That thought was a comfort to her as she sat on the back of the priestess Gamela's mule. They had returned to the shrine of Terichone with a few dedicates of other gods, agreeing that the gods might well model the charity that they encouraged among their followers.

Gamela was meeting with her high priestess now, as Shabane remained mounted outside. As they traveled, Gamela's drugs and the mule's own agreeable temper had accustomed it to the smell of death, and now it only offered a huff of irritation when Shabane shifted her weight on its back. There was a kind of peace in its acceptance of her death.

Even now, after the insects had departed from her flesh and the muck had been cleared away from her skin and covered with a rough-woven grey saddle blanket, Shabane watched the forest move with the wind and hungered to be part of it. She remembered the movement of ants on her back and thick, sucking mud in her mouth, slowly atrophying her resurrected muscles and bringing her just a few steps closer to the death that she could not remember. It was a sweet feeling, to become one with the high crowns of snakeblossom vines and the warm leaf mould and every crawling insect.

It was a sweet feeling, and yet so many miles remained on a course unknown. They stretched out before her in agonizing shreds of seconds, a long, winding carnage of time that would see her body decay to uselessness.

The grey sky was already almost black by the time Gamela returned from her meeting, carrying a lantern on a pole, and she rubbed her eyes with her free hand as though the sockets pained her. "We move to the capital," she said for

Shabane's benefit, although she could have gone anywhere and Shabane would have followed unquestioningly.

"We'll go back to your house and spend the night there," said Gamela, as though she had read and misinterpreted Shabane's mind. "Come on—it's not far away by mule." Obligingly, Shabane moved her body forward just a bit in the saddle, and Gamela put a foot in the stirrup and swung up behind her with her lantern pole as a brace.

They rode again in the quiet of trickling streams and softly crying night-birds, the mule's hooves gentle against the earth. Shadows shrouded the trees like the scarf across Shabane's head; Gamela's lantern discarded the firm shapes of the boughs and instead drew out the arc of an alligator palm frond or the briefly seen, staring eyes of a squirrel; the forest that Shabane had never properly known seemed still stranger to her in the darkness, like a shaky echo reflected back from mountains beyond the scope of vision.

She didn't count the hours in breaths or prayers or heartbeats, and so the time that they journeyed through the faint, tussock-lined swamp-paths was instead clocked by the passage of trees.

Shabane didn't fear the night; of all the things that might emerge to destroy her body and render it back to the earth, none gave her pause. She herself was perhaps the most fearsome thing in the darkness, and that thought troubled her more than the eerie impressions of flowers like waxen hands.

Finally, after they'd ducked the embraces of countless trees, the woman and the corpse reached Achane's cottage in the clearing.

The small house lay silent in the half-light of Gamela's lantern, imposing scarcely even a shadow on the surrounding forest. The hearthstone still rested on the porch with cooking pans hanging from the eaves, all of the cast iron now spotted with rust that Shabane had used to clean off with a bit of rough stone. The broom still leaned against the doorframe, where it had been on the morning that the sisters had departed for the temple; the dried fronds of the alligator palm crossed over the door just as they always had, advertising Achane's skill as a healer to all who might come to her with their sick and were yet wary of a woman who didn't wear a healer's black shawl.

It was home, just as it had always been, but the place where Shabane and Achane had made their home appeared suddenly false, seen from the eternal outside of half-life.

They tied the mule outside the cottage and walked or staggered under the crossed palm leaves, bearing the lantern with them into the darkness.

The lantern destroyed any illusion that remained to Shabane that her sister might be resting on the bed they'd shared in her lifetime. Lamplight dispelled the shadows hanging around Achane's dried herbs and reflected dully from the cottage-shaped censer that Achane had placed carefully back on the shelf over the fireplace.

Shabane had no eyes left to weep, and so she lurched to the porch and bore the cooking pots in, one by one.

Gamela carried the hearthstone back to the fireplace and placed it carefully in the slot there, and Shabane had no voice to tell this so-unfamiliar woman that the hearthstone was backwards in the floor. The shrine had a cheery pot-bellied stove; why should the priestesses know how to lay down a hearthstone?

She stared unseeing at the rafters and knew that she would give up that dissolution into the earth that she so craved if only her sister might have this place—her place—to live when Shabane was truly and finally gone. When at last Achane stood at the funeral bed and smiled softly, she would say like the bereaved little boy at the lighthouse, "You look like my sister."

><=

The night slid before Shabane's empty eyes without even the passage of trees to mark it.

She paced for a time, soothed by the regularity of the timber floor and the relative ease of walking it. Floors had no hills to trip her body's feet, nor fallen branches or dangling vines to catch at her body's limbs. Achane had built this place all but alone, refusing to let Shabane exert herself in anything more than nailing the floorboards to the floats or carrying the lightest of boards. She had done it without ever having built anything before, but Shabane's sister, who had once had every fairy story memorized, had turned her formidable mind to studying the design of cottages both inside and out. She had drawn no diagrams but the ones that had charted out spells to hold the walls upright as she had joined and braced them; she had taken no advice on how to support the steepled roof that she had wanted so badly, and so it had fallen in on their first night in the cottage.

Achane always learned quickly, though. Soon enough, their little home had been built deep within the forest, and Achane had begun establishing herself as a swamp witch even as she had tried to be mother and father and sister and doctor to Shabane at once.

They had been Shonè and Aenikus to one another, Achane repairing the house and bringing in firewood, Shabane keeping the hearth. When Achane had been out tending the sick, Shabane had cleaned the pots and tended the garden and cleaned the house and cooked soup and porridge; while Achane had stayed up late at night reading texts on healing by candlelight, Shabane had begged her to go to sleep and stop fighting something that couldn't be fought. Achane had just raised her eyes from the scroll and said, "You're my sister."

It had been almost as bad as being ignored by Mother, except that Achane ignored her in a way that meant cooking her breakfast even though Shabane could cook for herself. Achane had ignored her in a way that meant joking halfheartedly with her instead of listening when Shabane tried in all seriousness to convince her to stop this constant hungering for a cure. It had been in many ways the happiest and freest time of Shabane's life, and yet the aches had been deeper as well.

Now Shabane walked in slow circles from the bed to the hearth, from the hearth to the doorway, and from the doorway to the bed again. Herbs still twisted amid the rafters and a little golden incense-burner shaped like a cottage sat on their shelf; all of Achane's magical scrolls and inks and candles rested safely in their box at the foot of the bed. The flood that had washed over the riverlands had not touched the cottage where the sisters had spent the last seven years of their lives, and where they had stayed even though it might have been cruel to their mother and brother in their cottage by the river or to their father, wherever he had settled.

It had been too many years since Shabane had seen the rest of her family—Achane had never much cared to see anyone but Aerus, and their mother had not much cared to see Shabane. She consoled herself in thinking that no one but Achane would want to see her like this.

Shabane looked to the bed again, where Gamela lay asleep (or pretending to sleep, as Shabane had done so many times, so that her mother would stop pretending not to watch her). The priestess's solid body looked nothing like Achane's slender lines under the blankets, and yet something of Achane showed in Gamela's eyes when the priestess was trying to be kind; something of Achane showed in everyone who fought against fate to meet an impossible task.

They didn't even know where the king had taken her. What could they do against a king, except make pleas that Achane had surely made a hundred times over?

Although the priestess's snores sounded more real in the darkness than they had minutes earlier, Shabane painstakingly drew out a chair and forced her unwilling muscles to allow her to sit. She stared at the herbs on their strings as they swayed gently in the wind, and time moved by with only their pendulum swing to clock it.

Heat. Heat heat heat he was moving heat. Cold/ heat he was moving scent scent scent rat. Rat. Rat. Rat.

Rat rat rat *that thing death smell no heat* rat.

Rat.

Burrow burrow heat rat. Wait. Wait. Wait.

Move.

Grasp. Scales earth scales earth grasp heat. He was moving heat heat rat. Air airtouch touch touch heat. Scent. Scent *death scent human scent* heat he was moving. Hungry hungry heat heat rat.

Cold. Cold. Cold. Cold air he was moving heat. Rat heat, scent, burrow *that thing death smell move.*

Rat.

Rat rat rat rat heat heat cold. Cold. Cold. Scent.

Grasp scales grasp flicker flicker flicker scent. Heat scent flicker.

That thing death smell no heat.

Scales grasp heat heat heat heat ratratrat. Scent cold. *Move.*

Snakes do not contemplate. In their reptilian brains, they process the senses and the needs of the body just as humans do, and come to many of the same conclusions; they seek the heat or the scent of prey or the den just as humans do, although we are quaint enough to call them "firesides" and "food" and "home." Snakes, though, do not pause in their travels to wonder *why* they want these things. They move with a certainty denied to humans because they do not care about such things as *whys.*

A snake sees no reason to deny himself something that he wants immediately. He will follow the rat until he has caught it and swallowed it, and then he will rest in a dapple of sunlight until the urge strikes him to find better sunlight or to find new prey.

The way to control a snake, therefore, is to place wants into its head—to trick those finely honed snake senses and instincts into desiring a thing that the snake has never encountered before; to fool it into perceiving a prey which does not exist in order to guide it onward.

As the distant ratsnake ventured through the nighttime woods and the steamer paddled ever further away, Achane wrapped her mind deeply within the snake's own mind and guided it deeper into the tree-shadows toward her own den. She had felt, as swamp witches often do, when her furniture had been moved in her absence; it was something like feeling tugs at the scalp as Shabane had braided her hair, in a time that already felt like long ago. That the furniture had been returned to its proper place instead of stolen told her that Shabane had somehow returned to the cottage, perhaps to wait for her there, and if Achane couldn't cast herself over the rail and onto the shore, she could at least send one small creature to the cottage among the trees.

She would not be returning home, but neither would she be cooperating.

That thing death smell no heat.

Achane's hands were tied. She felt grit in her eyes like sand that she couldn't wipe away without twisting her arms in the scarf that bound them; she had almost fallen asleep to the gentle thrum of the steamboat engine, but she couldn't guide the serpent if she was asleep, and so she said her prayers over and over again to stave off oblivion.

The goddess of the alligator palm sat propped against a barrel of dried dates with her eyes closed, like so many of the other passengers, but she nonetheless cracked open an eyelid at the sound of her name and nodded at the familiar words of the address.

"Terichone, goddess of the alligator palm, you who give to your people in their tribulations, I ask only the strength to love as you love and to give as you give. When my will bends as does the palm in the hurricane, let it conquer the tempest and stand straight again. When my soul is weary as the land in winter, let me find the strength to revive myself and provide of my bounty to others.

"Terichone, as you hear all prayers, hear this prayer."

With her eyes fixed on the way the faint, cloud-shrouded moonlight illuminated the steamboat's wake, Achane couldn't see Terichone move to stand behind her, arms crossed in contemplation.

Achane felt a hand on her shoulder, and started.

She looked into the eyes of a beautiful, thickset woman with her grey hair pulled into a bun; the woman had an age-wrinkled face, nut-brown but with cheeks as red as hands long lent to laundry, and she wore her skirt pinned over the knee and her sleeves rolled up over her broad, hairy arms.

Nothing in this woman must seem beautiful, for beauty is too often defined by delicacy. But for those who understand what compassion and love look like when they are ingrained into the fiber of a body—when every muscle is filled with love so that every gesture and step becomes an act of goodwill—for those people, this woman was the most lovely woman alive.

She said not a word to Achane, but only smiled at her and kept her firm fishwife's grip on the swamp witch's shoulder.

Achane opened her mouth to ask a question or formulate a greeting, but she realized as she gaped that no greeting was necessary.

Terichone did not untie her hands. That was Achane's job.

When the beautiful, aged woman returned to sit again beside the barrel of dates, though, Achane felt inexplicably stronger and more awake. The darkness seemed softer in the light of the prow lantern and the midship lantern; the path before the ratsnake seemed somehow clearer.

That thing death smell no heat.

Heat heat grasp slide scales heat flicker flicker taste. Scent. Scent. Scent.

Scent.

Wet wet wet wet wet scent grasp slide slide slide scent scent *scent, slide* grasp scent *scent.*

Grasp, slide, wet wet wet. Scent. Scent. Heat heat *scent, slide.* Flicker flicker taste.

Scent. Wet wet wet.

Slide.

Shabane didn't notice the little black snake until the light of morning came through the cottage windows. The ratsnake lay curled in the corner of the floor, a trail of black ink leading to its coiled form and pointing toward the thick bulge halfway down its length.

As the light woke Gamela as well and the priestess rose from bed to stretch, Shabane noticed the other shapes on the floor. She drew Gamela's attention with a pointing finger that was blackened at the tip from the candle flame.

They examined the black marks on the floor that the ratsnake had drawn with its own body, soaked in ink.

King took to mountain fortress.

Shabane tried to muster a smile that her decaying body refused to display.

Achane had found a way.

What makes a man a legend? In the places where human beings gather to talk of one another, what distinguishes the figure of myth from the subject of gossip?

The line is a fine one, sometimes so fine that it could be said not to exist at all.

For the purpose of this story, Gauff Staag's story, we will call that distinction Death.

Any family that lives in the depths of the grey forest, away from a holt and its communal living and communal backbiting and communal tensions, becomes immediately subject to the holt-dwellers' communal ridicule. Perhaps borderlanders considered it rude to enjoy the company of bears and wolves more than that of blacksmiths and weavers, or perhaps they feared the dark parts of their own souls that sought a woodland solitude; perhaps a man who made himself and his family Other only presented an easy target. Let it be said in the defense of bears and wolves, therefore, that neither animal rips out a man's dignity as well as his throat, nor preys on his son more willingly than on his flock.

Jeiger was his father's only child, and so he had no allies when the boys at the holt market threw stones at him. Gauff Staag had asked him once, as he waited for the tanner to tally the value of the pelts that the hunter had brought to market, whether Jeiger would like to throw stones as well; Jeiger had nodded mutinously but held his silence even when a little girl had shrilled insults at him and tossed a handful of pebbles.

A hunter's chiefest virtue was his patience. The father had told the son this truth every morning as they had walked up to the brow of the mountain to watch the sunrise, and every afternoon as they had waited for game to walk by and stood side by side on a rough platform of branches lashed together high in a tree. Jeiger's mother had often returned from a day of checking her snares emptyhanded and muttering on patience, and she and her husband had brewed herb tea together and made soup without the slightest worry that their patience might one day see them tranquilly starve to death.

Jeiger learned to pay attention to the woods, and the mountains, and the sky, for each one indicated his continued health and happiness in the solitary world of the hunter. So, too, did he learn to pay attention to the words that the other young men and women spoke at the marketplace—the words spoken around him rather than hurled at him, for even stone-throwers grow with age to prefer more subtle pastimes. In that way he learned how life was conducted where people lived together with other families, and how these people who held his family in such low regard did so because they together nursed each other's children and tended to each other's sick and buried each other's dead. They together knew each other's jokes and each other's secret loves and each other's little vanities.

It was from the gossipers, and not his father, that he learned about the white stag.

In every legend of a great hunter, there is always a white stag, and it is a colossal beast with many-pointed antlers as black as coal and hooves that leave no trace on the leaf-mould or the game-trails. Such was the beast, the furrier told his sweetheart as Jeiger listened, that Gauff Staag sought in the wilderness with a wild-eyed obsession.

Like any young hunter who has heard of a strange beast making inroads on his own family, Jeiger began to search for traces of this mythical beast on the slopes of his father's life. Such a monstrous animal would leave no spoor, no trail of footprints or droppings or scratched bark that he could read as some people read books; instead, Jeiger watched how his father's hunts more frequently ended without a kill, and how dark hollows grew under Gauff Staag's eyes like the dens of beasts. Soon, the patient hunter began taking dried meat and a hip flask of mountain ale into the forests with him and staying for days on end; the hunter's patient son checked their sunrise-watching place every morning and haunted their platform in the trees, but while he brought back deer and rabbits and wild, grizzled mountain goats to fill his mother's stewpot, he did not return with his father.

Gauff Staag came back in his own time, always emptyhanded, always shaking his head gravely at his wife and son as he gulped tea like a man parched to death. He had brambles twisted in his hair and caught in the fur of his leggings, and when Jeiger checked his father's bow, it had been subject to all manner of cold and damp and hadn't been unstrung for days.

When father and son went to the market to trade their furs for bread and fruit and fine wool, metal arrowheads and cookpots and a barrel of good ale, the gossipers whispered about the gashes in Gauff Staag's jacket of tanned rabbits' fur and the twigs caught in his sandy, tangled mop of hair and his ill-kept beard.

It was a trail that even a blind man could follow, and yet when Gauff Staag disappeared in the height of the dry season, his son did not realize it for many days.

The story of Jeiger's search for his father and the white stag are his own to know, and he has only ever told one man the details of how he tracked a madman and his mad quarry through the forests of the borderlands. The perils that he suffered, and the revelations that he received on that journey, he told only to the Weiger scholar who understood how important it is to write down stories, lest they be changed by time and retelling.

The only story that most men in the border holts know is that, a week after Jeiger Staag set out to find his father, he returned with the man's bow in one arm, the skin of the enormous white stag draped over the other, and the look of one who has seen secrets in his eyes.

In the borderlands, men and women live with lines every day of their lives. There are the lines of wire in the brush that trappers such as Jeiger's mother set to catch the unwary rabbit; there are the lines of boundaries that demarcate one holt's territory from another's; there is the all but imperceptible line between being One of Us and being Other, and when Jeiger took up residence in the border holt where his father had always sold his furs, presenting a white deerskin of surpassing size and purity to the holt patriarch and his wife, the young man who had been an outcast all his life crossed that line.

On that day, both Gauff and Jeiger Staag crossed the gossamer line from gossip to legend—the first, through his triumph over the mystical white stag that had killed him, and the second, because he had walked to the edge of the line called Death, stared across it, and returned to his fellow men.

On this tenth Day of Viertmont, 580 Years after Ascension, four Erekoi Men were killed and thirty Erekoi Men were captured full Surely by the Men and Women of the Mountains, whereupon the Border Men pressed their Advantage to an Erekoi Encampment.

The next page was smooth and blank as the future of this pale, clouded dawn; Erlen dipped his pen again in the inkpot and began to sketch the encampment's layout. His hands moved swiftly over the page, left to right, plotting each tent and cannon's placement as well as the sentry posts and the smoldering cook-fires. He had learned an unbelievable amount about how best to guard a campsite by studying his enemies.

They had been watching the Erekoi encampment since the lightening sky had suggested the sunrise, and in all probability they would continue to wait until the opportune moment came. If impatience had brought the disenchanted Weigers to the borderlands, the mountains had chastened them and made them as patient as stones.

Erlen pressed his drawing square against the page so that it covered the entirety of his diagram, then closed the figures in a tidy box and penned an explication beside the box in his smallest, neatest handwriting.

The Erekoi generally make fewer Campfires of greater Size than the Border Men's. They hold Wood over the Fires before they begin to burn the Wood, which is I think an old Habit from the wetter Lands wherein Wood is seldom Dry. If they suspect Mischief, the Erekoi set their Fires outside the Area of their Tents so that they will not make Shapes against the Flames for Archers to target.

He had not yet diagrammed the campsites of the borderlanders; in the back of his mind, he knew that such information would one day be used against the people whom he loved like mountain air.

Erlen breathed deep of the rough scent that had gotten under his fingernails and into the grain of his pen, earth and blood staining it darker in his hands than the blackest ink could. It had been a gift from his advisor, Master Tuefweil, who had pressed the wooden pen with its metal core and nib into the hands of a scholarship student who could afford nothing more durable than goosefeather quills. *I traveled to write my treatise, too, and you'll have need of a pen that's difficult to break when the world is trying to break you. See that you keep it capped, lest you stab yourself.*

"They'll be least prepared after dinner," said Marla the knocker, breaking into Erlen's reminiscing. "They'll be gathered around their cook-fires in the daylight as though their circle strategy protects them in the day."

"We'll have to take them from the trees—they're bigger than we are, even surprised," replied Jeiger, who leaned against a tree with his elbow braced on the rough bark. "They have two cannons, and the first crossbows we've seen since the warring began, as well. I hadn't thought the Erekoi *had* crossbows."

"They learn, like dogs learn to carry," hissed Marla against a piece of jerky that slipped in her tight-clenched teeth and made them click together. The borderlanders couldn't risk a fire for either warmth or light, and certainly not for cooking.

Had Erlen been drawing their current position into his book, he would have first drawn a cross-section of the land on which they stood—the site of the Erekoi camp first, a comparatively flat stretch of land dotted with scrub at the top of a small hill, with the sheltering slopes of the hill descending like the feet of the letter *neibrig* on either side. Those illiterate in Weigengraff, who would not know *neibrig* from any other letter, must instead be content with imagining only the shape of a hill into this hypothetical diagram, for pictures are the oldest and clearest form of writing and have a power that transcends the walls of languages.

While the *neibrig* hill rises on the left or the west of the page, the valley to the right slowly grows and rises again to a taller hill all covered with thick evergreens and stones painted with pre-literate humans' doctoral dissertations. At the crest of this hill dips a small, invisible gully, hidden behind branches like hands over a child's eyes.

Draw into this small depression in the sloping diagram five figures, and you will know more than the readers of Erlen's book ever will of how borderlanders stage an ambush.

"How long will they camp here?" Erlen asked; he had brought a spyglass with him over the plains, and now it worked in the service of the resistance. "We may not be able to afford to wait until dinner."

"They won't break camp very quickly," answered Jeiger; Erlen made a note on a loose leaf of paper. "See the tents? They've taken time to drive the supports into the ground and weigh down the edges with stones, and they've set up a hanging rack for their cook-pots. Look—the sentry just coming off watch has tied the horses to a new tree for fresher fodder. Even if they'd begun breaking camp by now, they wouldn't be able to leave before noon." Jeiger smiled at the quick scribbles that danced across Erlen's page; he knew that his name was listed as an author's on the front page of the book because Erlen had read it aloud and explained what the symbols meant, but hunters didn't need to read anything but the land. Erlen's sigils and symbols and words meant only ink on paper to him

Ink on paper, or blood on his palm, when he had no ink for writing; the ache in Jeiger's missing finger hadn't gone away, no matter how many times he stared at the place where it had been. The sigil had stopped the bleeding but not the hurting, and, watching Jeiger rubbing the knuckle, Erlen mentally vowed to teach the man to write a healing sigil with proper penmanship. A few changes to the shape of a word could also change its meaning, and in the meaning lay the spell itself.

"What are they waiting for?" Erlen muttered, looking up from his careful script. "There's nothing here for them.

They may as well be up north in the Great Bowl, fighting Weigers." He didn't think it strange that he could refer to his countrymen as though they had no connection to him at all.

Marla looked up at all four of her companions, and her eyes traced the hill behind their gully.

"Nothing, perhaps, but us."

The hillside stood empty of all but trees and a lone, lost goat, but Jeiger walked only slightly less ill at ease for knowing it. His earlier reconnaissance had shown him none of the familiar signs of Erekoi invasion, none of the roads of wooden planking for carts or the scents of strange spices rising from the cookpots; there was nothing here to defend and nothing to conceal.

Erlen's book rested sheathed in his satchel, and he crossed his arms over his chest with his fingers hidden in his armpits. Whether this was reaction to the morning chill or commentary on the lost digit of Jeiger's hand, Jeiger didn't much care to discover, so he leaned over the long-ago-illustrated stones with Erlen's spyglass in his hand and peered at the Erekoi encampment.

Breakfast was being cooked now around the encircling fires, where the uniformed Erekoi prepared for morning with the same sleepy efficiency of the men and women of the holt. The sight had always drawn a sad sympathy from him for the people whom they fought, even though he seldom wondered any longer if the Erekoi looked on the borderlander preparations with the same reflective eyes.

He had respect only for a code that said, *First, kill no one who has't tried to kill you.* Whether or not that was one of Death's secrets, he didn't care to discover, either.

A hand that he knew as Erlen's touched his shoulder, so Jeiger passed him the spyglass.

They both knew how much harder capture was than murder of the unprepared. So, too, did they know the relief of clear consciences when they released their Erekoi captives to walk naked as the just-born to the nearest fortress, clear of any blood that would have clung to them like a caul.

Jeiger was a hunter, though, and he could reconcile himself in time to the necessity of destroying a predator so that it wouldn't destroy his prey. He could, in time, justify the killing of Erekoi, who came to the mountains only when they wanted to rip out chunks of coal or iron ore, silver or gold, and so disrupted the ways of life for every existing predator or prey-beast or human living in the borderlands. It would ache to think of other men as unreasoning beasts that did not know the profundity of their incursion on this land, but he could bring himself to do it with time and a slow hardening of his heart.

But Erlen was not a hunter—he was a scholar, and Jeiger still remembered the way his face had looked the first time he killed a man in battle. They had never spoken of it to settle the morality or immorality of the idea, but Jeiger watched the other man as they talked often enough to know when guilt drew a shutter down behind Erlen's eyes. It had since become easier, he thought, but never easy.

"The big one has come out of his tent with his lieutenant," Erlen whispered. "Can you read their lips?"

"Not when they speak Erekoi—not well, at least."
With that, though, Jeiger took back the spyglass and pressed
it up against his eye. "The next book we write will have to be
a book of languages with Weigenspeich and Wig and Erekoi
all in lines, so that they can be learned at once."

Although his ears were still slow to understand the unfamiliar Erekoi language, it did not matter at such a distance;
Jeiger could nonetheless make out a few words by the way the
lips moved, in conjunction with the way that the arms flailed
and gesticulated.

One word was "copulate" and another was "whore,"
and that the lieutenant was both angry and a woman made
the words a harsh joke at the expense of the commander.
Soon, though, the lieutenant's tight, goose-hissing posture gave
way to a straight-backed speech with words like "move" and
"watch" to give clues for the content of the conversation.

The commander didn't seem like what he heard, but
perhaps the "whore" conversation could be faulted for that.
Whether a man is being called a whore, or called the son of a
whore, or being called to task for attempting to make one of
an honest woman, he seldom enjoys the accusation.

In a few brief gestures, the commander sketched
out the borderlanders' stretch of the mountain and a long,
straight line to the north. His mouth cried a "set out" that
Jeiger couldn't hear, and the rest of his words vanished away
in a silent cacophony of the lips.

A month ago, Erlen and Jeiger had learned to pay
no attention to gestures of purpose. They had spent too long
in escaping an Erekoi fortress to risk such a heedless expedi-
tion again based on no more information than the advice of a

pointed finger and a particular twist of the lips.

In the depths of the Erekoi stronghold, the concoctions that had been meant to make them talk had instead made Erlen babble that the stones of the fortress had voices and screamed out for the mountains from which they had been hewn; he'd shouted that they were asking him to heal them and to take them home. Jeiger still remembered that the first time that he had trusted Erlen enough to take him in his arms, the Weiger had been screaming incantations that had made the air shimmer with the force of his hallucinations.

Better not to listen to the voices of stones or false men.

"Wigs," said the commander, and turned away—perhaps consciously, to block his telling lips from sight, perhaps not. A borderlander was a Wig, a bastardized and demystified Weiger, both in the slang of the Erekoi and in the border self-conception. The word was an insult, a bland commentary, and a badge of pride all in one. It was the first word that anyone had given the borderlanders to name themselves, and so they clung to it as their own.

There was no more to be had from the commander and the lieutenant, so Jeiger abandoned their conversation to search for others in the spyglass's scope. When it became clear that no one else was speaking in the enemy camp, he checked once more for signs of departure, collapsed the spyglass in disgust, and gave it up for a bad job. "Go take a turn, if you think it will yield anything," he whispered to the others in the gully. Marla rose in his stead to take the glass—Jeiger spared her a grateful glance for taking a post that his unease made him too impatient to fill.

He had done too much thinking on things other

than the coming attack. That in itself worried him, and some combination of sense-memory and instinct and hunter's training made him feel as partway-incomplete as a man who'd forgotten his own name. A piece of his full picture of the forest was missing.

"I'm going back into the woods," Jeiger told the others. Erlen nodded at once and rose to follow.

His mind rested uneasy, and when a hunter's mind rested uneasy, there was a dangerous beast in the woods.

Every landscape is the unexplored body of a new lover; its curves and contours, its flat places and hollows are different from every other's. Many hasty humans choose a loveless relationship with their land, living on it like indifferent husbands and wives in arranged marriages; some take what they like from the earth's giving body and leave the despoiled land behind.

Some lie quietly, their hands pressed against the curves of their land, and listen to the echoes of footsteps on the earth's surface like little fingers tapping skin.

Erlen watched the hunter incline his head against the slope of the hillock, well aware that he should be scanning the trees around them and nonetheless frozen by the scene.

He watched as Jeiger gently touched his ear to a stone half-buried in the leaf-mould. The world condensed to that soft and slow contact, the motion of the head against the breast to check for the expected heartbeat.

With more fierceness than was perhaps wise or necessary, Erlen forced his eyes to the trees. All of the shapes around the pair were the same regular shapes of the trees and the stones, like columns and couches in the Husmann's palace; all of the movement was the same gentle movement of leaves brushing leaves and branches tracing the outlines of other branches.

No flicker of a bird; no furtive twitch of a squirrel's tail as it sought to avoid being seen. Only the expanses of grey-brown bark across the slope.

Erlen suddenly understood why Jeiger had insisted that they return to the woods. He could not decipher the meaning of this unnatural quiet, and yet it made him so wary that he all but startled when Jeiger rose from the leaves and stones. His face had grown grave in the half-shadow of the trees.

"Let's go to the outcropping that the others checked," he whispered, as intimately close to Erlen's ear as he had been to the stone on the ground and as quiet as whatever he had heard there.

They moved across the leaves, ducking the fallen limbs and extricating themselves as they went from the brambles' embraces. Erlen had by now ceased to be amazed at Jeiger's easy footfalls; Jeiger had by now ceased to be annoyed at Erlen's lack of woodland grace.

At the crest of the hill, both glanced instinctively over their shoulders to assure themselves that the camp was well-hidden from view from above, and they smiled briefly as their glances met.

The downslope was at first more steep than the slope to the hill's crest; after the arduous slide down the first treach-

erous armspans, though, the land relented and curved gradually to a rocky outcropping under which Marla and the others
had searched earlier. It had seemed a decent campsite when
first they had scouted the mountain, except that the entire
front lay exposed to the mountainside before it.

Jeiger didn't lead Erlen underneath the outcropping;
instead, they filed carefully around it, down the thin, mostly
flat sliver of a goat trail.

When they were on the leeward side of that ceiling of
stone and peering into its shelter, Jeiger stopped in the shadow of a rock and took a deep breath.

In a moment, Erlen realized that the other man was
scenting the air, and he pressed himself deeper into the shade
of the outcropping. He could feel the roughness of the stone
through the cloth of his shirt, as well as the peculiar coldness
of untouched rock.

Jeiger closed his eyes.

Erlen tried to catch hold of whatever it was Jeiger
could understand from the air, what shapes the scent of
leaves and rock and animals made on his mind—he who
wrote down everything that he found important and noted
patterns and images tried to enter an ephemeral, unwritten
world that was as barred to him as his own world of letters
was to Jeiger.

He felt Jeiger's hand on his own and ducked closer
to hear what the other man whispered. It was only one word:
"Goats."

Then Erlen looked closer at the rock floor under the
outcropping, and for the first time he noticed the goat droppings scattered about. Faint as a whisper on the light breeze

came the caprine aroma of dung.

Goats did not travel alone, in Erlen's admittedly in-
complete experience. That solitary goat that they had seen on
the mountain, sojourning apart from its kind like the stragglers
of the borderlander herds, had to mean more goats nearby.

Jeiger sketched something unintelligible on his palm,
and Erlen shook his head at the shape that Jeiger had drawn
with his fingertips. Shrugging in agreement that this was a
poor diagram, Jeiger instead led the way further down the hill
to where the thickest trees stood near a thin trickle of a stream.
They no longer followed the goat path, but this time edged
along above the path of the streambed as it carved between the
grey, painted stones.

The two men paused where the stream dropped off
into a filmy waterfall that fell gradually down a stairway of
stones, and Jeiger scanned the woodlands once again.

Perhaps it was the conductive powers of the water or
the way that Jeiger's cheek twitched at the half-heard sound;
perhaps it was just the scent of animals that had grown suddenly stronger around them, even though the change was only
perceptible because Erlen had begun paying attention.

Perhaps it was the cartload of coal that sat concealed
in a thicket, guarded by two Erekoi soldiers and surveyed by
Jeiger with closed contempt. A blankness had come over his
eyes like the blankness of the hunter gutting his kill; he had
begun to eliminate the elements of humanity from his quarry.
Across the valley, a goatherd led his flock to the green pastures
that presumably lay beyond the shelter of the trees; the men
who stood ostensibly watching the coal cart instead watched
the herder depart and laughed quietly between themselves at

some joke that Erlen couldn't hear. He concentrated on the soft splash of the stream that fell away beneath him, but his mind was consumed with another sound altogether.

The faintest clink of hammers imaginable rose from the ground, and the great, gaping hole of a mine lay bare against the ravished earth of a mountain.

This is not one of those stories in which the heroes dramatically dupe the guards of a secret underground lair, sneak into the bowels of a mountain, and foil an evil plot. Such tales thrill the part of us that longs to set out on adventures, and yet most people who enjoy adventure stories wield no weapon more dangerous than a kitchen knife and meet no guards without the general alertness required of a tollbooth operator.

Adventure stories are well and good, but ordinary people such as Erlen and Jeiger do not trust their personal prowess enough that they don't worry what might happen once they're *within* that coveted mountain fastness. So it was that the two of them retreated cautiously, but not hastily, to the relative security of their little crevice in the earth on the other side of the hill.

"A mine—here!" whispered Marla, less in incredulity than in indignation. Her long, brown braids hung down between her ears and the ears of those who crouched beside her; they gleamed like polished wood in the dull light of early morning. "We should have guessed. Why else would soldiers that looked so ready to pack up on an order be so *entrenched* here?"

Jeiger nodded assent, his close-cropped hair brushing Marla's left braid. "They'll have been keeping it quiet, putting the coal carts on the roads from their other mines so that we might not find this one."

One of the other men, whose name Erlen couldn't remember, touched two fingers to the ground. "It takes a long time to build an operation such as this. Odds are they've guarded it more carefully since our raids, and we won't have a frog's chance in a furnace of storming it. We're only five."

The five of them sat in long consideration of that truism.

Of all of them, perhaps only Erlen understood the difference in war-making between the Weigers and the borderlanders and the Erekoi. Somewhere in his loose leaves of notes lay two paragraphs that he had committed to memory a month ago, when first he had killed an Erekoi man in battle.

The People of our Land (by which he meant Weigers) *customarily wage War by the destruction of Property; this is, I think, a direct Result of the magical Strategy practised by our People. The Weiger method involves Infusion of Magic into Symbols (viz. Sigils, Circles, and the written Word) so that the Caster be not drained by the Practise. To destroy a magical Working, one need only destroy the Symbol. The Erekoi therefore seem Barbaric to such People as ourselves owing to a* Love *of* Killing, *which is, I think, also related to their magical Methods. The Erekoi use Symbols only to* imprint the Spell upon their Selves, *and thus the only Means to break a Conjuration are two, which are Persuasion of the Mage or Killing of the Mage.*

The Border Men are something of an Hybrid between

the Two in that they infuse their Spells into Symbols *and also* maintain their Magic by the unified Design of the Whole, *therefore, their Means of War is to disrupt the Unity of the opposing Force.*

The paragraphs lay unspoken in the recesses of Erlen's mind; he didn't like what they imported—if he and his friends chose to storm the mine, they would be killed. The Erekoi wouldn't think, "Oh, we must disrupt their spells!" because no one really thought like that; they'd simply follow the strategy that they had followed for perhaps hundreds of years. Weiger universities held dozens of decrepit textbooks from the first days of Erekoi settlement, and even the colonists back then had been murderous before they'd settled down and intermarried with the local communities. The children of those colonists had stormed the Weiger-held land to the west of the Great Bowl, massacring the territory's old masters and driving out those they didn't kill out of hand.

If the Erekoi worked best through persuasion and killing, then—

"I have an idea."

The borderlanders looked over at their scholar, who hadn't been engaged in this war as long as they had and didn't know the forest as they did—who, only three months ago, had been one of the white sheep of the Weiger family, before he had dyed his wool to mingle with the inveterate black sheep of the borderlands.

Marla peered over at him from behind one shining braid, and the man whose name he didn't know studied the way his fingers pressed against the ground. Jeiger, who could read minds no more easily than he could read books, cast a heavy-lidded frown at his companion, but quickly smiled to belie his misgivings.

The last of the borderlanders—a woman whose short, white hair was barely visible under a scarf and whose eyes focused on the world through a network of wrinkles—looked Erlen over. Her name was Eppa, and she was the keen opposable thumb of the group of five.

She nodded. "Tell us."

Erlen reached behind him for his satchel and from the cracked leather case withdrew a book that he hadn't written: *The Wayes and Custommes of the Ereckoy.*

There was more than one way to skin a cat, as the popular saying reminds us, but what would one do with a dead, skinned cat? Like cats, human beings are far more useful alive and with their skins intact.

As Erlen explained his strategy, Jeiger covered his mouth with his hands to hide his smile and Marla suppressed her laughter only by biting her soft leather bracer.

Eppa laughed like the mountains—low and deep and all but inaudible.

≥≤

Kemaeros had been told since his youth that his eyesight was uncannily good, and the compliments had puffed his childish ego up like the chest of a bird about to break into song—until, of course, his attempts to find gainful employment with his eyesight had sounded a harsh and displeasing note. The goldsmiths had found no use for a boy with well-honed eyes and enormous, clumsy fingers, and so Kemaeros had been passed on to the town militia to train with a bow.

When the arrows had shattered one by one on the stone of surrounding buildings, splinters flying into the streets of their hill-town, the militia had been forced to concede the boy's utter untrainability. It had made a very grave youth where once the puffed-up boy had been, and Kemaeros had taken to watching people and following them to see how they used the pouches at their waists or their daggers with the mesmerizing filigree.

Soon enough, those in the town who had trained their eyes in the same way had begun to notice quiet Kemaeros's habits. They had followed him with stealth honed through long practice, until the young man had learned how to watch for stealthy movements as well; they had followed him through the city and into the forest until Kemaeros had learned how to sense a man with dark intent even when he couldn't see a man at all.

When at long last Kemaeros had shuffled into the town watch's office, haunted-looking and grim with dark circles from his cheekbones to his eyebrows, to report someone following him, they had laughed and opened their arms and embraced him.

From that day on, Kemaeros was a watchman, and he was the best watchman on the force.

From another never-to-be-forgotten day mere weeks ago, when one of the watchmen had come back to his familiar cobbled streets in the back of a cart with his right arm missing below the elbow—from that day on, Kemaeros had taken his post guarding a concealed mine in the mountains.

Long years of waiting for the world to need him had

made Kemaeros a devout man, one who prayed to Loukaros
every day to lift the storm from over his head and allow his
life to flourish like a field after the rain season. The devoted
know that Loukaros is only the god of war because war is the
swiftest way to change the world, and Kemaeros understood
that he was a stronger man now because of the years of despair that had marked his life. He knew that this trial-time,
too, would strengthen him and his people, but the idea was
hard to remember when missives came daily from other encampments to report Wig attacks and comrades humiliated,
wounded, or even killed. Today, as he watched the forests
for any trace of man, he prayed for the god of the hurricane
to bring the lightning and the high winds down on the Wigs.

The goatherd led his flock through the valley again—
a long stream of grey and brown bodies and the shine of
eyes and the curving shapes of horns and crooks—just as
Kemaeros caught the faintest glimpse of a pale flicker from
the corner of his eye.

A naked man rose from the stream to stand at the
head of the falls, hands on his hips, straddling the stones
and the thin sheets of water that washed down from the top
of the hill. Although no one but Kemaeros had eyes keen
enough see it, the naked man smiled before he stepped down
from the height.

Naked men had never entered the general watch
training procedure, except as a necessity of communal living
with one's fellow watchmen. As this man placed his feet carefully in each separate pool into which the water fell, following
the course of the stream to each indentation in the stone that
caught it, Kemaeros thought he knew why.

The man's hair was almost white and fell long about his shoulders; his skin was as pale as new cream against the dark stone and moss of the hillside. As he reached out to steady himself on the stone, the man revealed the pale hair beneath his arms; even the hair at the juncture of his legs was pale. Every movement that this man made seemed at once cautious and assured; every glance or smile seemed designed to project benevolence over the watching guardsmen.

As the nude man came closer, Kemaeros could see designs inscribed in white clay on his pale chest—they were letters in Old Erekoi that read *Please lift the clouds from our land* and *O ye who guides the tempest, send our village sweet and gentle rain* and even, plainly, *Loukaros, slay our enemies.* A white scar in the shape of a lightning bolt raked across his shoulder, over his collarbone and halfway down his chest.

All suspicion that this man was a bathing Wig fled. Kemaeros could only tap his fellow guardsman's arm with one trembling finger and point, because the pale, pale man had reached the stream and stood ankle-deep in its cold waters.

With his eyes like eagles' eyes, Kemaeros could see the slightest pattern of chill-rash on those ankles—but the gods, he had been taught from his youth, came to man in the guise of man, with all of man's frailties. Even Loukaros of the storms, who chose to visit the camp in the shape of a pale, slender man with prayers written on his chest just as they were written on the statues in the god's hill-temple.

When Loukaros spoke from the shallows, fish darting swiftly about his narrow feet, there was no guard or miner or carter in the camp who did not hear him. Even the goatherder leaned on his crook to listen to the words of the god personified as the benevolent godly visage clouded over with fury.

"Stand still, and hark ye to the voice of Loukaros," he said in perfectly unaccented Old Erekoi. Loukaros had been one of the gods from the motherland, and so, perhaps he was obstinate in his refusal to adapt to the change of the language. *"In this place thou dost the work of the king, and yet thou displeas't the gods."*

Kemaeros felt a cold chill run through him like the stream in which Loukaros stood.

"We shall destroy this mine and all who remain in it!" Loukaros shouted, pacing now closer to where Kemaeros stood. His eyes burned pale, pale blue, the uneasy shade of the sky that shows intermittently through stormclouds, and his face was afire with hate. *"By sundown tomorrow, thy works shall be drowned with the fury of the storm; the mines shall fill over with the waters of this stream in which I now stand!"*

The miners began to whisper amongst themselves behind their guards as the god stalked steadily closer across the fallen leaves. He did not seem to know or care that he was naked; he did not brush back his flowing hair from the angular planes of his face.

He was not beautiful, for his cloud-whiteness marked him an alien thing, but in his movements there was a kind of terrible power like the sharp, jagged bolts of the lightning.

"Thou may'st leave this place tonight and be spared; thou may'st leave this place on the morrow and be dogged by disaster; thou may'st remain here, and be drowned. It is not for the gods to choose how man meets his own doom."

With a few steps, Loukaros would be close enough for Kemaeros to touch him—would his white flesh be cold as the autumn rains? Would those so-human-seeming muscles yield no more than stone under probing human fingers? Without thought, Kemaeros backed away.

Loukaros closed the distance swiftly; he raised his fingers to the sky and drew an arc downward like a descending storm. Seemingly to Kemaeros alone, he whispered, *"Thou hast been warned."*

And all of an instant, Loukaros turned on his heel and strode back into the stream. The waters closed around his ankles; silence closed over his head; he disappeared into the trickle of water even before he had left Kemaeros's sight, and the watchman studied that retreating, ghostly shape until it had passed beyond even his magnificent vision.

That night, the miners disbanded their camp.

Jeiger wrapped a blanket around his naked companion and clasped their hands together to warm him; for the first time since Jeiger had lost his finger, Erlen didn't appear to notice the absence in his haste for warmth.

"Did they believe you?" asked the borderlander. He set to toweling Erlen's cold, wet feet dry as the scholar wiped the clay prayers from his chest and shivered.

Despite the chill, Erlen smiled through his chattering teeth. "They didn't chase me, if that means anything."

Jeiger smiled in return, standing to press his wind-raw cheek against the pale cheek that had so stymied the Erekoi. "You're a very god come down to the land, and you bless me in your presence."

"You flatter," Erlen laughed, for a real friend tactfully directs his sarcasm away from the cold's effect on the more mortal and less godly aspects of a naked man who has just spent several minutes in a cold stream.

The blanket scratched at his sides; his feet ached with cold, and yet Erlen found that he couldn't stop smiling at the thought of the guards' faces. When Jeiger handed Erlen his clothes again so that he could dress, he felt warmer than mere clothing could have made him.

It does not serve a man well to impersonate a god so close to Erekos. On the seashore and in the mountains, where Loukaros holds court, the storm-eyed god is always watching the patterns in the clouds for the weapon he needs or the gift that he might bestow—and when the time is right, he seizes it from the storehouses of the sky and goes walking.

This time, he carried a staff of white cedar, and the sap ran over his pitch-dark fingers.

Loukaros is not a pale god, for white gods bring only destruction to credulous believers who have waited lifetimes for such a deity to appear. White gods bring with them pestilence and war and disillusionment, and of the three, the last is often the worst.

For all his rages, Loukaros loves and tends to his people as often as he smites them.

Loukaros has skin the color of thunderheads at midnight, and he moves so stealthily that not even Kemaeros could perceive him. Certainly, Erlen and Jeiger did not see him circle their meetingplace as he felt the soft forest earth with his staff.

Certainly no one watched him ascend to the hilltop and reach his sap-stricken staff to the skies, and no one could have seen the grim grin on his face when the blow he struck sent a faint ripple speeding across the skies.

The storm-god is the god of war as well, and he can be petty in choosing his enemies.

chane had finally gotten to sleep on the steamboat's thrumming deck; she lay curled up on her side against the wood planks with her head pillowed on her scarf-bound hands. All around her, the birds were beginning to wake to the hint of sunlight over the mountains; they sang abbreviated snatches of tunes like drunkards wandering home half-asleep.

Terìchone didn't need to sleep, so she leaned against the railing to watch the slumbering swamp witch and thought of old stories.

Storytellers will often tell you that there is no tale without conflict. That there is no story in which suffering does not take place, because humans have an unholy fascination with suffering that makes happiness bland without pain to counterbalance it.

In some of the hill-towns of Erekos, though, where the ways of life are settled and the children are occasionally as innocent as they look—where dozens of families still gather around a communal hearth and break bread together as their tale-tellers design their characters against the wood and stone of the walls—in these places, there is one tale with no hint of suffering in it.

The storytellers don't withdraw this tale from their memories before midnight, when the room is warm and the fire is dying; when the early winter winds creep through the cracks in the mortar and mothers shiver and pull their shawls closer about their shoulders, only then do the story-tellers sit back on their chairs and say, "Let me tell you a happy story."

The gathering breathes out softly, like a collective sigh.

"In the times before Erekos was Erekos, when it was the wild land of a gentle people, Shonè and Aenikus went by different names but shared the same hearthstone. They lived in the mountains together, and every night, they shared their bed; every morning, they woke beside each other."

When the husbands and wives who are listening hear this part, they always touch each other's hands, even if they have spent the last night apart and the last day fighting with each other. They are half-asleep already and have forgotten this morning's urgent squabble; they smile at each other with the half-ashamed expressions of truce.

"Shonè walked three times around the house to be sure that it needed no repairs, and then she walked through her garden, casting life from her skirt like seeds. The garden grew strong with corn and beans, which Aenikus cooked ev-ery night in a pot that he had forged himself. They lived sim-ply but happily together, bestowing the grace of the fire and the hearthstone on their gentle human children."

By this time, the human children around the fireplace have fallen asleep in piles like kittens, or with their heads resting against their parents' knees.

"In time, new people came to the land that was not Erekos yet, and by the time they reached the hills and the children of Shonè and Aenikus, they were peaceful and loved the children of the gods. In time, these new people married the gods' children, and they became the sons and daughters of the gods as well."

Some of the faces in the audience are paler than others, some browner, but none of them look like the faces of the conquerors or the conquered because those two faces had melted together long ago. The people of Erekos do not mind the differences in their shades or their faces very much, even though some families will not marry their daughters to paler sons while other families seek out paler in-laws. Although the statues of Shonè and Aenikus that the hill-people carve of smooth-grained, dark wood still bear a greater resemblance to their native ancestors, some of the newer gods bear long-forgotten conquerors' noses on their marble features. The priests have never forgotten that Loukaros came across the sea with the pale men.

"When Aenikus and Shonè found the lands of their family expanded to the shore, they decided to visit the house that their children had built for them on an island far away— and they liked it well, and still visit it when their children fill it with the sounds of home."

The fire always crackles for a long moment before any of the audience stands from the warmth of their chairs;

the scent of woodsmoke drowns out the smell of cold that
sneaks through the chinks, and for that instant, not one of the
people in the hall feels less cheered than melancholy.

Then they stand. They say their goodbyes, they warm
their hands one last time over the dying fire, and they leave
before the spell can be broken.

At last, the storytellers are the only ones who are left,
and they read the future in the sizzle of a pocket of sap in
one branch on the fire; they smoke pipes and they eat the last
crusts of bread and drink the last sips of wine, and they study
the atmosphere of an empty room. A kind of devastation is
always present in a room that had been full and now stands
dark and empty; those who remain crouching in corners and
picking up scraps always carry a kind of guilt like that which
survivors feel.

The storytellers don't ask one another what it means,
that people shy away from the only happy story in the world
just as they shudder and shrink from the cadences of sorrow.
It isn't a question that they dare to ask.

Why is it that people are so unwilling to lose themselves in unadulterated happiness? Does it make them suspicious? Does it make them hesitant, scanning the storytellers'
faces for some wrinkle or glimmer in an eye that will make
clear The Catch? Are human beings simply incapable of be-
lieving in perfect joy?

Must even the gods suffer in order to make themselves truly real?

It was almost dawn on the steamboat, and Teìchone
knew that she would have to pass the swamp witch into other
hands before long. The hills where Shonè and Aenikus had

first lived would be harsh, but they had been harsh for the young gods as well; harsh places were not always unhappy. Indeed, the home of the gods had been a very, very happy place to grow up, even though the work had been hard in the days after the great flood had made every survivor terrified and suspicious.

The echo of the turning paddle wheel sounded against the hollow trees and shook the last of the snakeblossom vines, and below decks, the king was stirring.

Terìchone's people needed her in the swamp and the shore lands back down the river, and Achane had not yet learned how to untie herself.

Achane woke to a rush of white cloth against the mist-draped trees, and she threw herself to her knees quickly enough to see the descending grey hair of the woman who had touched her shoulder the night before.

It looked so very like a suicide—but as the woman had vanished into the dark water, Achane could have sworn that she had been laughing.

The king and his entourage arrived in state at the capital, in an open carriage drawn by four grey mares; a bugler sounded a trumpet to announce the arrival of the monarch, the guards on the capital walls rolled down gaily-colored banners leaping with rampant pumas and swaggering rams with curving horns, and even the sun peered out lazily through the high-noon clouds to see whom the children cheered in the streets.

History will determine whether King Milaus becomes a heroic or a villainous figure; history may or may not remember that he plucked a young swamp witch from the very doorstep of a temple and dragged her away from her dead-and-walking sister. In time, the texts of Erekos may even forget the zombi army that grew and raised weapons and marched in the fastness of this king's mind. So much of the truth becomes lost in the retelling and the revising, and it can never be reclaimed.

Be not so quick to judge him, therefore, and remember that on this day, the people of Erekos ushered him home with cheers.

The capital never gets called "Telessa," although that is its name; like a monarch for whom "the king" suffices, Telessa goes by "the capital" throughout Erekos, and no one mistakes the high-walled city on the river for any other.

One who has never stood on the hills and peered down at the capital's limestone fortifications can scarcely imagine the impression that the blue-grey stone makes as its walls straddle the young river and the mountains rise green and purple behind it. The road to its gates winds through the hilly farming country that stretches between the forests of the swamp and the forests of the mountains, and at one hill that has been called Dead Man's Hill since before the capital lost its name, the pathway widens in an overlook that affords a view of the river valley.

The capital itself rests on an island that rises out of the river's widest tributary in the shape of an enormous eye, with the city for an iris and the king's palace like a pupil in the very center. Hundreds of years ago, when kings had still built temples to their memory, some ruler whom history has lost had built a great limestone wall along the riverbanks. It bordered the river on the outer banks and spanned the width of water with stone arches, beneath which stood a row of enormous floodgates. Those floodgates now regulated the flow of water over the paddlewheels of mills and small factories on the fringes of the city, but long ago they'd thwarted the last of the maritime Weiger invasions. The only passage from the banks to the citadel was a drawbridge that was rebuilt and refurnished with each new king's crowning.

To the watchers on Dead Man's Hill, the capital was a marvel of cloud-grey walls with the river dashing whitely against the feet of those walls, a wonder of breathtaking scenery and excellent military planning.

The watchers on the hill, though, had never paced the parapets by lanternlight, as Milaus had; they had never run their fingers along its stone balustrades worn smooth from hundreds of years of touching hands, and they had not seen moss grow in the chinks between the stones over the gates. As the king passed under the first gate with his own carriage under him rather than a swamp-country post-chaise, though, he had no eyes for the children who laughed and threw their hastily gathered wildflowers in his path; neither did he have any patience for the gaily fluttering banners that reached down over the limestone walls and danced with a circus of heraldic animals. His mind was on cracked mortar growing thick with moss, and he rode with one hand on the decorative rail of the carriage and the other clenched at his side over the aching scar of his old gut-wound.

Since the Weigers had been driven from these lands, they had never yet come over the mountains to attack Erekoi strongholds—never more than they had in the past few years, the Wigs worrying his flanks and destroying his fortifications—and yet Milaus could not forget the way his horse's hooves had pounded on a different drawbridge far to the north; each beat had driven the shards of iron embedded in his flesh just a hairsbreadth deeper as his brother Adriolaus had shouted for healers to attend to the heir.

There had been moss on the stones of the Weiger fortress, too.

Strange, how that moment in time remained last of all his memories of that campaign.

On the other side of the carriage sat the swamp witch, whose name he still didn't know and rather feared to know; she held her tongue as she had since her capture, even though her face had grown thinner and slightly more lined and her many thin, dark braids were beginning to fall loose. Ilaumeleus had taken her meals and fed her painstakingly with dried fruits and bread dipped in gravy; she had eaten only a few mouthfuls, in silence, and let the adjutant wipe her face with his handkerchief after each inelegant bite.

As a prisoner, she was ideal; as a sorceress, he had already seen her worth.

The king waved at his subjects and smiled, and the queen cast her eyes demurely downwards so that the people wouldn't see the frightening intensity in her gaze. Ilaumeleus practically stood in the driver's seat of the carriage, and his laugh rang out over the crowd at each flirtation or familiar face.

The houses passed around them as the current of the crowd drew them inexorably closer to the city's center; the feigned smile, as familiar to the king as breath and sleep, grew to a jubilant laugh that echoed Ilaumeleus's; the celebratory flowers were slowly trampled into the cobblestones and abandoned there. The gates of the castle opened for Milaus and his queen, and they spilled into the courtyard trailing commoners like river weeds waving in the wake of a steamboat and catching in the paddles. Grooms came to return the king and queen's horses to their proper stabling and to lock the carriage safely away, and guards came to remove the swamp witch to quarters that were simple, tasteful, and utterly inescapable. Ilaumeleus bowed and begged leave; the river of bodies rose to a peak of flood, and as suddenly as it had touched the courtyard's full capacity, the flood dispersed through a hundred minute channels of doors and passages.

Milaus and his queen linked arms and walked across the flagstones—in silence, in mutual agreement, and in state.

When Shabane had survived eight summers and her mother had grown resigned to an invalid daughter, her father had taken her through the swamp to a river-town and boarded the two of them on a steamboat.

It had been more than ten years ago, but Shabane's soul still remembered the way the engine had thrummed like the greatest great cat ever birthed, its reverberations shaking the deck. She had coughed at the clouds of coal-smoke that the still air had draped over the passengers, even though the smokestack had been cleverly positioned to keep the worst of the smoke from the passengers' eyes and noses. Her father didn't notice how she had pressed her fingers to her mouth to soften the sound; her family had grown used to her coughing.

They traveled across the water as though on the back of an enormous, purring beast, and Shabane held tight to her father's hand as the speed of the ship and the current drew them down the river to the delta. Daughters of the grove had passed the steamboat by in instants where they might have lingered for long moments if Shabane had walked beside them; their long, leafy tendrils blew grey-green in the wind.

Father and daughter were going to look for a healer again.

She couldn't remember how long they had waited on the deck for the delta to meet them, but when they emerged into the watery fields and the rice paddies, the sky was a clear, bright grey. The steamboat engine had stilled, and in the comparable silence of the paddle wheel slowly spinning to a halt, Shabane caught her first and last glimpse of the port-town of Palamea. As soon as her eyes fastened on the spire of the meeting hall, her father put his hands over her eyes and whispered, "Don't be afraid."

He had wrapped her up in her shawl just as Gamela was even now wrapping her up in a warm cotton jacket and a pair of skirts to hide the decay of Shabane's body.

Shabane's father had carried his young daughter off the steamboat and through the streets; she had heard bartering and laughing and carriage wheels on cobblestones all around her, but none of this had really *meant* anything to her ears. The only sound with meaning was the beat of her father's heart against her cheek and the rustle of his clothes against her own as he shifted her weight; the only feeling that mattered was the tight, slimy feeling in her throat that she had never been free of in all her eight years.

Finally, Shabane's father had shifted her over to one arm and knocked on a door, then called out a name in a voice like need and fear all at once. The hinges creaked, and her father carried her inside and set her down on the floorboards. He shut the door behind them, and Shabane looked around herself for the first time since her father had covered her eyes.

Shabane first of all saw the tall, olive-skinned woman who took her father's hand and drew him to her breast for a welcoming embrace. She watched as her father kissed the woman on both cheeks; he enfolded the woman's thin fingers in his own sturdy, dark ones and gave that woman a look with more love in it than he had ever shown anyone but his children.

This woman, Shabane always remembered afterward, wore her hair entirely covered by her long, black healer's shawl. Witchcraft was a serious business in a part of the world that needed healers, and so witches learned to be practical and healers learned to be even more so. It didn't do to dip one's hair in either medicine or vomit or shit.

The woman had bent down to study Shabane's eyes; she placed her shawl-covered ear against Shabane's ribs and her slender fingers against hers back and asked Shabane to breathe deeply, then to cough, then to hold her breath. She asked Shabane to bend over, to spit on a thick and shining leaf, to go to the latrine cup and fill it up.

Each time, Shabane had complied with a kind of terror of making a mistake, until the healer finally told her to sit quietly on a rug and wait. Her father came to hold her hand as she cried—her tears just as quiet as the woman desired her to be. The healer cast her a sad and hurting glance over her black-shawled shoulder, her thick eyebrows drawn together into one long, questioning line, but Shabane's father shook his head, and the healer returned to her vials and potions and urine.

After what might have been moments or an eternity, in which the rug had grown warm with the radiated life of Shabane's father, the healer had knelt before them and pressed her mouth to his ear. He closed his eyes and listened to the slow stream of rustling syllables that the healer had passed on to him until silent tears moistened his lashes, but he blinked them away and nodded over and over again.

His hand held the healer's and made pale spots on it where he pressed the flesh too hard.

Finally, Shabane's father had leaned back and pressed himself against the wall, his eyes still closed and his tears unshed. He pressed Shabane's hand with his as his fingertips touched the healer's, and there the great man sat, broken.

No cure existed, in herbcraft or in prayer or even in magic.

Now, with the priestess Gamela's heavy hands straightening the healer's shawl over Shabane's body's shoulders and concealing her face and hair much as the black shawl had concealed the healer's hair long ago, Shabane could remember her father's face as clearly as though it were drawn in the same ink that still stained the floor from the ratsnake's writing.

Later, her mother would scream at her father to leave their house and their family for his healer whore; the sisters would pack their few belongings and set out to build their own home in the swamp, with Achane supporting her ailing younger sister every step of the way and constructing a house alone for Shabane's comfort; their younger brother would watch his family slowly vanish as their mother stroked his thick, black hair and whispered endearments.

Now, with her second steamboat voyage mere hours

away and another kind of healer tending to her dead body,
Shabane remembered the last words that her father's healer
had said as she had wrapped up a decanter of medicine that
had been meant to soothe the hopelessness of a grown man
more than the sickness of an eight-year-old girl.

*"Your body is a vessel for your soul, and one day you
will realize how much stronger is your soul."*

he woman who came to treat Achane wore
the black shawl of a healer, draped to cover all
of her hair as well as her neck and lower face,
and yet she used no medicines that Achane knew. She untied
Achane's hands for the first time in two days, and left them
untied for the first time in four; her dark face grew grave at
the bruises on Achane's wrists, but she only ran her fingers in
patterns like vines across the knots of dark flesh and watched
the purple shadows fade slowly.

The healer untied the sashes and laces and pins that
held Achane's clothes on her body, and the witch shuddered
at the chill memory of the queen's hands on the pins of her
skirt and petticoat as that cold woman had undressed Achane
so she could urinate. She remembered the grey-brown eyes of
the queen assessing the bruises on her legs, so different from
the gentle sympathy of the healer's fingers drawing snakeblossom patterns across the wide, purple bruises on her thighs.

"How did you get these?" the healer asked; she didn't look up from her work, and her black shawl hid her expression.

Achane tried to speak, not realizing until her tongue touched the roof of her mouth and stuck against the raw dryness there that she hadn't spoken since the king had told her his purpose. For a moment, she stood working her tongue against her dry lips. It gave her space to find an answer.

"I tried to go home," she said at last.

The vines of the healer's spells sunk their holdfast roots into Achane's skin and twined up her legs to her arms; she could almost imagine leaves brushing her face as the healer's fingers did, clearing away the damage of days of travel like old bark. She felt her body become heavy; the weight embraced her, until only the spells held her up.

For the first time, the healer met Achane's eyes, and hers were a pristine shade of blue so incongruous in that dark face that they seemed windblown flowers against the silt left by flooding. "What else is wrong?" she asked. "My work can't cleanse you of all that ails."

My sister is dead, bloomed the thought in Achane's mind, but she cut it away as swiftly as it grew. "The king took me from my sister," she whispered instead to the healer. "She needs me."

They contemplated this together in the quiet splash of the basin of warm water that the healer pulled closer; every time the healer's dark hand dipped into the basin to wet a soft cloth, Achane remembered Shabane's last, wild steps and her fall into the shallow pool left by the storm. She remembered the king's army of zombi as the healer washed away the vomit still crusted on Achane's plaited hair.

The water cooled quickly in the light breeze that came through the arrow-slit window, and the hairs rose on Achane's legs where the healer's cloth had cleansed her. Far away, someone opened and shut the door to Achane's house; it felt like a mouth opening for a breath.

Achane wondered, in this hard, stone room furnished with deadwood and the wool of many-years-gone sheep, whether this hill-country healer felt the changes of each part of the castle in her marrow. She wondered if this castle could be the healer's home.

Her hands were still numb from the bindings, and yet she felt the pressure of the healer's hands on her own. The healer didn't speak. She didn't try to sully the pure quiet of the stones with excuses or sympathies or even true comfort; she only rubbed Achane's palms with her fingers until the blood began to rise from its sluggish riverbeds and fill her veins. In the healer's blue eyes, there was no trace of the snakeblossom vines or the dendrove trees or the pumas that always lurked behind the eyes of a swamp witch; only the faint silhouettes of eagles and tall pines reflected in the woman's dark pupils. Fish appeared to swim for an instant in those clear circles like both sky and water, and yet they were not the flat-bodied river fish that Achane's father had brought home from his days in the canoe; these sleek, slender creatures darted like arrows in the mountain tarns.

They were two very different women, Achane knew, and when the king at last decided what he wanted to do with her, they would inevitably stand on different sides. And yet... and yet, they had the same speaking eyes and the same touch for healing bruises, for all Achane wrote her spells in neat,

angular script across the bruises to impress the magic on
her mind while this healer drew vines and leaves and bud-
ding blooms on the wounded skin with her fingers. For all the
healer didn't free the swamp witch, neither did she bring her
greater pain.

"You may change into some fresh clothes now," the
healer offered, pointing to the neat stack of what must have
been another set of hill-country clothes and a healer's shawl.
"Or, if you prefer, you can sleep. The king will wake you
when he wants to speak with you."

"Do you know why the king wants me?" Achane
asked it without thinking, without judging whether it was a
wise question to ask. She asked with the perpetual innocence
of one who has never had spies at the walls, listening for every
hint of leverage.

The healer had long since lost such illusions. "I don't
know, nor do I want you to tell me. The king has done many
noble deeds for our city and our people, and he must've
brought you for a purpose." She straightened to her full
height, just a few inches taller than Achane; her eyes were
unlined by time, and the river of experience had not yet worn
deep grooves across her forehead, and so she might have been
said to be young. Her eyes, though, reflected a world as old
as Achane's.

Achane bent to the pile of clothing, whispering thanks
as she did. Without looking further at the woman in the black
shawl, she crawled into the white jacket and the heavy brown
skirt, and then she draped the black healer's shawl inelegant-
ly over her fraying braids, pulling the loose end over her left
shoulder to her neck.

The test passed, even if it had not been a test, Achane sat on the edge of the bed and rubbed her wrists gently with her fingertips. She smiled bitterly at the shadowing folds of soft, black cotton over her arms and remembered that her father had left her mother for a healer woman; she could never forgive him for it, but neither could she forgive her mother for refusing to be healed. The woman had cried every night after she'd thrown her husband out, and she had denied the doctors and witches and healers their turns at Shabane's bedside until Achane's sister had lain wasted and ashen on her pallet.

No, Achane could never forgive her mother some things. But neither could she wear a healer's shawl without a deep, sick feeling in the hollow of her chest.

The healer pressed her palm against Achane's shoulder and whispered, "Terìchone bless you." The blessing fell as warm about Achane's ears as the healer's hand resting on the smooth, dark fabric of the shawl; in mutual contemplation of the wood of the floor, they stood and sat together.

Achane nodded to break the charm of their contact and breathed in reply, "Shonè and Aenikus guide you home."

It was a long time after the healer departed that Achane curled up under the thick, close-woven blankets and shivered herself to sleep.

The shawl fell from her brow as she slept, and a single silver hair glistened in the light that spilled through the arrow-slit window.

hose people who keep an exact accounting of days will notice that we have left Erlen and Jeiger unattended for an entire day; we laughed as they drove the miners up from the cold, black earth, and then we dropped the two of them like woolen gloves discarded in warm weather.

While we weren't watching, Erlen put on his trousers and his wool stockings and his woolen shirt and his jacket, then he laced each boot properly so that it wouldn't chafe his feet for the long walk ahead. After they had examined the mine in the glow of left-behind oil lamps, guessing at its depths and its usefulness to the Erekoi, Erlen and Jeiger had returned to their encampment and watched for a time as the soldiers who camped on the little *neibrig*-shaped hill took down their laundry and packed up their cookpans. If Jeiger had been able to speak Erekoi or if Erlen had been able to read lips, they would have known that the soldiers were even then anticipating Loukaros's lightning bolts.

Instead of watching them, though, we watched Achane on the steamboat. Because of this, we didn't see the borderlanders break their camp and walk across the hills to the higher northern mountains where they had their holts; we didn't see how Marla the knocker-woman and Erlen and Jeiger spent the entire night and all of the next day walking from the longhouses in the forests to the proud mountain cave-holts as rain poured down around them. They passed a night without sleeping so that they might reach the very northernmost and very southernmost holts; we have ignored their travails.

Perhaps it was best that we didn't watch the border-landers as they began to converge on one long hall in the hills, for there is no novelty in grizzled, bearded men walking to discuss weighty matters. The hand over the forehead to shadow lined and deepset eyes is nothing new, nor is the herd of goats that cannot be turned over to the conniving neighbors and so must be brought along. Every proper council of war has "an old man in a battered hat who leaned upon a thorny staff"—this one merely has several dozen who do not like or trust each other very much but love their world's nations less.

We will not be allowed to speak here in the great Mittler Holt where these men meet to shout at one another. Our voices wouldn't fill the longhouse to its high rafters or touch the roof of shakes, but this is for the best. The holt-holders love their own voices too much to listen to us, anyway.

When the holt patriarchs and their goats and their attendant sons and daughters had at last settled around the central fireplace and begun to argue in earnest, the oldest old man rose to his leather-booted feet and stepped onto the armchair that his grandfather had carted across the mountains a hundred years ago—his bald, tanned head didn't gleam in the firelight, but his light green eyes did.

He was Gaerthe Mittler, most recent and longest-reigning patriarch of the Mittler Holt, and if he hadn't decided on a cold winter day twenty years ago that the Wigs needed to shape up and stop snubbing one another, none of the other holt-holders would have been there.

"Our comrades over there," he began without introductory harrumphing or hallooing, instead merely pointing at Marla and Erlen and Jeiger as the instigators of the gathering, "Our young comrades got all of us collected together to work some holt-magic, and so they would serve best to justify themselves in that request."

Erlen stood, grasping at protrusions on the wall and levering himself up on Jeiger's shoulder, heaving toward the spiraling smoke and the droplets of rain that spilled through the smoke-hole. Marla clung to the wall at their side, hand braced on a beam.

Erlen had never before been to a meeting of the holts, and as several dozen squinting eyes fixed on his own dark hollows, he swayed with inexperience. "The holts closest to the Erekoi lands have been fighting Erekoi invaders for almost a year. The Erekoi work daily to build new fortresses in the mountains from which to launch attacks against us, without meeting with the holt patriarchs to parley or even sending challenges to the holts. Our holt, Brogen Holt, has moved its children, its aged, its herds and herders, and some hunters and farmers to the forest so that they won't be found while

our fighters hold the buildings. And why do the Erekoi fight
us? Why do they build up garrisons in our land?" he asked, as
though those who had not fought could answer.

"We think it is because they have mines in our lands
that they would give their own lives to protect. Two days ago,
we found a mine down in the Ridges. It wasn't on our maps,
and the Erekoi had hidden it well—probably for over a year,
judging by the wear on the support beams. We convinced
the miners to clear out, but we have no idea how many more
mines there are in our mountains. We have no idea what kind
of effort it will take to clear the Erekoi from our land."

The weathered, windbeaten Wig elders exchanged
significant glances and puffed on their pipes at hearing a
man who spoke with a Weiger accent, but called the mountains "our mountains" and the land "our land."

Jeiger looked to his own holt patriarch, who sat with
Eppa, his wife, on the pelt of the enormous white deer that Jeiger's father had killed and that had killed Jeiger's father. Jeiger
was a legend and the son of a legend, a fourth-generation citi-
zen of the mountains, and he had spent every morning of his
life looking east to where the sun rose over the forsaken motherland; he dared every holt-holder to blow sarcastic smoke-rings
at him as they had at Erlen. "The Erekoi want our mountains
for the coal and the ore. If they can't get their mining done here,
they will have to move on to some other mountains, and they'll
leave us alone. We want to find every mine and every fortress
in our mountains and shut them all down, one by one—to find
them, we want to work holt-magic."

The gathering did not grow silent at this pronounce-
ment, for such a gathering is never silent; Eppa whispered

fiercely to her husband, and three patriarchs conferred in a corner, hissing their responses to every suggestion and gesticulating frantically with their arms. Sons and daughters knelt to gain their fathers' ears, and over the rustle of whispers and coughs and cloth agitated by harsh gestures, the goats cried plaintively for their homeland. Gaerthe Mittler watched the subdued chaos from his seat upon the armchair of his ancestors, serene in the knowledge that this one was well and truly out of his hands.

At length, in the center of the room, the northern holt-lord Halgirth pulled himself to his feet with his enormous, fur-clothed arms crossed over his armored chest like two hunting dogs lying asleep in front of a barrel. "We in Halsgard watch the Erekoi and the Weigers at war in the Great Bowl beneath our mountains," he proclaimed; the dry rasp that had crept into his booming voice hinted at his love of the pipe. "The Erekoi are great killers, and where they don't just blow the Weigers down with their cannons, they put the heads of defeated soldiers atop their standards when they leave a battlefield victorious. They've taken and retaken the Weiger forts along the border of the Bowl a dozen times since I became patriarch of Halsgard; we see the puma and the ram flying over the ramparts almost as often as the Weigenland wolf. How is it that your little holts in the forest have fought the Erekoi so handily, when trained Weiger soldiers fall before the Erekoi guns?"

Eppa laughed her low, deep mountain-laugh as she helped her husband to his feet. The years had been unkind to his body, which trembled like a struck drum and made his voice shake. "We've had a lot of luck, and some good tactics," he said as loudly as he could, which was still so softly that even the goats grew quiet in order to hear him. "Our young men and women," and he touched his wife's wrist as well, "have fought like cornered cats, taking only the targets that they could see their way clear to defeating, and making a good deal of sacrifices to stay disciplined against the Erekoi.

"But most importantly," he continued, "We've never had a full army against us—only patrols, small garrisons, sometimes up to forty in an attack. The Erekoi are too busy with the Weigers in the north to turn a full army to us, and I shouldn't like us to face a full army."

Gaerthe Mittler nodded and gestured to Halgirth, directing the conversation back to the northern lord.

The patriarch of Halsgard blew his lips like a horse, then uncrossed and re-crossed his weighty arms. "I fear if we become a bigger enemy than the Weigers, we may face a full army—all of the holts against a full army, and not just the four or five holts now holding the borders. This we might do by threatening their mines, for all they *are* on our land. Better, perhaps, to negotiate a treaty, with the Husmann's grace and the Huswife's blessing."

"We're not a sovereign nation in the eyes of the Erekoi and therefore cannot negotiate a treaty!" shouted Erlen, and all eyes turned toward him.

It was not the time to summarize his classes in international politics; neither was it the time to be making claims that he couldn't explain. Instead, he took a deep breath and reached into his satchel for *The Wayes and Custommes of the Ereckoy.* Those sitting close enough to see leaned in to peruse its pages, and those against the walls leaned back with expressions of skepticism.

"The Erekoi feel that these mountains are *their* land," he said, opening the book to the map in the center and holding it up just as Master Tuefweil had done a lifetime ago in a building like a cathedral, where knowledge was worshiped above even the Husmann. "They draw their maps with their border following the mountains—on the eastern side, well past our lands. By their laws, we are invaders in their land, and the only treaty that they would negotiate with us would be over how quickly we need to leave their territory."

He paused to let any holt-holders who disagreed formulate a response; when only resentful whispering ensued, he continued, "Erekos has nothing to gain by negotiating with us except a temporary end to hostilities, and every one of us knows that it would be temporary—as soon as the war with the Weigers hit a lull, the full force of the Erekoi army would be in our mountains to wipe us all out."

Jeiger clasped Erlen's wrist with his four-fingered hand, picking up the thread of the argument. "The time to force out the Erekoi is now, while the Weigers have them occupied up north. Get them out of their fortresses and their mines now and force them to move on to a new place, and they'll be so firmly planted elsewhere when the war with the Weigers dies down that they'll have no interest in our lands."

For perhaps the first time in their twenty years of meeting, the holt-holders fell silent.

Because almost all of them were old men, almost all of them had attended the first meeting of the holts in this very longhouse; some had been holt patriarchs, and others had come as strong-armed first sons to ensure that their holts were prepared for the brawl that they had expected. All of the men gathered here, and most of their children, knew that no person could ever lack interest in the neighbors, whether those neighbors were the next nearest holt or the next nearest nation.

Every patriarch in Mittler Holt knew that even the bold strategy that Jeiger Staag and the Weiger at his side proposed would only postpone the next confrontation; not even the hands of the gods could *prevent* it.

Better, then, to postpone the confrontation to a time in which the enemy's fortresses were in Wig hands and his memories of his neighbors made him wary rather than cocksure.

Halgirth of Halsgard broke the silence first, twisting it to pieces in his heavy hands even as he said, "Be it a fool's errand, I'll be a fool. Halsgard will work holt-magic for you."

"As will Mittler Holt," said Gaerthe Mittler, standing from his armchair.

Like the raindrops that pelted the roof, the cries of assent came; the three patriarchs in the corner hissed yeas even as Eppa called a yes for her husband, and over the voices of dozens of patriarchs, the goats raised their voices as though they, too, wanted to draw the magic of the world through the community and into one great purpose.

For when the holt patriarch speaks, he speaks for the goats as well; he speaks for the men and women and children, for the sheep and the fowls penned up in his holt, for the turnips and onions and mushrooms and potatoes in the ground, for every smithy and potter's wheel and chapel and home under his hand—he speaks for the whole of his holt, from the ground to the heavens. The patriarch's magic comes from the

assent of the community, and the community is so very much
more than the sum of its people.

In the thrum of anticipation, Gaerthe Mittler paced
to the wall of the longhouse, where a thick, woolen curtain
hung. He drew the curtain aside with his long fingers, feeling
as he always did how heavy the cloth had become over the
twenty years that it had hung on the wall of Mittler Holt.

In the light of the fire around which the holt patriarchs
and their followers sat, shadowed by every gesture and every passing body, a great vellum map of the mountain holts stood illuminated. On the far left, Halsgard had been inscribed in heavy ink
and placed with an X at the border of the Great Bowl to the north;
on the far right, another X marked the domain of the Stettenbourg
clan, at the very last crag remaining before the mountains became
hills in the south. Somewhere in between, amidst the falls and
the encampments and the Erekoi mountain fortresses, an X represented the longhouse in the mountains where the holt-holders
gathered even now—an X labeled *Mittler Holt*.

Each patriarch sat or stood in contemplation of his
own X, of the name that had long ago been inscribed above
it and the clan for which those little marks stood; some patriarchs couldn't read any words but the ones on the map that
spelled out the names of their holts, and yet they knew those
letters so well that the curves of them entered their dreams on
tired, aching nights.

Every patriarch remembered every person and beast
and building and garden in his holt, and in his mind, each
sank down into the earth and rose up into the sky and filled
himself with the voices and tastes and smells of home in order
to bring the entirety of his holt into the circle of holt-holders.

Somewhere in the crowd, a daughter began to beat a drum; somewhere else, a son began to hum a low and lonely tune of home, and the goats muttered uneasily as they did when their herders brought them into their pens for a storm. They could feel the power brewing in the air even before the hairs began to stand up on Jeiger's arms.

Jeiger found himself whispering the words to a song that his mother sang as she peeled potatoes and dressed meat, and even Erlen let his precious book fall from his hands and instead only stared to the east as though he were remembering the first sunrise that he had watched in the land that he loved. Marla sat cross-legged, tapping her foot on the flagstone floor of the longhouse as though she were pressing the treadle of her too-long-neglected spinning wheel, as Eppa stroked her husband's hair and whispered to him about their children.

Around each holt patriarch coalesced the idea of home, until the entirety of the borderlands took shape within the longhouse and the circle of the spellcasters.

Gaerthe Mittler's youngest granddaughter brought a box of white chalk to the map, and one by one, the patriarchs came to take a piece of chalk from her and draw the X's of mines near their holts. Each felt the way the earth thrummed in resonance with the gardens and the people who worked them and the foundations they dug into the ground, and he knew by the alien echoes of Erekoi metal and Erekoi men in the earth where the mines had been laid.

For what might have been an hour, the patriarchs stood and made their marks and sat again, until the shadows of homelands began to fade away and the home songs began to die around them.

At last, in the plain light of the Mittler Holt fire, the patriarchs and their people beheld the chalk marks of invasion on the yellowed vellum of their lands.

Secure in the knowledge that, for the first time in months, other people would willingly take on the formulation of strategy, Erlen, Jeiger, and Marla slipped out of the longhouse, across the rain-whipped road that cut a ledge in the mountain's slope, and to the sanctuary of their beds.

he troubles inherent in finding a mountain fortress—a particular mountain fortress, containing a particular person—were too many to number. Gamela knew full well that a fortress kept watch over each of the major mines in the mountains, which made three that she could locate on a map with reasonable accuracy; another two had been designed to bridge critical valleys in the south and prevent Weiger invasion, and a final, towering edifice in the southern hills kept guard over a long, curving wall of thick limestone that might have been meant to keep the Weigers out and might have been meant to keep the Erekoi in. All together, that made six fortresses that Gamela knew existed; there were also a good half-dozen fortresses and garrisons in the Great Bowl which changed sides between the Erekoi and the Weigers according to the tides of war, and the towering Fortress of Storms that guarded the Erekoi side of the Bowl.

The first trouble, therefore, was discovering how many other fortresses existed, and so Gamela flirted with the steamboat captain and tried to make him forget that she was rough-skinned and only beautiful if beauty were measured in compassion. She tried to make him forget that the black shawl she wore hid her body from forehead to waist and made her only one more anonymous healer, torn between the floodplains of the south and the northern battlefields.

Steamboats carried soldiers, and so captains might know where those soldiers were bound.

As she kept half an eye on the corpse and the rest of her gaze coquettishly lowered, Gamela wondered again why she hadn't given up the search for Achane. Terichone knew, so many people in the swamp needed her efforts more than the witch did—even the corpse, who wrenched at Gamela's heart with her steady refusal to lie down and die, needed her less than the flood-wracked.

And yet, in the corpse's insect-eaten eyes, Gamela saw her husband's sightless gaze questioning her from beyond death, and she remembered the coldness of his hands in hers as she had begged him to come back to her. She remembered how a long night of weeping and pleading had made her eyes ache, and how, in the end, the body of her husband Nereus had staggered deliberately to his coffin and lain down inside, drawing his shroud across his face.

She remembered letting him go, and the memory reminded her why she couldn't abandon Achane or her sister's corpse.

When Gamela was reasonably certain that the steamboat captain had no more to give her—and he had given her precious little but heavy-lidded stares and sneers with his thin lips drawn in a straggling beard that couldn't hide his receding chin—the priestess of Terìchone bought two tickets and a livestock pass for the northbound trip, thanked her goddess that she had come just before the scheduled time of departure, and shifted her shawl to cover her shoulders more warmly as she led corpse and mule onto the ship and got the mule settled in the livestock berths of the lower decks.

The breeze from the river was chill for this time of year, and a long, grey evening stretched ahead. Across the clouds flew formations of birds, startled from their perches by the heady throb of the engine coming to life; the shapes of wings rose to meet the pale midday sun like hands raised in prayer, but the distant congregations drifted slowly away when the thrum of new life resolved itself into a dull, mechanical groan.

They'd been lucky to buy passage to the north, when the entire world sought to escape Loukaros's early rages; even the steamboat itself was a kind of blessing, for by the wrenched-looking ropes where once lifeboats had hung, it had met with the storm as well. The lifeboats were gone from their places, too, although Gamela didn't know why—the captain ran a high risk, cutting loose his lifeboats and then taking so many passengers. Gamela kept her arm linked through the corpse's and thanked Terìchone that she had been given the foresight to wrap that decaying face up well; although no covering save a blindfold could hide that the girl's face had no eyes, the long, black cloth wrapped over her rotten mouth and nose and her thin, brittle hair at least concealed the extent of the blight.

The shallow-drafted steamboat pressed surely against the current and toward the mountains that birthed the river. Around it, the land began to heal.

Broken boughs still shone whitely against the moist bark of the dendrove trees, but the dazed birds who hadn't known where to rest when their nests fell spinning to the earth now jostled, shrieking, with their hospitable neighbors; just-fledged hatchlings chased one another through the still-proud branches of the daughters of the grove without knowing that the empty space through which they now flew had once held the daughters' crooked, moss-twined fingers. A few snakeblossom vines were sending out new shoots as they had in the wakening seasons, and the tender tendrils clasped the sure, rough spurs that lined the bark of the alligator palms.

The world built itself anew, in different shapes that were no less pleasing than the last, and the fallen boughs became home to ants and termites and eventually dissolved into an effusion of moss and soil and toadstools at the feet of the trees.

Gamela listened without hearing to the hopeful whispers of the job-seekers headed to the cities and the craftsmen coming back upriver from repair work in the delta with bags of cutlery and well-wrapped plates under their arms for their troubles. Even the poorest Erekoi knew how to be generous in gratitude—sometimes more generous than those who had more to give.

A man shaded darkly copper-red from decades of drinking in the sunlight pulled a straw hat over his sparse, grey hair and smiled at the women in their black shawls. "Done with 'n work down south?" he asked, and in his raw voice the coast echoed like waves against stone. Gamela dipped her head gently, checking the fold of her shawl across her neck even though she had no cause for modesty. The coast-man nodded, laughing a little into the mist of rain now soaking his hat and resting in diamond droplets on his hair.

"My family still lives down along the river, tryin' to forget that they ‹ns were once children of the coast. They dun't always mix right with city folk, but they en't got the sense to go home." He caught a question in Gamela's eyes and laughed again, staring out over the riverbanks where cautious deer startled from their splay-legged crouches and leapt from the water with their white tails flashing at every cough of the engine, interrupted in their drinking by the great alligator with sails and smokestacks. "And why am I away from home, eh?" he asked the trees. "Very good question, that 'n. Very good."

He smiled with the benevolence of the wise or the mad, looking through the trees to the mountains that lived miles and miles beyond them. "As well to ask why you en't at home, or why she en't at home," the coast-man murmured, whistling the sibilant sounds like a bird of the sea. He smiled, a grin with three teeth missing and two rotted at the front, and Gamela realized that his skin had always been a warm, comfortable copper—even before the sun had burnished it. "As well to ask why none of us can rest easy when we get uprooted."

To banish the unnerving openness of the man's black eyes, Gamela turned her gaze to the dull waters and the wake that brewed behind them; she watched bobbing waterfowl follow the boat with their legs paddling as though they expected bread from the passengers, but soon the larger paddle left the birds behind.

A flash of white at the riverside caught the priestess's eye, and she glanced up; only a stand of alligator palms stood where the white flash had been, though, and Gamela breathed out to realize that she had only seen another startled deer.

The steamboat pulled away from the alligator palms, and Gamela took the corpse aside and helped her to sit against the rail. She lowered herself down beside what remained of a woman, shawled in black and shrouded in skirts, and took out the prayer scroll that had guided her to Terìchone long ago. With one arm up to shield the papyrus from the gentle rain, Gamela began to read.

Above her, the old coast-man smiled into the stand of alligator palms where just now the goddess Terìchone's white skirt had flashed, tugged his hat brim, and nodded once.

He was going home, anyway. He could afford to watch two lost souls on his way.

Morning carries with it a kind of gravity that the sunlight knows how to wear; as that great, distant colossus looks on, the world turns its head for a glimpse of that burning glory. For a moment as long as a day, the world, too, shares in that glory—its rivers made magnificent and golden by the first light of day and transmuted into silver at high noon, its forests caressed by the benevolent hand of majesty and made green and brilliant. Even the high peaks raise their stern faces to feel the warmth of the sun's presence, and behind them suddenly flow black cloaks lighter than gossamer but utterly impenetrable.

Morning is a myth-time, a time when the world awakens at once and becomes its best self, and so men have long followed the world's example and awakened with the dawn.

When men turn the world upside down, though, they cannot be blamed for waking while the moon holds court over a bony, pale land that rests uneasily. Erlen's eyes opened on this dark world when the wooden clock in the guest lodge called two bells past midnight; although he had slept only six hours to replace the dozen that he had sacrificed, Erlen felt inexplicably awake. Although he didn't know it, the sound of the long rain pausing for breath had told his body half an hour ago that the world had changed, much as the impending dawn had nudged him to wakefulness every other morning.

A long shaft of moonlight fell through the smoke hole to illuminate the stones a few paces from the fire pit, and the contrast only made it clearer that the fire had died down to mere coals since last it had been tended. Erlen slid one leg out from under the blankets, casting a quick and guilty glance back at Jeiger still asleep on the floorboards.

Without a second thought, Erlen belted on his short sword and his hunting knife. Defense had become habit long ago.

He laced his boots and pulled on the fur-lined jacket and waterproof satchel that he had bought three months and a lifetime ago, and while his companion slept with the peace of one awaiting morning, Erlen walked through the pool of moonlight and into the night.

Although the rain had abated, the night sky lay blanketed in clouds above him. The moon peered down at the rooftops of the holt like a half-open eye, lazily regarding the shakes and shingles and silvering the thin smoke rising from the meeting hall's smoke hole.

Every pool of collected rainwater threw back the moon's image; every thin and wavering column of smoke caught her light and became a pillar in her palace.

The light that spilled under the doors and through the

shutters of the meeting hall told Erlen that the holt-holders were still awake and making weighty plans; he shunned their designs and went walking up a thin path that wound through the sparse and wind-twisted trees.

It was perhaps a trail that goatherds and shepherds walked, their animals trotting single-file up the path of stone and packed earth at sunrise; it was perhaps a trail that lovers followed to hard but secret beds amid the mountain's moonlit stones. Tonight, it was Erlen's trail, and it bore him steadily closer to the cloud-shrouded moon. Even when the way grew overgrown—even when it ceased to be a pathway, but only such a winding track as a lost lamb might follow into the jaws of a mountain wolf—Erlen walked surely and unafraid to the bare summit of the mountain.

In the deep quiet that came to a place devoid of trees and unknown to night-birds, in a moonlit night empty of the rising sounds of life from the holt below, Erlen sat among the high mountain stones and looked down across the valley, to Mittler Holt, to Erekos, and beyond.

The holt seemed a mere collection of huddled kittens from this vantage like the moon's; each indistinct building's shape exhaled filmy breath into the chill air and slumbered on, unaware of any watchers above. Erlen hadn't known how precarious the placement of the holt was before now; he could see from his perch that it balanced on the only stretch of flat land on this mountain, and that the cartroads that had been cut into the mountainside dropped away sheer at every ledge. The twisting, turning road that he had walked so easily yesterday morning seemed suddenly as threatening as lightning, a perilous zig-zag of switchbacks that dropped

from the sky to the feet of the peaks, or rose up from the base
of the mountain to the smoke-clouds.

And beyond that—Erekos.

Erekos, he thought, and laid *The Wayes and Custommes of the Ereckoy* on the stone before him.

Land of rivers and swamps, land of gods; a savage
people lived there, the Weigers told themselves, but a savage
people possessed of the secret of steamboats and cannons
and enormous mechanisms to operate fortress doors. A savage people who did not stop at the fortress doors that they
conquered, but instead dashed inside with their broadswords
waving and their eyes wide as they hacked the surrendering
defenders to pieces.

A thesis was a lonely thing, when pitted against the
reality it attempted to describe.

The nobles and merchants' children at the university
had disdained to attend lectures on the Erekoi language because they had felt that diplomacy with such a savage country could only be fruitless—but while they had studied natural
philosophy and ethics, Erlen had been one of five students
to study the vocabulary and grammar of the land across the
mountains. At the time, he had only meant to keep himself
out of the war a little longer by delaying his Great Work, but
Master Tuefweil of the shrewd political judgments and the
flawless Erekoi had plucked the scholarship student from the
bored young aristocrats in the advanced language class and
made Erlen his favorite.

Master Tuefweil had understood Erlen's inability to
make friends with the well-heeled students at university; he
had understood how a young man might have become so dis-

enchanted with his country and its laws and its people that he really had no desire to give his life for that country. He had understood, and he had pointed Erlen gently towards study of the migration to the mountains, and he had explained gravely that the borderlands were a far safer option for a man who could speak fluent Erekoi and who studied politics, but who also didn't want to politick himself into an early grave with his Great Work. The Erekoi might give a Weiger scholar an all-too-personal education in mechanical instruments that would leave him changed forever—perhaps changed to a corpse.

In the moon's quiet company, with the worn limestone summit around him and a light, misty rain beginning, Erlen could forget what the Erekoi did with those cunning mechanical instruments in the bowels of their fortresses. He could forget how the stones of the fortress had screeched for healing, had begged to be returned to the mountains from which they'd been hewn, even as his own soul had screeched for the cold wind that drew the mistfall in whorls around the trees below him.

Jeiger told him afterward that, in his madness, Erlen had drawn sigils in the air that filled the room, and this did not surprise him at all. Every part of his own aching body had wanted to heal the mutilated stones.

He ran a thumb across the thick scar across his collarbone that scrawled its way down the slope of his chest just as the road below him scarred the mountainside, and he didn't think about how he had received it.

A sudden jolt of white light made him leap back; in his surprise, he slipped on a rain-slicked patch of stone and felt his legs fly out as he tumbled down the long slope, scrabbling at space with hands as blind as his lightning-dazzled eyes—

—an eternity later, his fingers caught on a branch, and even though his arm screamed at the contact as his body hit the mountainside, he didn't let it go.

When at last the afterimages of a scar across the night sky had faded, Erlen dared to open his eyes to the darkness and moonlight.

He had fallen four times his height from the summit of the mountain to a stunted tree rooted in the rocks; his hand grasped the trunk as his body lay across a river of broken stone. No bones seemed to be broken; the sliding scree had been kind to his falling limbs.

Erlen levered himself up from the wet rock shards and carefully returned to the summit. Rain lanced down in earnest now; the last, failing moonlight picked out the water-filled gullies in streams of silver that warned him of his own precarious footing.

At the top of the mountain, the renewed rain had already soaked into the charred remains of The Wayes and Custommes of the Ereckoy. The lightning-struck book had burned fast and hot at the center, fire consuming the words and rain dampening the ash. For a long moment, Erlen stood in contemplation of the knowledge that had been irretrievably lost there; something rose beneath the knotted scar on his breast, but it was neither rage nor grief nor fear. It made him think of the anticipation for battle and the heaviness afterward. It made him aware that he was utterly alone.

As the humbled scholar heaved his lighter satchel onto his shoulder and began to make his way down the mountain again, Loukaros smiled from the darkness. His thunderhead eyes followed the pale flicker of Erlen's hair;

his smile, too, was dark in the moon's pale, echo-glorious court. Only the god's lightning-tipped fingers glittered like smoke and silver.

Over the capital, the castle bells tolled two hours past midnight. The clappers were muffled for the night, for only kings and criminals are awake in the small hours of morning to hear them, and neither cares for the time.

Although Loukaros was even then lying in wait for a young man on a mountaintop, we mustn't imagine that he wasn't watching the capital city as well. The storm god's eyes are everywhere the wind touches the brow of the earth: in the citadel and in the untrodden lands far out of the reach of the two muted tones of the castle bells.

Tonight, the king rested uneasily in his library with accounting ledgers spread out before him across a grand desk of dark, heavy wood. While the queen reviewed the progress of the Weigenland war in an armchair, a porcelain lamp throwing her eyes into shadow even as it illuminated the reports that she read, the king tried to make sense of the war's

cost. The value of plunder, he knew and understood; the cost
of outfitting units with decent gear was a necessary expense
to save the cost of recruiting and transporting new soldiers.
He knew how to tabulate the cost in lives, which had their
own kind of value in the currency of politics; indeed, he even
knew the value of land, which was primarily tactical and determined in accord with its defensibility.

Everything had a cost, and everyone had a price.
Even the witch would have a price, and he only had to sound
it in order to cheapen the cost of the entire war.

He had grown up hearing legends of zombi from
his nursemaid, but his mother had always dismissed them as
idle swamp tales—"It would win us the war to have a single
unit of them," his father had muttered, when Milaus had put
the question to him in a fit of boyish curiosity. He had never
imagined that he might *see* a zombi, or that he might have
before him a woman capable of raising the dead.

It was true, her zombi had been a roughly formed
one. It had lacked grace and agility, strong as it might have
been; surely, though, it was possible to train such creatures to
move as smoothly as real human beings. When healers grafted the limbs of the dead to the bodies of the living, it took
time for the soldiers to learn how to use their newly whole
bodies again, and a zombi was nothing more than a living
man with dead limbs grafted on everywhere. Proper training
would create regiment upon regiment of soldiers that could
not be killed; what was more, they would be soldiers that required no provisions, no armor, and possibly not even weapons to defeat the enemy. Such soldiers could tear the world
apart with their bare hands, then return to their graves to al-

low humans to put the world to rights again.

And the flood, which had cost citizens so much? With an army that cost so very little to maintain, more funds could be diverted toward the citizens themselves. More young men could return home to their families to help them rebuild. Those people who threw themselves against the walls of fate so that their king might conquer the citadel of fortune could finally reap the benefits of their endeavors.

The only cost that he had yet to learn was the cost of his nameless witch's cooperation.

Milaus rose from his chair, feeling the tightness in the center of his back from long hours of leaning over scrolls to peer at the minuscule columns of figures. He left a heavy brass bar on his papers to tether them to the desk—perhaps so that they wouldn't blow away and perhaps so that they wouldn't dog him as he slept. The king only thanked Aenikus that he was not yet as old as his father had been when last that venerable king had sat in the same chair.

The portrait of dead King Imlaus gave mute assent from its place above the fire. The portrait's heavy brushstrokes carved yet greater severity into a face that could only be described as a stern visage, as the writers of histories and legends had long ago deemed it. Not one of the many lines drawn from Imlaus's grey brows to his thick beard had come from laughing. At best, Milaus recalled, the particular wrinkles of the age-spotted skin at his father's right cheek were reminiscent of the grim smile that the old man had worn when first he had ordered his sons into battle.

In war, the old king had said, there were only brothers in arms, but Milaus's younger brother by blood held the impregnable fortress at the edge of the Great Bowl, and he had long ago hidden their father's other portrait in the dungeons where it could terrorize the Weigers imprisoned there. Adriolaus had never much held with stern visages, preferring instead a well-deserved laugh at another's expense.

If Milaus were to die, Adriolaus would sit in the chair that the king had just vacated and survey the room by the light of one great fireplace and dozens of decorative lamps. Adriolaus would put up a portrait of his brother over the fire and at last succeed in evicting their father from his life; the thought made Milaus smile as his accounts had not.

The clock on the mantel reminded him that it was now two and a half hours past midnight. An hour for criminals, and for kings, to take themselves to bed.

"Will you be sleeping soon?" Milaus asked; the queen looked up, the polished stone at her brow gleaming in the light of the fire. Her lips drew up a little at one corner, the closest to a smile that ever crossed her sculpted face, and she shook her head.

She didn't need to say a word. Her light eyes told of a time of conquest, a time when compromise could not be considered. Their every message was a message of war.

At one time, she had been a laughing and carefree daughter of a noble family from the coast, and Milaus had truly loved her. That love still remained, held close to his breast along with her iron ring, and yet it had grown up as fast and hard as the woman who was once Carisica had become the queen. He didn't mind any longer that she didn't follow him to bed; he only said another devotional before his eyes closed and repeated to himself that the marital bond was sacred to Shonè and Aenikus. If they had intended his marriage to be a chaste one, he would honor their decision.

Imlaus was bound to the battlefields of the next world; Adriolaus to the courts of this one; Milaus, to the gods who might bridge the gap between the two.

Milaus passed his hand over his eyes and walked the silent halls. Arrow-slits in the outer walls let in faint bars of moonlight over which he stepped with careful, booted feet. The idea that some enterprising army might one day breach the cannons mounted on the moss-covered outer walls, the river barrier, and even the city walls themselves to stand within bowshot of these arrow-slits seemed very real in the dream-time of two-thirty in the morning. The king undid the buttons on his jacket as he went, feeling his way across the thin chips of polished shell that held his own outer shell in place. As he swung open the door to his bedchamber, shrugging the finely embroidered jacket from his shoulders, he smiled a little at the pool of moonlight at the foot of his bed.

If he stood in that little patch of light, the moon's harsh, white rays would shine on the harsh, white scar carved deep into his side. He could examine the grisly mess in a full-length mirror exactly as though he were a wandering carnival grotesque; he could try to divine some metaphorical meaning from the puckered flesh that his father's war had made.

He dropped the jacket in the moonlight and undid his boots before crawling beneath the bedclothes, feeling the first shock of blankets unwarmed by human contact and lying quietly until the cloth warmed around his shape.

It was his war now, and he didn't care for metaphors.

Imagine the most beautiful woman in the world—not defined by the beauty of her kindness, as are the priestesses of Terichone, nor a ruination of beauty, a beauty diseased, as Shabane had been even before her death. Imagine instead a truly lovely woman with nothing of the supernatural about her, dressed always in embroidered violet and green and grey to set off the grey cast to her eyes. Her skin is flawless and pale as milky tea, attesting to many years of smart marriages made between noble families from the motherland across the sea; her high, sculpted cheekbones flush easily when she has exerted herself in dancing or riding or laughing, and she is always dancing or riding or laughing, even if she only laughs to herself.

She reads fluently in several languages that no one speaks any longer in Erekos, and her favorite texts are of military strategy, even though she cannot imagine a time when she might see a battlefield. When she wears her long hair loose and curled, its dark brown curves reflect the brassy candlelight as they spill across the scroll open before her and obscure the terrain that strategists drew there long ago. Her hands are perfectly shaped and only faintly calloused from the rope of her small skiff, and she brushes her hair from the papyrus and half-listens to a conversation between nobles as they sit around her, smiling with her face still radiant and glowing from a day spent in the world that she loves so well.

Imagine this beautiful woman as she dances in the marble-floored ballrooms of her father's estate. Her lavender gown billows around her as she spins; men with skin as brown as nuts, men who control great shipping companies along the coast, take her hand and twirl her around until she is laughing and halfway dizzy with the sheer joy of the flute and the fiddle that guide the dancers. She has the flowers of the daughters of the grove in her hair, held in place by dozens upon dozens of tiny pins, radiating a soft perfume that lingers where she has been.

Imagine that no man who touches her hand does not instantly love her, and that no woman who sees her, with her diamond necklace sparkling and her long, curled hair glistening with flowers, does not wish to be that brilliant flush-faced beauty. Imagine that the musicians who play in the corner do so to gain her favor rather than her father's— that the man who cups a silver flute in his fingers presses the keys to match the pace set by the grey-eyed woman's delicate, slipper-clad feet.

Such a woman is no fable, for all she possesses the grace and charm and striking beauty of princesses in fairy-stories; such a woman does not live in a dream world, for all that her father denies her nothing and her company is composed of only the most charming and beautiful people that can be summoned to her side.

Such a woman, a real woman, understands as she spins in the arms of a shipping magnate that one day one of these men will be her husband, and that every moment that she spends in their company is only spent to make her seem more desirable to them. She understands as her dear cheeks blush prettily that every bit of money that her father spends on her is an investment, and that one day she will pay for this loose living with her hand, her virginity, and her life in marriage.

She spends very little of herself at the events of eveningtime—the balls, the lavish dinners, and the parties that

make her marriageable. Instead, she loves the simpler plea-
sures of daytime. She prefers to ride through the lands on
which her father's serfs farm rice, even though very little of the
rest of the country has lords or serfs any longer. The thought
makes her feel cold inside, so she warms herself by bending
in the rice paddies to tend the plants that give her father's serfs
their livelihood. She prefers to sail out in her skiff all alone
and dressed in fisherman's oilcloth, and then to dock secretly
in a fishing village, or once or twice in the city of Palamea.
In these places, she drinks date wine with the fishermen and
flirts with them as she cannot with the men her father offers
to her. She has kissed a few of them with the temerity of the
nobility, who do not expect the world's less courtly men to
want more than kisses; she has always slipped away when the
fishermen put hands on her thighs and drinks on the counter
before her.

She falls in love, once, with an almond-eyed sailor
from the motherland who shares a pipe of tobacco with her
on the docks of a coast town and confesses to her his lifelong
love of scholarly works and of the many wondrous beasts
of the sea. They meet for a week like villagers walking out,
and she cries and holds him close when he tells her that he
must sail back with his ship and that he may never see her
again. He gives her an expensive trinket that she wears to
that night's ball, dancing in the arms of an olive-skinned
man whom she had never met before. He compliments her
on how well the moss agate she wears at her brow sets off
her eyes, and she replies that it was a gift from a dear friend.

Her father sits with her as she reads the next morning, and she twines her slender and beautiful fingers in her

curling ringlets and listens with only half an ear as he tells her that she danced last night with the new king of Erekos. She doesn't listen at all after that, because she is more interested in her text than she has ever been in knowing to whom she is engaged. The scroll discusses the early naval strategies employed in a sea-war that no one remembers any longer; she understands as she reads that within a month, she will be helpmeet to the head of all Erekoi military forces, and that she may find herself surveying battlefields after all. The idea makes her smile inside, but her face is as set as stone.

There will be no more charming sailors; there will be no more sails on her skiff; there will be no more talking with farmers or drinking with fishermen. She will need to find other pastimes to engage her, because being a wife—even being a queen—will make her no happier than being the most beautiful woman in the world.

She reads a scroll on naval strategy that is written in a language that she never hears spoken, and she smiles with genuine warmth for the last time in her life.

Imagine that this woman's name is Carisica, and that she has decided in this moment to build a fortress of herself to keep out the marshaled forces of domesticity and arranged romance and marital bliss.

That night, she kneels at an altar that overlooks the choppy, moonlit sea. The moon draws no warm highlights on her hair as she asks Loukaros to help her to make a wall between the joy of her life as it has been and the emptiness that she perceives ahead.

Imagine, if you will, that today, the queen sat awake until late at night in the library of her husband, staring at military reports that she had read and analyzed and interpreted hours ago. Imagine that she told her husband without words that she would not go to bed with him, and that she smiled to herself in this brief, stolen private time as she remembered rope against her hands, a young sailor who spoke of whales and dolphins, and the sea wind blowing her toward the rice paddies.

Morning came to Achane with the scent of hot tea in the air to remind her of peaceful home mornings an aeon ago. The memory was false, though; she had always brewed the tea for herself and Shabane in the morning, while Shabane had breathed in the scent with lungs that always rattled with phlegm.

The idea of home was a lie even before she opened her eyes to the stone walls that confirmed it.

A young man who wore the same sort of brightly colored livery as Ilaumeleus sat at her bedside, staring out through the window as though the spectacle of city roofs and smokestacks interested him a great deal more than the woman he had been sent to keep company. His dark eyes traced a light latticework over the city; he might have been checking old haunts or following some young lady with his gaze, and he might have been feigning indifference to put Achane at her ease.

The witch sat up in bed and saw the healer's shawl puddled on the pillow that was not hers. She draped it over her head and around her shoulders so that it concealed her vulnerable neck and lower face with the old armor of modesty. Likewise, when she stood, she adjusted her white jacket and heavy skirt to cover her entirely but for her hands and eyes, for she no longer walked the swamps that knew her, and every exposed fingers-breadth of flesh was a liability.

A breakfast had been spread on the table beside her bed, and she regarded it with something akin to wonder. For a long time, Achane stared at the plate of coarse-grain bread spread with butter and lined with shining nuts already removed from their hulls. Even the plate gleamed, its glaze polished clean by some unknown servitor deep in the castle's bowels, and the teacup beckoned to her with the slow and undulating dance of steam over the surface. She felt her mouth watering.

"You can eat all you like." Achane turned at the voice, and the adjutant smiled at her with eyes that glimmered brown as the nuts in the fresh morning light. "It's all for you. I tried to get the kitchen staff to put a bit of lamb on your plate as well, but they said you'd not be used to anything so flavorful in the swamp and it would most likely kill you." He grinned again, all of his teeth white and straight and only slightly grooved. "Being from the swamp myself, I can vouch that lamb is far nicer than pork, and the kitchen staff hasn't got any place keeping even a prisoner from the finer things in life."

Through the all-concealing shawl, Achane muttered, "Thank you," and left the plate untouched.

The adjutant smiled for a third time, as winningly as before, and stood from his chair to snatch a nut from the plate. "See? Not poisoned," he commented, tossing it into his mouth, chewing, and swallowing. "And it would hardly be *worth* poisoning you after you've been brought all this way.

You may as well eat up." He tore a crust from the bread and dabbed at the butter with the edge to make his point, then ate that as well.

"And the tea?" Achane asked, although she hadn't suspected foul play before the adjutant had mentioned it.

"As you wish," he answered. He sniffed it, remarked, "Honey," and took a generous sip before passing it to her.

Achane scented the honey as well, even through the cloth of the shawl; she could smell a dozen herbs that she didn't recognize but that were nonetheless distinct, and she had a sudden vision of arranging the nuts into a protective circle when no one was watching that made her bold enough to drag down the end of her black cloth armor and expose her mouth to the edge of the cup.

The taste was bittersweet as the hot, honeyed tea spilled over her lips and into her mouth.

She swallowed even as the adjutant called, "Your Majesty, the witch is ready."

From behind the door without a handle on the inside came the man whose arms she had suffered to be around her for days, whose hand she knew better when it was clenched at his waist than when it pushed open the door before her. He smiled at her, but she knew the calculation behind that smile as she hadn't known it behind the adjutant's disarming grin. The boy had gulled her as readily as the king had stolen her, and it was no consolation to know that he would suffer the effects of whatever drug he had placed in her tea as he'd smiled with those clean, white teeth.

Teeth, after all, were only bones for chewing up the world. Strange, how she kept forgetting that lesson.

The adjutant patted her shoulder gently, as though the betrayal had grieved him. "Truth serum in the tea, I'm afraid," he whispered as he kissed her cheek. "You will not be harmed—you have my word on that." Turning from Achane, he bowed low to the king and walked out the door.

Achane looked up and met the king's eyes. "What truth could you want from me?" she asked, feeling a slackness overtaking her limbs as the teacup fell from her fingers. She clutched at the table with its treacherous breakfast in order to steady herself. The woodgrain beneath her palms felt at once more deeply etched and more distant than it had before.

The king sat on the bed and studied her as she struggled to control her loosening limbs. "You will be able to stand easily again within half an hour as your body becomes used to the serum," he said rather than answering her. "Our healers have assured me that hallucinations or paralysis are very rare, especially if you bloody well stay calm—sit down." He gestured her to the wooden chair in which the adjutant had been sitting, and Achane stumbled to the narrow, unshuttered window and sat.

"We will discuss magic until you are well enough to walk, and then I will take you to a part of the castle that may interest you." The king reached over to the small table and pulled forth the plate of bread and nuts, which he offered to Achane. "A full stomach will help you recover more easily from the serum."

She took it and rested it on the heavy cloth across her thighs, staring mutely at the contrast between the deep, reddish clay of the plate and the deep brown of her skirt. The fibers were spun from some kind of animal fur, but she had never encountered such an animal.

She did not eat. Once burned, once learned.

The king tried a kind smile that didn't fit the harsh angles of his face, but when Achane only met his gaze and didn't move her hands to the plate, his brow furrowed, and he looked away.

"What's your name?"

"Achane of the swamp, sister of Shabane," she answered immediately, words tumbling from her lips like water overflowing the edges of a cupped leaf; her hands flew to her mouth and upset a pair of nuts, which rolled across the floor to lie at the boots of the king.

He paused to digest the family she had named, for if few people didn't claim their lineage as part of their identity, fewer still claimed a brother or a sister instead of mother and father. "Have you a husband?" he asked, the harmonics of his voice framing the question more gently than Achane had ever heard it asked by her mother.

She was twenty-six years old, and Achane's mother lamented somewhere that her oldest daughter would never marry. The herbs and spells to which a swamp witch wed herself led to numerous grandchildren, but they were all someone else's.

"I have no husband."

"Do you work magic for your living?" asked the king, now harsh to match his prisoner.

"I do." She could have tossed the plate at the king and tried to make good her escape, and yet she couldn't hit him with her muscles slack and unwilling; she couldn't leave through the door without a handle; she couldn't find her way through a castle that wasn't hers to escape across the most effective fortifications in the world. Even throwing nuts at him would only have been childish.

"How many zombi have you raised?" the king pressed. Achane remembered the nightmare request that he had made on the deck of the steamboat, with the grey sky reflected on the churning wake so like the churning in her stomach.

It was best that she hadn't eaten. "One," she answered, and hated that the word had trickled out because it implied that Shabane wasn't alive; she hated it because it was true.

"Could you raise more?" the king asked, and Achane despised every fiber of herself when she nodded.

She hated herself all the more when a tiny, glowing place inside her like the end of a match flared brightly as it realized that, with practice, Achane might learn to raise the dead to true life and then pass that life on to her sister. Lingering like sweetly scented smoke in her mind was the hope of embracing Shabane again, as whole and beautiful as she had been before her sickness had destroyed her.

"I won't raise your dead," Achane breathed. "You can't force me to raise your dead."

Once more, the king's hand made slow but steady progress toward his waist; he looked down and dropped it to his lap, smiling softly as he did. "Is your zombi still out in the swamp?" he asked.

"I think she is, Terichone help her." For although the hearthstone had been moved, and the door had opened and shut again, who was to say that Shabane hadn't tripped on a stone or a root and fallen to the earth mere steps from the cottage? Who was to say that Shabane's body didn't hang mutilated from a tree with a puma's paw claiming it as the great cat licked its lips? No good could come from such thinking, and so Achane gripped the armrests of her chair and forgot the image of bloodstains on feline teeth. She didn't realize that the lid of her left eye fluttered.

The king searched her eyes, but found only throbbing grief there. "If I didn't ask you to raise a man from the dead for battle," he began, "but for my sake—because I missed him dearly—would you raise such a man?"

"Who would the man be?" spilled the words, honeyed as the tea that had betrayed her.

"My father."

Achane closed her eyes so that she couldn't see whether or not his face was sincere. Many men and women had loved those close to them so deeply that they couldn't let them go; so many more missed those whom they'd let go so deeply that they would scrabble for any chance to bring them back. The king could have been one such man, and yet he had done nothing to make her believe him.

Minutes later, she opened her eyes to search for truth in his hard face.

His eyes were far-distant, focused on the world beyond that which the window framed; he smiled slightly, although if it was at a memory of the departed or a passing fancy, she didn't know. He didn't wear a stone upon his brow as the queen did, but he wore a silver circlet on his hair, and he wore the mantle of humanity as uncomfortably as did every legendary figure.

His knuckles gripped whitely at the fabric at his waist, though, and Achane had learned already that the king only did so in the throes of a great passion—anger, she had seen;

could this be grief?

"I can try."

The king stood in a rush from the bed and walked to the door, where he knocked twice and called, "Let us out." He glanced back at Achane with a kind of terrible ache etching his face. "You should've recovered sufficiently by now. Follow me."

Achane rose to still-unsteady feet clad only in worn stockings without toes, and she stumbled after the king as Shabane had once followed in her wake. The wooden beams seemed to cut deep grooves into her feet with every slight dip in their grain, while at the same time they were miles and miles away. The page-adjutant fell into step behind Achane and helped her up when she stumbled; he had recovered more easily from his own sip of the serum-laced tea, and now he lent his hands to help her walk the corridors behind the king's long steps.

They traveled stairways and hallways, hallways and stairways, through halls decked with tapestries and dirt-floored passages barely wide enough for the king's broad shoulders. That this was all one building, Achane did not quite grasp; it seemed that they might as easily have been traversing hundreds of one-room buildings that were nothing at all like the cottages she remembered, each one locked onto the next to form a vast neighborhood in which hardly anyone lived.

At last, though, Achane passed down a great stone staircase into an enormous, low-ceilinged room lined with pillars and lit by a single oil lamp that hung by the stairs. She knew without even breathing the air laden with the scent of embalming fluid that no one at all lived here.

The king pulled the lamp from its hook and bore it across the granite tiles of the floor to a marble dais at one corner. Achane followed, grateful only that her years as a swamp witch had destroyed the old superstition that one should not breathe in a room full of the dead, lest one take in a departed soul.

The body on the stone lay quiescent in its well-made, heavily embroidered cotton clothes; its skeletal hands clutched a sword to its chest even as a long shield of wood plated with iron and copper covered the lower body of the last king.

Achane laughed a hollow laugh that echoed in the tomb of kings, resounding from every pillar and ringing in the old king's all but empty skull. She collapsed to her knees and laughed as though the world were ending, and the dust of the floor spun around her before settling again to the stone.

"I fail to see why you are laughing," the king growled, the *damn you* implied by his flint-struck glare.

The swamp witch stood slowly, guided to her feet by instinct rather than the aid of the adjutant who moved to stand at her elbow. "You're a fool," she laughed, and gestured with one dark hand over the body of the king's father.

"You're a fool to think that even magic can make a man walk when his muscles have long since shriveled away."

In the tomb of Erekoi kings, a bloody history resounds from the walls of stone. No marble dais is unmarked with scenes of horsemen and foot soldiers massed across from each other on its grave face, their tongues crying soundlessly for battle; no king's bones rest without a shield to guard the body's legs and a sword laid across its chest.

The marble faces of the earliest king's soldiers have long since been worn away by the frequent touches of small princes learning history, and now every one of those lavishly depicted men has become as anonymous as the bones on the slabs above them.

Milaus knelt before the dais that bore his father's body, tracing his kingly hands across the stone in search of his own face among the mounted warriors. The stone had been polished to such an extraordinary smoothness that its grain didn't catch on his fingers as he moved from general's shoulder to horse's flank, from the amused smirk on Adriolaus's face (so well captured by the sculptor) to the frown on his own.

Much had been invented, each foot soldier drawn from the sculptor's imagination rather than from the ranks; in all his time with the army, Milaus had never witnessed so many smooth-shaven, unscarred, and poxless foot soldiers in one place. The six cannons on the Erekoi side were fluted like flagons and chased with fanciful whorls, although Milaus knew full well that there hadn't even *been* cannons at this battle, let alone such fantastic creations as these. Much had been invented to make a better picture for future generations to survey—and yet by the recognizable nobles in armor and the generals ranged alongside them, Milaus could still place this particular battle in his memory even without the words chiseled into the base of the dais: *Linachè Valley.*

He remembered this battle.

Grey pre-dawn with the sun just lining the horizon with faint seashell pink; Milaus with his second horse, a bay gelding, stolid and unafraid in its saddle. He was a prince, which, in the days of Imlaus's kingship, meant that he and his noble father led the battle and made the men ashamed enough to follow; Adriolaus was sitting astride beside him and making half-hearted comments every now and again about how the women would treat a wounded prince's scars.

Adriolaus seemed very pale in the grey morning, even though he was the darkest of the men in their family. His edgy mare was shifting from hoof to hoof as Milaus's gelding breathed the first scent of the approaching battle with the men who massed across the valley. The king looked to his sons each in turn, and his eyes made them feel colder than the coldness of knowing that they might die, because his eyes reminded them that even should they survive, they would have to rise again and lead the charge against the Weigers in the next battle.

Their attendant general sent riders out to either flank with their strategy, and King Imlaus bellowed a challenge across the shallow, barren length of Linachè Valley.

Milaus hadn't yet been wounded in his side, and so the only sensation that filled him as he listened for the Weigers' reply was a hot tingling throughout his whole body, as though Death were holding him tight and whispering to him to let go.

The king raised his sword, and he cut the invisible string holding the army back.

Pound pound pound the gelding's hooves ate the ground—ate it and swallowed it whole as the army was running and riding behind him; it was a battle without cannons, and so instead arrows fell all around Milaus and his father, all around Milaus and his horse as they rode toward the army that came toward them just as willingly and met the

arrows with all but identical shields and all but identical terror; he could see a woman's face pulled back like a mask behind a helmet and then he struck the Weiger line as though
he himself were the weapon.

He was through the mounted warriors in all of an
instant, hacking at their arms and their steeds as he rode
and blocking every strike against him with his shield or his
sword; he twisted the weapon out of one Weiger knight's
hand and then slashed the man's arm nearly off in one whirling strike that left him open to the pike of the next rider—he
could only press it back enough to divert the thrust to his
shoulder and then he was surrounded by foot soldiers who
hamstrung his horse and hacked at him as he fought to dis-
mount. He had lost Adriolaus; he had lost his father; he had
lost his horse, but he didn't care because he was screaming
at men who were screaming at him and he was going to
kill every last one of them if they didn't kill him first; he
was striking at necks with heavy blows, he was blocking dag-
ger strikes and pike thrusts even as one Weiger leapt onto
his back and tried to bear him to the ground. Horses were
screaming; dawn was breaking like the bones in the arm of
the man that clung to Milaus's neck as the prince smashed
his shield against him to make the damned Weiger let go.

There was no time. Time had long since been
slaughtered.

Each strike caught on his shield vibrated up to his
wounded shoulder; each hard blow he dealt threw shocks up
his wrist and he couldn't tell if he was shouting because his
throat had been scraped raw and aching by the sound, but he
couldn't stop screaming, couldn't stop fighting because he was

dancing with Death in Loukaros's court, and he passed on his grim partner to every man he met.

The castle bells tolled just as the Weigers blew retreat on a bugle, and Milaus looked up from the carvings on the stone to his father's shield and sword and bones.

It had been the most critical victory of Imlaus's kingship. It had been his greatest contribution to the bloody history of his predecessors, and it had won them three miles of territory and a crucial fortress in the mountains of the Great Bowl. Milaus's father had survived to sit on his triumph and gloat, and his youngest son had survived to call it the most idiotic victorious battle in Erekoi military history; the eldest son had survived to kneel as a king by his father's dais, and remember.

He touched his own shoulder as carefully as though it had just been wounded there in Linachè Valley, and then King Milaus wiped his eyes to erase the memory of that grey morning.

eiger awoke before dawn to find Erlen gone. Other individuals, their affections wound tightly around the moment, might have felt tragically forsaken for as long as it took to harden their hearts against speaking to the offender; Jeiger, on the other hand, only stretched his back until it cracked, then crawled out from under the blanket. Rushes from the floor were stuck in his hair and his sparse beard like burrs in sheep's fleece, and the camp blanket had long since integrated a small garden's worth of dried plant particles and mud into its tightly woven wool. One day, Jeiger would need to drag a comb through his hair and find a new blanket, but today was not that day.

He rolled up the blanket and thrust it in his pack, checking for his bowl, his spoon, and his lightest cook-pot as he did—for a proper Wig never trusts his neighbors not to borrow items permanently and without permission. Last of all, Jeiger laced on his boots and unrolled the tanned-leather vest that he had used for a pillow. The soft rabbit fur on the inside kept him warm enough; someday, perhaps, he would tan enough hides to attach sleeves, and even make a sturdy pair of gloves. Today was not that day, either.

Today was the day that Jeiger shouldered his pack and headed back the meeting lodge, where he found the children of the holt-holders in congress over the strategy that their fathers had created last night. Erlen stood there in front of the great map of the mountain holts, shouting amongst the borderlanders, in deep dispute with one of the stern-faced, thirty-year-old Mittler grandsons. It warmed Jeiger's heart that the two of them seemed ready to come to blows at the slightest change in stance or tone; it was almost as though Erlen had become a member of the coarse and fractious borderland family.

When Erlen spotted the top of Jeiger's head, elevated a few inches above the tops of other heads in the room, he immediately waved him over with a shout of "Now listen to him! He'll tell you that we don't know anything about boats!"

Jeiger spared a last glance back through the door, where he could see the very tip of the sun peering over the mountain's shoulders even as it cloaked them in gold. The sunrise under his belt, he made his way through the press of men and women as cautiously as he might have navigated a thicket of sharp and plucking briars.

"Boats?" he asked against Erlen's ear when the flow of people had brought them together; Erlen nodded.

"The Mittlers want the people of the western holts to take over the steamboats on the river—I have no idea what

their logic is," he flung a glare at the current Mittler represen-
tative, "because I'm the only one of us who has even *seen* a
boat, and that hardly means that I know how to sail one—"

"But you know more than we do, and it needs to be
done," answered the holt-holder's grandson. "If the Erekoi
keep their steamboats, they can bring soldiers to the mountains
in an instant, no matter how many of their men we incapaci-
tate. If the holts are to drive the Erekoi out of our mountains, it
will have to be without the threat of more of them at our
backs." He looked over at Jeiger with an arch to his eyebrows
like a bristling question, and despite the early hour, it was
light enough already to see sense.

"We *will* need to keep them from bringing soldiers down
on our heads," Jeiger agreed, and the tide of righteous anger that
Erlen had clearly been riding for well over an hour made him
open his mouth to protest before Jeiger caught his upper arm in
one hand and touched the small of his back with the other. "And
if we knew how to sail, who's to say that we wouldn't be leaping at the chance? But because we *can't* sail, we would probably
drown ourselves before we even found a steamboat."

Quite suddenly, something changed in Erlen's posture; Jeiger was not a man of metaphors, and yet in his mind
it had the same meaning as a taut bow suddenly relaxed. It
meant a focus dropped; it meant a question to be asked later,
when everything didn't depend on the reactions of the moment. "We'd need an expert who understands boats in order
to have any hope of succeeding," Erlen explained, and by the
tensing of his arm, Jeiger knew to let him go. "Can you provide us with that?"

"I can," called a voice from the throng, and through

the thickets of people came a woman with skin as pale as the Wigs', a thick braid of grey, and eyebrows of Erekoi-black. "I know something of boats, or did some years ago; if you can find me a boat fit to take on a steam engine, and men fit to take orders, I can help you."

She wasn't a woman Jeiger knew; she spoke with an accent less familiar even than Erlen's cultured Weigenspeich, perhaps because it hadn't even an undertone of the forsaken motherland in it. Her eyes seemed younger than the wrinkles in her face suggested, and the part in her hair lay arrow-straight.

Erlen didn't look at Jeiger for confirmation of his decision; he had long since moved beyond the point of deference to one who had fought this battle longer than he had. "We can take orders if they're worth taking," he told the woman with flint edging his voice. "How did you come to know about boats?"

The woman only chuckled, and her laugh was lost in the din. "You'll need to take orders without questioning them, and quickly, too, if you want a boat to respond as you need it to. And as to what I know," she smiled at him fondly for his distrust, "much of my family is Erekoi, or part Erekoi, and they love their boats You needn't think you're the only ones this war has brought to hard times—he people of the mountains *do* marry, and sometimes they marry Erekoi if they've a fancy for them."

"And the Erekoi in your family don't 'have a fancy' for the king?" Erlen's smile was a bright, brittle, sleepless smile, and his eyes were still ringed with dark circles.

"Not many of them. Every family will have its dissenters, of course." She put out a hand for him to shake, and the man who had been a Weiger three months ago took it in the Wig manner—clasping her wrist and shaking once. As Erlen took her wrist, Jeiger noted the apparent firmness of her grip. "We'll have to leave soon, though, if we want to find a good boat," continued the woman. "At this time, with the flood just dealt with, most steamboats will be headed north—upriver, toward us. We can catch a great lot of them if we move now."

Erlen glanced at Jeiger, but this look only said, *Are enough of us ready to make the journey?* Jeiger mentally counted off those of the border holts who could be trusted to capture a steamboat, subtracted the number that would be needed to guard their own homes, and ventured a careful nod. His hand was already on the hunting knife at his side, even though the steamboats were far away.

"I'll let the others know, and we'll meet you when we can," Jeiger said instead of asking how they would take over a steamboat crowded with ordinary people. And instead of asking how much blood the old woman was willing to spill for her Erekoi kin, he asked, "What's your name?"

She chuckled, as though that were another good joke. "Don't ask me my name, child. Names are for friends."

He wondered what in the Husmann's name she was, if she wasn't a friend.

Very few of the bravest people in the world have the nerve to stay put. Their souls always cry out for Where They Must Be, and this place is inevitably one step further away

from the homeland. One might suppose that these coura-
geous souls who seek out the battlefield in distant lands have
something from which to run—something terrifying at their
backs that hounds them even as they face the world's mon-
sters with steely eyes and feet firmly planted.

Let no man speculate on what pulls so many coura-
geous men and women out across the dangerous slopes of
the world; let no man question whether fear of mediocrity
or terror of comfort makes a journey seem the more valiant
option to every hero.

Erlen had long ago stopped asking himself why he
had gone away from home, first to the university and then
to the rocky borderland slopes. When one is trying to be the
hero, one cannot be the doubter as well. There is no victor in
a battle against oneself.

The old woman who declined to give her name knew a
secret trail through the mountains that would lead them to her
family's village on the river. That it was a secret trail seemed
only logical, given the woman's refusal to give away her name
or her origin or even from which holt she had come; that the
trail led directly from Mittler Holt to the village seemed equally
plausible, given that the woman's knowledge of boats had come
as if from thin air. Jeiger had once told him a story of a hunter
who had found the Path That Led Everywhere, and if this was
that path, it would not have surprised Erlen in the least.

Their footfalls were silent on generations of leaf
mould. Thirty Wigs glanced uneasily from side to side as
they walked, though, and they had muffled their cooking
gear and weaponry so that no jingle or clank would betray
them to the Erekoi.

Marla had gone back to the holt to protect it and to stage attacks on the mines nearby; Eppa had hovered over her husband, the holt patriarch, as though she knew that his death would soon come, and Erlen had known that this time the white-haired woman would not return to the battlefield with her companions—she had a different battle to face in the north, with the massed forces of the holts. The man whose name he couldn't remember walked at the end of the line with his pack hanging all but empty on his back so that it wouldn't hinder his arm when he reached for his bow.

Jeiger was beside him, as always, and they didn't need to speak to be comforted by each other's presence. Each brushed back the branches that stretched across their path and held the young wood back so that it wouldn't strike the other; in a long line of men and women who walked single file, with several paces between each person and his nearest companion, they alone walked abreast, directly behind the old woman as she led them across streams and down slopes, over stones and through thickets. The trail never ceased to be clear beneath their feet even when it faded into the bracken, carved as it was in the empty places between the trees. No glow of light or power illuminated it, not even in the comparative darkness of the trees; no ancient footsteps marked it, or if they did, their marks had long since been covered over by the cast shrouds of the branches. In his chill myth-thoughts, Erlen wondered if perhaps the trail was older than both footsteps and light.

Through the thick shadows of the leaves, through the green boughs that hid this path from the dim light overhead, came an all but imperceptible mist of rain.

"It won't be long," the old woman called softly, perhaps to the sky and perhaps over her shoulder. She spoke as warmly as though she were addressing an old friend, and her hands were always returning to the ring of tiny keys at her belt as she walked. "Not long at all."

In time, the old woman brought them to a narrow bridge across a river glutted by the recent rains, and she turned to face the Wigs when their long train gathered to a thick and cautious cluster. Bridges had become dangers since the Erekoi had come to their lands; bridges were exposed ground, potential traps, even when they weren't railless paths a cubit across. That narrow walkway was braced with only a few long logs, pegged together and sunk into the earth on either side of the swift waters.

"This river comes together with others in the mountains to make the great Erekoi river," the old woman told them. "Brave these waters, and the waters of the Erekoi river won't make you at all afraid." She laughed softly at a joke that no one else understood, to the applause of drifting branches thumping against the bracing beams of the bridge.

The bridge was barely wide enough for the woman's narrow feet, and it swayed as she walked across it. Never did she stumble, although once an entire floating tree smashed its dirt-clotted roots into the wood as though bent on snatching it downstream; the old woman only stood as still as bated breath until the bridge stopped rocking, and then walked past the finger-thin roots that tried and failed to pluck her sleeve.

Jeiger stepped onto the bridge next, and for a freezing, shattering moment, Erlen realized that he wouldn't be able to follow until the other man had crossed the bridge and made it to the other side.

Surefooted Jeiger, the lean man who crouched for hours on pine boughs above the trails where the deer and wild goats walked, and who never lost the instinctive balance of his feet—this man put his feet to the aging planking that might have been as old as the trail, as old as time. This man bent his knees and held his arms out loosely as he walked so that he could center himself on the wet and rough-hewn wood, and step by step, he made his way to the woods on the other side. When at last his foot touched the shore, an eternity after it had first touched the bridge, Erlen let out a long and heavy breath to make room for the relief that swelled in his chest.

It is never an easy thing, to see a loved one enter the hands of Death. It's almost harder to see him walk out again.

The wind smashed at Erlen when he left the cover of the trees for the unprotected bridge, but even when the once-misty rain began to batter him in earnest and slicked the planking, he kept his eyes on the other shore. He fell on the wet wood as he had last night on the mountain, but this time his hands were ready, and he caught the edges of the bridge and held on tightly even though it shook like thunder. If the rest of his journey was a crawl, no man or woman would laugh at a crawling man when he or she stood next in line.

Erlen stood as the wood of the bridge met the ground, and although he was cold and wet, he didn't care because he was *alive*, and Jeiger draped his coat over the other man's shoulders to share a warmth only partially physical.

As each Wig crossed the bridge alone, the grey-haired woman smiled, and her black eyebrows furrowed closely together as she looked up at the cloudy sky.

That night, the Path That Led Everywhere deposited

the thirty-one men and women in the old woman's village at the foot of the mountains. Everyone in the houses slept the comfortable sleep of those who wake hours before dawn, and so no one watched as the Wigs climbed aboard the largest fishing vessel and set off silently into the night.

They learned the old woman's commands by lantern light, and although they used the same light to search for any sign of an owner—a captain's log, a tally of the day's catch, a scarf thrown casually on a chest or a chest on which to throw it casually—they found not a trace.

By lantern light, Jeiger whetted his hunting knife, and Erlen stood with his hands resting on the other man's shoulders and thought for the first time about what made him run.

amela woke on the deck while the sky was still dark overhead. The corpse was shaking her with stiff, gloved fingers clenched in the fabric of the priestess's black shawl, and Gamela's half-open eyes followed the corpse's other pointing hand to a dark shape on the water. It was a fishing boat; even in the darkness, without lanterns to illuminate its deck, Gamela could tell that it was just a large fishing boat—

—and any fishing boat out in this darkness would have its lanterns lit. In the time that it took to realize this, Gamela was standing and raising the corpse to her feet as well, and with her heavy arm slung around the corpse's slim waist, she led them into the darkness between the prow lantern and the midship lantern.

It would buy them only moments. Gamela knew in the animal parts of her soul, the parts that didn't censor their needs, that they must get away quickly and quietly, without

being noticed—but hadn't they seen yesterday that the steamboat carried no lifeboats? The corpse couldn't swim, of
course; there would be no escape that way. The sails bellied
and cracked overhead in the stiff breeze, but otherwise the
deck was silent. Not even the engine groaned beneath them.

They're looters, Gamela told herself firmly so that she
wouldn't have to think of any other possibilities. There was no
room for other possibilities on the deck. *They're poor men who
are looking for a quick way to repair their fortunes, so they'll
go after the plates in the dining hall, as well as the cashbox.
They'll steal food and medicine. They'll steal good iron tools.
They'll steal the coal so that they can sell it back—what won't
they steal? What's so valueless that they won't cut down a person who hides with it?*

Her eyes fixed on a coil of rope, for every person who
grows up in the fishing villages along the river knows to carry
more rope than he or she will ever possibly need, because one
day that rope will be vital. If there were anything in the world
that a crew of looters in a fishing boat would have in excess
and fail to steal, it would be rope.

"In here," she breathed to the corpse, helping the
dead woman to curl up inside the wide coil of thick rope between two circles of light. She arranged the dark scarf and
dark skirts over the body so that not the faintest gleam of light
on decaying flesh would alert the looters to a dead woman
huddled in the rope.

Gamela thought as she crouched in another rope coil
that she ought to have told one of the crew about the fishing
boat of looters; she thought that such desperate men as those
on the fishing boat would surely take the temple's mule that

even now stood docilely in the hold, and they'd either keep
him for farm labor or sell him off to someone who had lost
livestock in the flood. *But wasn't that the point of the temple's
mule? To provide labor for those who needed it?* She quieted
the religious sentiment long enough to see the first hook catch
on the steamboat's rail and the first pale glint of hair as the
first looter hauled himself onto the deck.

Gamela had never in her life seen a man with
pale hair.

More men followed, though, as the hull of their fishing
boat scraped painfully against the hull of the steamboat. It was a
strange and terrible thing to see these pale men and women with
their pale hair and flashing eyes as they rushed across the deck in
the near-silence of two hulls scraping together and sails creaking
and worlds colliding. It was somehow less terrible to see how
they held glittering knives and swords to the throats of the crew-
men and walked them slowly to the edge of the rail, because if
these people used weapons, then they were at least ordinary humans; if they let the crew leap into the water and swim to shore,
then at least they had mercy.

One man whose right hand had only four fingers began waking the passengers asleep on the deck, his left hand
over their mouths as they woke so that they wouldn't scream
at seeing a strangely colored man holding a knife loosely in
his mangled hand. He spoke to them softly but urgently in a
strange language that meant nothing at all to Gamela; when
he saw only terror in just-awakened eyes, he asked quietly in
accented Erekoi, "You swim?"

Some nodded and some fought, but his hand was firm
on each mouth even when some tried to bite his fingers and

others kicked at his legs; some burly men tried to wrestle him to the ground and pounded the deck with their feet. He was impossibly tall, though, and his limbs were as long as they were strong; he only held the passengers away until they'd ceased to struggle and then asked again, "You swim?"

In time, each passenger he woke nodded submission, and he pointed with his knife to the rail. Each passenger leapt into the water, and their shadows stroked across the dim waters to the shore.

As the rest of the pale invaders—*they were looters; even if they were strange people from a strange land, they were looters and they would be gone if only Gamela waited long enough*—descended the ladder to the lower deck, another man came to speak with the man who had sent the passengers into the waves. They whispered quickly and intensely to one another, and once, the newcomer shook his almost-white hair back from his eyes and cast a glance toward the rough coils of rope. Had Gamela ducked, he would have seen the movement, so she only closed her eyes to squinting crescents so that their glitter would not betray her.

The moon-pale man turned away again. He breathed something that might have been a foreign curse and began searching the deck for any passengers who remained.

In time, the other looters came up the stairway that sailors called the ladder, their greater height allowing them to hold knives easily at the throats or the guts of the crew-members and passengers who walked before them. Gamela watched in silence, for there was something ethereal in the silent procession on a moonless, starless night; no longer did the heavy men try to rouse attention with their boots pounding on the deck. They knew that no one remained to rouse.

Once more, in a long row like a parody of children gathered at the riverbank to dive, the looters pressed their captives to the railing and forced them to leap through the thick night air and into the embracing river.

An old woman who looked Erekoi breathed one harsh syllable as an invader raised his hand to push the coast-man with the straw hat over the edge. The stranger paused, conversed with the grey-braided woman for a moment, and then pulled his short sword away from the coast-man's grey hair. He muttered what might have been an apology, and then the invaders gathered together on the deck.

The white-haired man hadn't seen either Gamela or the corpse, and he went to join his fellows.

Gamela could understand nothing of their conversation but the Erekoi word for "donkey"—and that from the mouth of the woman who looked Erekoi and had rescued a man of the coast from the river that could have borne him home.

The old woman took the helm as a great many of the pale invaders returned to the fishing boat; others tossed down the heavy iron hooks, and the boat gave a pained, scraping shudder as the smaller vessel pulled free.

Suddenly, Gamela realized that the pale invaders had come for the *steamboat*, and that they wouldn't vanish before morning.

In daylight, the coils of rope wouldn't conceal either her or the corpse. She fixed her eyes on the coast-man, who stood at the old woman's side at the helm, and made her decision.

*S*o many questions. The king had fired questions at her like a cheap conjurer asking platitudes of an imaginary spirit, like an archer shooting flame-tipped darts at the sea and waiting for it to catch, and then the visions had started and had wound through the questions like the hair of the sea-goddess winding into her spinning.

Why won't you raise the dead? Surely it's no more objectionable the second time than the first! The walls had shimmered around the king until they were as clear and distorted as sea-glass; the weak sunlight had filled that blue-green grey-violet glass with lavender echoes and half-shadows.

"I raised her because I loved her. I raised her because I thought I could bring her back to life." The king's reflection on the walls of glass had been old and harsh; it had been a young, laughing face almost his own; it had been the queen's face, and each had worn a crown of stars so unlike the silver circlet on the king's brow. "I won't raise zombi to fight in your armies. I won't raise your loved ones—they're long since beyond saving."

Achane hadn't seen her own reflection, no matter where she'd looked.

Think of the others who've lost loved ones, of everyone else who's seen death to keep our borders safe from the bloody Wigs! Can you deny them their loved ones? Can you deny the mothers of our land their own children, when you can save those children by raising the dead to fill their places?

A grey man had walked through the dizzy glass a thousand feet below, and he had filled the air with lightning.

"You're the king. Call off the war, and no more mothers' children will have to die." The grey man had stared up at the king's feet and scowled; he had knocked at the glass until it had seemed the glass must break for his knocking, but the castle knew that it was stone even if Achane found herself forgetting.

The king had taken on Shabane's face, and the high priestess's face, and the face of Achane's philandering father; he had been every man and woman Achane had ever known at once. *This is our land!* they had all screamed, a thousand chorusing voices that made Achane flinch and cover her ears with her palms for the loudness of them. Seeing her wince, they had pulled back and become only the king again. *This is our land, and one day the Weigers will take it from us if we don't fight them now. These are our people, and this is our land; these are our homes and our mines and our rivers and forests. Every inch of it is ours, and we will not see it in their hands! It's for this we need an army—for us.*

Far away, so far away that Achane had barely been able to make out the shapes through the warped glass-that-was-stone, the queen had been at her devotions. She hadn't set a house on fire, because the cottage-shaped incense burner was the symbol of Terìchone's generosity; she hadn't cooked gruel and burnt it as an offering, because such was the worship of Shonè and Aenikus. The queen had instead brushed her hands over the clear surface of a bowl of water and cast it against the stone-that-was-glass, and she had then put the bowl to her lips and drawn deeply of the cloudy liquid. Beneath Achane's huddled feet, the grey man had looked up and smiled.

"Hundreds of years ago, say the legends, the colonists from the Erekoi motherland came to this place," Achane had breathed against the heavy fog of her own exhalations. "They marked our part of the map *Ethelarus*, which means 'land of our enemies.' But in time they began to marry the people of this land, and the people of this land learned to read the Erekoi language. They asked what 'E' stood for on the map— what their new husbands and wives had called this land that they shared. The settlers were ashamed, king. They said that this letter was the land's name in their tongue. 'E'—which is said 'Erekos' in the old way of speaking. We're a land *named* for our shame of war."

The Weigers don't care for old legends, and neither do I, the king had answered, and his side had split open and bled across the glass of the floor. Far away, the queen had bowed at her altar and opened her palms against the glass-or-stone-or-glass and drawn lightning into them.

The grey man had danced, and he had been darker.

He had been dark and smooth and had reflected his shape everywhere throughout the castle—a thousand, thousand dancing grey men prismed and imprisoned in the glass; the castle
had been a jar with lightning trapped within it, and crackling
bolts had arced between the king's hands and Achane's.

Have you seen murder, Achane sister of Shabane? the
king had asked as the castle's servants and maids and soldiers
had walked through the busy glass walls beneath his feet, beneath the pooled blood seeping across the floor.

"I haven't."

*Perhaps the sight will help you to understand why we
need such soldiers as you can raise. You damned witch—if
you'd ever lost soldier after soldier, brother after brother, you
wouldn't stand there refusing. No man, woman, or child—no
god!—would refuse anything to halt the war, after seeing what
destruction it can wreak.*

No god, the grey man had said as his image had struck
the stone-glass-stone behind the king and struck shards like
diamonds from the surface; no god but Loukaros who glories
in the tempest and the times when the world has been shaken
apart and remade.

And now the stone reflected nothing at all; the light
spilled through the arrow-slit window of the room without
a door-handle, and Achane sat shaking apart on the quilted
comforter.

The king was taking her to a fortress in the mountains, on the edge of the Great Bowl that she had never heard
anyone speak about before. She hadn't known that it was a
famed battlefield; she hadn't known that it was anything but a
break in the mountains on the maps.

She hadn't known that over a hundred thousand

Erekos   203

men and women had lost their lives there in the hundreds of years since the Erekoi and the Weigers had begun to fight in that gap in the barrier between their lands, and the knowledge filled her with peculiar ghosts like the shadow-figures that had walked in the castle of glass—like the voices that had thundered *our land*.

After the world had ceased its trembling and flashing, Achane had made a circle on the ground with fibers torn from the hem of her dress and had drawn protection over it with her mind, and in the center of this circle she now huddled with her hands about her knees and her head bowed to face the floor.

Her fingers were thinner and bonier than they had been before; she was growing quickly wasted by her refusal to eat, and yet something in the looseness of the skin there made her deeply afraid. It reminded her of the old women she had tended in the rice-farmers' villages; it reminded her of Shabane's skin in the frantic, anguished days before her sister had died.

It reminded her of death, and she was only glad that she had no mirror to see that death coming into her own face. It would have been like watching Shabane die all over again.

When the queen came into the room that had no exit, her figure swathed in a traveling dress of grey, she only cast a dismissive glance at Achane's circle before she reached across it and lifted the swamp witch by her arms until both of them were standing.

For a moment, their eyes met, and Achane remembered with a shiver the sight of the queen drawing lightning from the stone-glass-stone.

When the king's procession left through the very gate it had recently graced with banners and laughter, no merrymaking accompanied it; only armed guards and a freshly trained unit of soldiers shared the quiet roads. No one danced and chanted nationalist anthems; they were too busy praying. At the bridge between the capital and the world outside, though, a few soldiers' wives and soldiers' widows, soldiers' husbands and soldiers' children watched them go.

Just as before, they threw flowers in the path of those who had come a great distance but had a great distance yet to go.

At the helm of the steamboat that they had stolen, facing north with the dawn on their right and the night still darkening the left, the coast-man and the woman with the grey braid held one another's hands and did not need to speak. It had been a long time since husband and wife had sailed together, but they remembered the way that a boat moved beneath them; they remembered stories of the water and what it meant, too.

It's said in the parts of Erekos between the river and the sea that once, long ago, the ocean flooded all of the land and drowned all living things. Such stories are not alien ones; every culture that knows the ways of water tells a story of the great sea-mother who smothers all of her young. This story came from the motherland across the waves, along with a language and donkeys and melon seeds and gods and an ideology of this-mine that-yours; it crossed the restless ocean and took root in a fertile land receptive to flood-stories. It bloomed with characters that only the first people of that land knew, and in time it settled into the shape it wears today.

The Erekoi say that the goddess of the ocean, she whose name can never be known, weaves the entire world together with a lacework of water. They say that she is the most beautiful woman ever to live, with long hair and long fingers and grey-green eyes that hold all of the watery world in their depths, just as witches' eyes reflect their homes. And yet for all this, the gods of the Erekoi are imperfect gods, and so one day as the sea-goddess was making yarn to weave the world together, her hair got caught in the fibers that twisted around her cyclone of a drop spindle. Because her hair was so long, though, she didn't realize that she had wound herself into the yarn until she had already pushed that yarn into the world-loom. Now the water that wove the world together was made of thicker threads than ever before, the gaps between them slender—plainly put, the world began to flood.

Many people drowned, but more than that, the animals drowned as well. Fish that had known only fresh water dried up in the rising salt tides of the ocean; fish of the saltwater expired as their bodies filled with the fresh water that surrounded them as they were caught in rivers. Flocks of birds tumbled from the sky in exhaustion and drowned; herds of sheep made their last stand, bleating, on the mountaintops, before they were swept away.

The sea-goddess wept, and behold—behind her stood Loukaros, the god of the storms, the god of war, the god of the world being destroyed and remade again. "Let me cut your hair," he said, and he held his knife at the nape of her neck. "You cannot unmake your weaving until I've cut you free."

"If I let you cut me free," the sea-goddess replied, and in her nameless eyes there was grief likewise beyond name, "If I let you touch your knife to my hair, so too does it touch the fabric of the world."

"If you don't let me cut you free, then there is no hope for the world. War brings change—war unmakes the ill in the world so that a new order can take its place." The goddess of the ocean wailed and cast about her for any other answer, but her flood had drowned even the old gods—all but two, who huddled on a mountaintop as the waves drew ever nearer to their gardens and their walls and their hearthstone.

At last, she let Loukaros cut her hair away.

The legends say that a great storm swept the ocean when the knife first touched the fabric of the world, and the surviving animals and people began to rend each other's skin, and for the first time since time began, the world knew animosity and fear.

Such, some say, is the price of repairing the damage of the world.

When the sea-goddess had unmade her weaving, though, and began the laborious task of unspinning all of her yarn and pulling all of her hair from the thick fiber, the world calmed again. Soon, the sea-goddess's long, once-beautiful hair lay in a pool on the floor, and she turned once again to weaving the world with a warp and weft of water. Her hair never grew again after Loukaros's blade sheared it short, and the world itself never lost the taint of fear, of lightning, and of war.

But as the floodwaters receded, Shonè and Aenikus looked up from where they huddled on their mountaintop, and they smiled grimly as they acknowledged the work that

they would have to do. They walked down the steep and slippery slopes that still echoed with thunder and, for the first
time, walked among men; they watched the angry and fearful
rend each other and then took them apart, and fed them, and
soothed their wounds. They showed the hungry how to plant
again with seeds from the gods' garden, and how to care for
their flocks, and how to kill plants and animals without mal-
ice but with respect for the life that would flow from the dead
into the living. If this washed-new world were to be one of
death, then each death must serve the continuation of life; if
war had become a dangerously seductive option, then peace
had to become equally attractive.

Look closely—can you see the place where two stories collided long ago? Can you see the jagged edges of one
ideology grafted messily onto another, justification of war
meeting a more nebulous ideal? These edges still grind together today; in places where their shade of skin marks the
local people as particularly unmixed, where the colonist or
the indigen is particularly close to the surface, the two pieces
of the story do not mesh until one has broken the other to fit

The king, for example, had never heard this version
of the story in all of his scholarship. He had researched Shonè
and Aenikus and their legends thoroughly on all of the lonely
nights when his wife would not come to bed, and yet this story
does not exist in the pale-skinned capital or on its dry scrolls.
There, the illustration at the very end of the story depicts only
a shorn goddess trying to reweave a devastated land.

Many centuries before the colonists had come
across the waves and named this place Erekos, the people of
the swampland had raised pillars of stone beside the roads
to remind every traveler of the flood story. A different god

brought the flood; a different god brought war, and here the other piece of the story is preserved almost unadulterated: the unmaking of the world, and the remaking, and at the end, the rebuilding.

Their language and their writing had been lost when the Erekoi language embraced the land, and yet these pillars remained. In a mixed-blood land, a mixed-blood story rules, but the native stones bear the last word. Their bas-relief promise of peace remains, for all who can read the legend there.

As a woman no longer young made her way across the deck, garbed in the black shawl of a healer and bearing a scroll of prayers to Terìchone in her pocket, the old man doffed his straw hat and shook his fine, grey hair free of stories. His skin gleamed like new copper in the red sunlight of dawn, and he smiled at his wife with her black eyebrows and her long braid. Such a woman knew the oldest pathways of the earth, and the places in human hearts that were deeply afraid, and the way that death shaded into life again, and she still called him husband. "That 'n is wound up with our daughter," he confided, and his wife laughed gently at him.

"Worse people to get wound up with, I'm sure." She patted his hand, and between them ran a love as old as the mountains and as dear as the sun emerging through the storm.

⊰⊱

As the steamboat ploughed the deep and tranquil river with its engine silent and its sails pulling it ever further toward the north, so too did it make its way across the pages of Erlen's book, drawn in careful detail with every part labeled according to the old woman's directions. She knew enough of the Weigenspeich for sailing to give the words for masts and sails, a helm and a rudder; for the smokestack and the boiler room, she had only Erekoi. Erlen's pen marked these words dutifully in both the curved print of Weigengraff and the angular Erekoi letters, and in boxes marked off with his drawing square, he began to transcribe the woman's directions for how a ship went together to become more than the sum of its parts.

Some have said that knowledge is power—if this is so, it is power like a great weight suspended from the branches of a tree. It is a latent power, a passive power, a potential power, waiting only for the sharp blade of circumstance to cut it free.

Erlen sat with his knees drawn up before him like a table, his back braced against the rail of the steamboat and his mouth in a grim underline, labeling in silence with Master Tuefweil's pen. When the old woman called him by name, he only noticed her because she threw a shadow across his diagram. He capped his pen and thrust it in his pocket with the ink bottle, holding his book carefully as he stood so that the ink would not smear onto facing pages.

"She wants our help," the woman said, gesturing to a broad woman shawled in black who stood between her and the elderly man she had rescued last night. "Her name is Gamela, and that one," she gestured to the far rail of the ship, where another black-shawled figure leaned, "is with her. They're looking for that one's sister, who is a prisoner of the king."

"The king?" Erlen looked between the two Erekoi women who were all but anonymous in their black shawls, and at the Erekoi man whose face was crossed with a lattice of sunlight and shadows where the dawn light filtered through his straw hat. "Why is he taking Erekoi women prisoner?"

For a moment, the grey-braided woman regarded him in silent consideration, and then she leaned over to breathe Erekoi words against the stranger's black shawl. The stranger only nodded once, hard. "You ought to see," their guide responded after a moment, in a voice as level as the great plains. "Please don't scream or do anything else rash."

The trio led him across the deck to a great nest of rope coils, and the woman named Gamela unfastened the pins that held the other's shawl in place—her fingers trembled so that the pins came away from the cloth only grudgingly, and when she had unwrapped the black fabric, she let it fall to the ground.

A beautiful woman had once worn the face revealed there; Erlen reached out unthinking hands to cup her cheeks, and the flesh was cold. Eyes that must have been deep Erekoi brown in life had rotted away days ago, just as that sunken nose and mouth had rotted away; the woman's—the corpse's—brittle hair did nothing to shroud the wreckage of her ears and neck. In some places, strips of the corpse's flesh had peeled away entirely, revealing blackened and congealed blood that made him want to remove her clothes reverently to understand the extent of the rot.

This woman was indisputably dead, had been dead for days…and yet she raised her cold fingers to rest them against the backs of his hands, and he saw that the tips of two of those fingers were blackened as though they had been burned.

She had once been a beautiful woman, or so her bones claimed against the evidence of tight-stretched skin, and yet no longer was she so.

"What is your name?" he asked her in Erekoi before he even wondered if her decaying mouth could produce sound. She gaped at him without eyes, her lips forming syllables that not even Jeiger could have read—he shook his head and stroked her cheek because if he did that, then he could pretend that this abomination was no more real than the voices of the stones that he had heard so many weeks ago.

There is a profound and primal disgust in abomination, certainly, but as wiser men have said before, fascination is by far the stronger force.

He turned to Gamela, who had unpinned her own shawl as well. "She is zombi," the woman explained, and he frowned at the word. It had been written in horror in that deceased book, *The Wayes and Custommes of the Ereckoy,* and yet Gamela said it with a profound sadness in her eyes as she beheld the true form of the word before her. The lines on Gamela's face, grooved as gently into her skin as the river had cut into this land, told Erlen that the woman had lived more years than he, even though her dark hair and proud bearing had refused to submit to time.

"Did her sister," Erlen ventured as carefully as he might have placed a foot at the top of a mountain, "Did her sister raise her from the dead? Is that why the king is holding her?" In his imagination, shadow-women shaped like the zombi before him rose from the ground; weapons flickered, teeth flashed in decaying mouths, and the image died.

Gamela looked to the once-beautiful corpse, whose skin tore open a hairsbreadth more as she shrugged her slim shoulders. "Her sister brought her to this state, but what the king intends, we don't know," she answered. Her voice was quiet; her Erekoi came slowly, as slowly as Erlen had heard it spoken in class by those who couldn't find words in a foreign tongue. "I haven't known much of anything in this business, but the high priestess told me to bring Achane back, and so here I am." She smiled and touched the corpse's shoulder. "Achane is her sister. A swamp witch, a healer. One of Terichone's, as I am."

The name *Terichone* meant diagrams of cottages, incense-burners, statues, and rough-barked palm trees to Erlen, as well as lists of attributes and a few common prayers, but he nodded as though he understood. "Where is the king holding Achane?" he asked, trying the name on his tongue even as he tasted its derivation. *Achane: Ae kane, the patient girl.*

Gamela shrugged as the corpse could not. "We don't know that, either. Little promise for this rescue, do you agree?" She laughed with a faint tang of acrid self-mockery in her inflection. "She is in one of the king's fortresses, but which one, we don't know. We lost the king's trail days ago in the swamp and so we can't follow him to one lair or another. We don't know how we might enter a fortress to discover if it holds her; we don't know how we might enter a fortress even *if* it holds her. We don't know how we might get her out even if we do get ourselves in. We don't even know if she's still alive, although she was a few days ago."

"She is," Erlen answered, and it was less an effort at comfort than an article of faith. So long as the corpse stood, her resurrector lived, and his thesis held.

The woman crossed her thick arms over the railing, and the corpse stood beside her and stared without eyes at the passing forest. "I don't know what you plan to do, young man," Gamela muttered, and Erlen stepped closer. "I don't know if you're a Weiger or some other foreigner, but there's no country I know that speaks a different language and doesn't hate our king. Tell me—do you and your friends plan to attack the king's fortresses?"

"Yes," Erlen answered at once; he felt the space beside him fill and saw that Jeiger stood there. He looked at the two women who leaned at the rail, and Erlen touched the other man's arm as he realized that this was yet another world of words that was closed to the borderlander. "A moment—don't be afraid," he whispered to the tall borderlander, dropping back to the Wig dialect as Jeiger's eyes met the corpse's sunken, rotting gaze. Jeiger blinked and swallowed; he hissed something that Erlen didn't hear as Gamela spoke again.

"If you plan to attack these fortresses, take us with you so that we can look for Achane," begged the Erekoi woman. Erlen's hand fit cleanly against Jeiger's whole left hand, and he held it so that the man wouldn't forget. "I can heal the wounded, and I can ask the goddess's blessing on you. We won't be a burden, and we won't stand in your way—only help us to look for Achane."

The old, grey-braided woman stood with her arms folded in her woolen shirt, and her husband watched with a face cast from the bronze of Erekos and a hat woven from its reeds.

It had been too long that Erlen had watched men die crumpled against trees and women breathe their last huddled against unyielding doorways. Too long that he had been the only person in the entirety of the resistance who could heal, too long that he had watched Jeiger trace the sigils imperfectly and thus heal only imperfectly, too long that he had been an instant too late because there were too many wounded for one man to heal—

—and they were going to rejoin the holt-holders eventually, when the others of the party had brought the rest of the steamboats north; was it so much effort to bring two women with them? A woman and a corpse?

Jeiger met Gamela's eyes, and Erlen remembered the legend that he had written down of Jeiger and his father— how the legendary hunter's only son had followed the trail of the man and the great white stag that he had hunted, growing steadily more desperate as the rocks of the mountains had yielded nothing. How, when Jeiger Staag had found the white stag's skin hanging from a tree where his father had left it to preserve it from hunting beasts, it had been a perverse sort of joke, because his father's body had been ravaged by wolves and bears already.

The borderlands had their own tales of anguished searches for family, and they had their own tales of corpses.

"We'll help you," Erlen said softly; Gamela breathed out in a rush and then looked away, which Erlen thought meant that she was grateful. "Thank you for your offer of healing."

"I'll heal both your people and the Erekoi," Gamela told her shadow as it arced across the river.

"So will I," answered Erlen, and the grey-braided woman looked up at her husband and smiled.

The ink in his book was long since dry; the time had

long since come to call the five members of the raiding party who had stayed aboard and gather them around the helm to discuss docking in the old woman's village. He looked over to the red-haired border woman who stood with her knuckles clenched white around the bars of the helm and a smile bright as morning on her terrified face and, closing his book, Erlen smiled as well.

A Wig sailing a ship; a corpse searching for her sister; an old woman who won't tell her name; I and my comrades going to wage war on the king who keeps a fair maiden prisoner.

If I didn't know better, I would swear that this was a story.

he king who rode out in grave state from the capital's gates remembered the last time that the people had thrown white flowers in his path. They had stood at the edge of the bridge and watched with solemn eyes that hadn't enough familiarity to weep; they had let the procession become subsumed in their press and scattered pale flowers instead of bright ones, because the runners had told them hours ago that the king was dead.

The king *was* dead—Imlaus had died in the fortress that loomed over the Great Bowl, choking to death on blood-red wine far from the battlefields that had been his only joy. He had died with his sons at his side, pounding and flailing at his back to force him to cough and draw air into his lungs, and then, when he had gasped his last at the head of the long table, Adriolaus had looked at his brother with a kind of cold terror that was nothing like his usual easy laughter and asked, "Are you taking him to the tomb, then, or should I?"

And so Milaus had led the procession back to the capital, and Adriolaus had taken charge of the fortress on the mountain, and the people had tossed the white buds of that awakening season to greet the ever-sleeping monarch and the son who led him through the streets to the tomb where he now lay.

Strange, that those who cast their botanical prayers for the soldiers at the front should do so when Milaus was traveling back upon that long road to the fortress on the mountain. He had been young on the first journey, but the years had hardened away his youth.

The queen rode beside him, wearing a coat cut like a military jacket, and before him rode a soldier with the witch Achane sharing his saddle. Some people might have said that only the queen's cold eyes on the back of that man's neck kept him from handling the captive woman lewdly; some people, though, always assume the worst of their fellow men and cannot bring themselves to believe that mere common soldiers could have been brought up with dignity and courtesy for others. The witch rode chastely between the arms of the soldier, her legs swung to the side rather than parted and all but her eyes swathed in the healer's shawl.

They had been younger eyes when first she had spoken to the king. Aging with journeys, Milaus supposed, was not the sole prerogative of the nobility any more than courtesy was.

The farming country stretched out around the roadway, such as it was—here, the luxuriant earth parted its forests and permitted the Erekoi to plant grain crops and beans that even now stood in full blossom in neat rows. The wind drove the scent of beanflowers against the grey procession of armed men, and those who had been farmers in their real lives breathed it in like the scent of ambrosia.

For many, the king knew, war was not real life. It was a bad dream to which the recruiting officers had called them; it was a nightmare of ploughshares-into-swords from which every man hoped desperately to wake.

Some never woke at all, but others arose from the hard camp beds and went back out to the fields when their tours of duty were up. Some of these men even now rose to their feet in the beanfields or the wheatfields, shaded their eyes against the watery morning light, and remembered with a shiver the clang of not-real weapons on not-real armor. Their hands went without thinking to the not-real wounds in their thighs, their sides, their cheeks, or their arms, and they tried not to consider that the blows of the nightmare had left very real scars.

Because war was a dream (and only a dream, even if they'd had such a dream once before), some of the men dashed down the rows of beanpoles to laugh with the new recruits marching in formation behind the king. They soon found out that it was the king who was riding in front, and then it was a flurry of recollections—*I was in Company Three a year ago, called ourselves the Alligator Boys on account of the commander was a river-man,* jockeyed with, *Held the fortress at Aekos Point for three weeks while the Wigs smashed themselves against the door, and it was catapults for days until our relief routed 'em;* some were about, *See here, Your Majesty, not meaning to be smart or anything, but you understand that we're a lot of honest men who've got the harvest to think of, and some of us have got boys out at the front; couldn't we have*

them back for the harvest season? while others shouted only,
Long live the king!

And each got an answer, as was his due, and not
a one asked about the woman shawled like a healer in the
front of the procession. A healer going toward the battlefield
was nothing new. A healer wrapped in black was the kin of
no one; he or she had sacrificed that identity to be kin to all
who came for the working of magic. No one cared—indi-
vidually *cared*—about a healer, even though it was such a
person's business to care for each person who came for aid.

Being a healer was rather like being a king in that
respect.

In time, the press of farmers broke like a flight of but-
terflies dispersing, and such a flight rose from the bean flowers as the men returned to the fields. Across the hills with
their limestone bones, the wheatfields rippled in a gathering
breeze.

A little less than a day's journey ahead, there would
be an outpost for soldiers headed north; half a day's travel
past that was the long, narrow road carved into the slopes of
the mountains. At the top of that road like a lightning strike
was the fortress that guarded the Erekoi entrance to the Great
Bowl, the Fortress of Storms.

He had sent a rider ahead—*Lord Adriolaus, your
brother is returning. He brings his queen, soldiers, and a prisoner; he bids you prepare housing for all of them.* And Adriolaus would have housing, for the fortress that he watched
sprawled across the peak. Lord Adriolaus feared no siege
in his high fortress with its deep well; Lord Adriolaus, who
loved the pageantry of the court, had Weiger lords and gener-

als to dinner in times of truce and spoke fluent Weigenspeich to better amuse them. Lord Adriolaus had laughed to his older brother that he had even had the redoubtable Halgirth of Halsgard and his fur-clad retinue to dine, and the mountain man had brought three roasted sheep to the feast as a sign of goodwill. Halgirth had a weakness for tobacco imported from the motherland across the sea, and for all his size and barbarity, he was a shrewd politician who ignored the Erekoi so long as they ignored him.

Lord Adriolaus knew that he had political currency among the soldiers because they knew that his fortress was built on the foundations of the first temple to Loukaros, and blue banners streaked with lightning lined every rampart and every switchback on the long road up the mountain. Lord Adriolaus privately laughed at his brother for his religious devotions and his pilgrimages, for Lord Adriolaus of the many-chambered fortress had no room within his walls for gods.

Such a man was far different from Milaus and his queen.

Such a man had better lodgings than a tomb to greet a king returning.

he steamboats came up the river one by one; at noon, the first one arrived at the fishing village in the hills, and the borderlanders tied it with ceremony to the trees at the bank. Thereafter, the remaining vessels used the fresh winds of afternoon to drift in a long, broken line to the northlands. Near this point on another tributary, many miles away, the capital hunched on the water as though to guard it jealously from usurpers, but here, a collection of cottages and houseboats and wide docks welcomed strangers without question.

The next steamboat to arrive had the word Ithucha painted on its side in letters that gleamed in the sunlight of early afternoon. It was a feminization and a slight corruption of the word for fish, and this filled Erlen with theories until the coast-man explained to him that the Erekoi named their boats just as though they were people, from the greatest steamboat to the smallest fishing canoe. If such an idea was absurd to those who didn't live with boats every day of their lives, then perhaps the Erekoi fishermen might have found it equally absurd that Jeiger had named his bow and whispered its name every time he strung it, or that Eppa had given her sword a name that began with the same letter as the names of her children—and she sometimes called its name when she meant a daughter. Names were only a way of making all things individual; they were only a way of making all things a touch closer to human in human minds.

In the slow press of clouds across the evening sky— clouds that Jeiger said boded storms, for all they seemed to be no more than wisps of vapor like locks of hair—the commandeered fishing boat and a third steamboat in full sail began to navigate the deepest stretch in the center of the river. It bore the name *Galana*, as well as a story of another named steamboat called *Tarancha* that had run aground and been torn to pieces by the trees that it had struck. It had been a strange, sad sight, the borderlanders muttered, as though the ship were awaiting funeral rites.

A woman's corpse stood in the shadows of the trees; she, too, was a strange, sad sight.

The woman was no horror, although she was horrifying enough to see; there was nothing sinister in the way that she stumbled across uneven ground and leaned heavily on the arms of the forest until she had concealed herself from the Wigs whom she might terrify. The priestess Gamela who traveled with the zombi had pinned the black shawl back over the corpse's face and upper body, even though she herself did not wear concealment any longer. Gamela only called her companion "the corpse," although she looked ashamed of the words when she said them.

Gamela was even now learning the words that she would need to speak in the Wig dialect—"Where does it hurt?" and "Please, hold still," as well as "I am a healer. Please, don't kill me." At least she could read; Erlen had written the words down on a piece of paper sacrificed from the back of his book, and she studied the letters religiously.

In the same way, Erlen studied the ships' logs that his people had found in the captain's cabins of each steamboat— even the water-soaked, battered log of *Tarancha*. How many steamboats did the Erekoi have? The logs didn't answer, for all the ink on the parchment told exactly how many passengers had been picked up or had departed in every port, as well as the quantities of livestock on board and what provisions had been bought at great or little cost. The logs recounted every repair made and every cart of coal taken in, and yet they didn't mention their sister ships.

The coastal vessels could be safely ignored; the coastman had explained in his all but impenetrable dialect that their bottoms rode too low in the water for them to navigate the shallower river, even though he had spoken in terms of deep or shallow drafts and other such words that Erlen had never learned. So, too, could the fishing boats be ignored; they were too small to transport many soldiers at once. But how many steamboats did the Erekoi have?

He had no ready answer, and the next steamboat coming north might well be bristling with soldiers.

In the fishing village and in the water around it, the people gawked at the captive steamboats as though they were enormous beasts brought to heel—the people in the university's menagerie had looked so when they had beheld the captive wolf pack or the puma imported from the west. There was a festival feeling in the air as young girls trailed through the village pathways in long chains, each of them with a hand on a piece of long vine with red flowers. Sometimes a little boy would dart out from the illumination of a doorway to clutch at the vine, but the girl-children only laughed and shrieked and pushed the invader away; they were invincible together, and soon the young boys had also formed into chains with their own vines.

When they met at an intersection, boys and girls encountering one another like ancient enemies armed with flowers and leaves, the brown-skinned boys ducked between the girls at the center of the female chain and then tied their vine around that of the young girls. Their shadows danced under the wisps of clouds and the first stars in the still-light sky; they danced in the light that spilled from open doors.

The girls tied their vine around the knot that the boys had made, and suddenly there were no invaders and no enemies; there were only children dancing in a circle and laughing as they spun around like wheelspokes.

Three wheels of children danced in the streets of the village, and mothers brought chairs outside so that each mother could watch her child at play as she mended the nets by the light of house lanterns. Soon there were five wheels, and then six; on every face, there was a kind of amazing joy.

When the vines at last broke from pulling, the children paddled into the river in full clothing to get yet another look at the steamboats that had made their village special for a day, and Erlen remembered his question.

How many steamboats? Had he ever asked the Erekoi outright?

He stretched his back out of the hunch that it had adopted as he studied the logs by candlelight, rolling his head slowly around his neck until the bones crackled like brush underfoot, and went walking through the evening streets.

None of the old woman's "family" in this village looked at all like her; somehow this didn't surprise Erlen a bit. He came to the docks, where the grey-braided woman and her grey-haired husband sat conversing quietly as the first fishermen pulled in and tipped their hats to the couple. If these men—and a few women, Erlen suddenly realized; he hadn't thought that the Erekoi let women work at fishing—if these *fishers* each gave him a suspicious look as they beheld his pale hair and his angular face, they only looked back at the old woman again and began to smile.

The copper-skinned husband looked up at Erlen first, drawing his wife's attention with his eyes and a barely noticeable squeeze to her fingers. He asked gently, "Can we help you with 'n, son?"

"How many steamboats are there in Erekos?" Erlen replied. The couple smiled at each other at the question.

"How many steamboats? Aye, about six shallow-drafted enough for 'n river," answered the man. "You've got three up here, and a fourth 'n wrecked downriver; two 'ns were down along the south coast last I was in Palamea, and aren't like to come upriver for weeks. There's business in floodin', grisly business though it be—especially for they who have 'n steamboat."

Something in the old man's face made Erlen sure

that this was a time for decisions. Here he waited in an
Erekoi village with the king in a fortress in the mountains; it
would be a long time before the Wigs could make their way
down the river to the coast in order to search for the remaining two steamboats, and it would be an even longer time before they could get those other two boats back up the river.
Indeed, it would be a very long time all told, and soon the
Erekoi would be searching for the stolen steamboats, if they
didn't know already where those boats were. The part of Erlen that was a Weiger still demanded that they destroy the
boats they had and be done with it; the part of him that was
a human looked up at the ghostly pink clouds that Jeiger had
said meant great storms were coming, and he thought of the
wreck of *Tarancha*, driven into the tearing trees by the floods.

He thought of the children who even now bobbed
on the current of the river, awestruck at the paddlewheels of
those captured creatures with smokestacks and sails.

There is always a moment when a man stands before
the divine with all that he is and all that he has done and sub-
mits to judgment; in that instant, he must prove that he is a
human and not an object with a name.

Erlen faced the old husband and wife and asked, gently as the first steps of a babe, "Do you have children who could
take these boats down to the coast and help those wrecked by
the flooding? If Jeiger's right, and there is a storm brewing,
worse than the storm that brought the first flood—a steamboat
can't carry soldiers if it's full of refugees."

The two nodded at one another first, and then at him.
The dock-lanterns drew their hair into silver and made their
faces ageless. "Our daughter is out on a fishing boat, but she'll

come in soon—she and some people she knows will take the boats down to the coast," said the woman with the grey braid.

"Does she know how to sail a steamboat?" Erlen asked, for that practice had stymied him when first he had set out on this adventure.

"She does," the old man laughed, and his wife laughed with him. "And she knows where to take those ‹ns who have nowhere to go. She's 'n sensible girl—solid, sensible girl."

Erlen smiled. "Tell her and her friends to set out when it's safe, then, and give her my thanks."

He felt as though he should bow to them, as his class-mates who had been the sons of nobility had bowed to one another respectfully on parting; such a gesture, though, would have been lost on the couple, and so he shook their hands as the Wigs did and then walked out into the evening-turned-night.

Evening and night here were almost as beautiful as sunrise in the mountains, when he was outdoors in that first chill before the sun touched the earth. They were almost as beautiful as the circles of mushrooms in the soft soil that caught in the gullies; they were almost as beautiful as the cir-cles of lichen that grew on the bark of trees that he could only barely see in the grey morning light.

They were almost as beautiful as that first morning of freedom after they had escaped the Erekoi fortress, when Jeiger had taken him up to the top of the mountains and smiled over the long stretches of plains as the first sliver of sunlight crept over the rim of the world and bathed them both in soft light.

The clouds overhead were still lined with a bright, sandy glow, and the mothers of the village had taken their children inside and greeted fisherman fathers with warm stew and mended nets and the love of family. In the morning to come, the borderlanders would set out for the northern fortresses at which they would meet their kin for the first assaults; with luck, a few mines had already been cleared out and a few fortresses surprised and conquered.

In the morning, they would once again be facing a very real possibility of death, and intellectually, Erlen accepted that. It gave him more reason to be alive today, and to write what he could when he could, and to love his people well because he might never see them again.

He walked toward the village meeting hall where the Wigs were being housed, scenting potato soup on the air as he went. A familiar silhouette sat in the entrance, peeling potatoes with a knife that had skinned all manner of animals long before it ever encountered the potato; Erlen's step quickened without thought, and he smiled against the darkness when Jeiger looked up at him.

"We'll leave in the morning—the steamboats are going to be taken far away from the king and his people," Erlen said as he seated himself just inside the door and took a potato. Jeiger only nodded and flicked a curl of potato skin out the door, but he smiled as he hadn't before, and his hands were all but imperceptibly steadier.

There were talks that the two of them hadn't had, and probably would never have; they didn't need to discuss whether this was love or what it meant that they slept beside one another, whether it meant that they were comrades or brothers or lovers. On that first morning, when the sun had risen on their new freedom and the two of them had sat on the mountaintop with their hands touching, Erlen had opened his mouth as if to speak, but the way that Jeiger had looked over the plains halted any words that he might have thought were important.

By taking him to the top of the mountain and granting him the gift of the sunrise, Jeiger had said without words, *You make me feel this way. Like light coming into the world.* And that had been the first time in Erlen's life that he had ever believed in his soul that some parts of life needed no names to make them fully human.

*B*y the time the king's troops had reached the first way-station, a few cold stars shone in the high, pale reaches of the sky. Darkness swelled on the eastern horizon, and the wind from the distant sea blew the scent of bean blossoms across the fields to the sharpened stakes that ringed the deep, empty trench around the fortress.

It was a grim place, even amid the lush hills overflowing with wheat and beans, and it made the hills look just as grimly upon the world as that stone face. There were walls of grey rock lining the fields where wheat met beans, too low to keep out animals but just high enough to tell the neighbors, "This is mine, and that is yours." Achane hadn't noticed the walls before.

The soldier who held her was muttering about enclosure as his horse took quick, heavy steps like drumbeats across the wooden planking of the drawbridge; his hands grew briefly tight on the reins, but the tension went out of him when he passed under the thick stone archway and into the fortress. To him, perhaps, this place meant solace. Perhaps it meant the country-love of the red and violet banners embroidered with leaping pumas and grizzled rams; certainly, his eyes scanned the banners and the cannon mounts as though they, too, were his forces as he passed through the courtyard. Perhaps this place only meant enclosure, and his sudden calm was the calm of surrender.

Achane stared up at the thin clouds that stretched across the sky like pink gauze, and she smiled a bitter, thin-lipped smile to realize that a storm was coming. Perhaps it would only drop thick rain on the bean blossoms, but more likely it would rip at the sails of the boats at the coast and drive the lightest ones into the rice fields, if not all the way to the trees. Houses just resettled on their own foundations would be lifted once more, drifting on their tethers to the edges of the clearings around them; mothers and fathers would stand guard at the porches on either side of the houses as those porches became decks, and older brothers and sisters would try to keep the children quiet with stories as they themselves shook with terror at the nightmare idea of the house falling down.

She could feel the storm brewing like an ache in her marrow; it would be a day, perhaps two days in coming, but come it would.

"Down you get, mother," the soldier whispered to her, lifting her with chaste hands from the back of the horse before he lowered himself to the ground as well. The drawbridge groaned as it was pulled roughly upright, but chains bound it there and it could not lie down again. "I wish the road had been easier for you."

"Thank you," Achane answered, although she didn't meet his eyes and she might as well have been thanking the ground.

"The king says that you'll retire with the queen," said the soldier.

If she didn't look up, Achane didn't have to see that he was exactly the sort of man whom her mother would have wanted her to marry; she didn't have to assess his plain and practical face and his hazel eyes lined with creases from smiling as kindly as he was surely smiling now. If she didn't look up, Achane could hear his words and the concern in them without thinking anything but that this soldier, too, feared the queen.

When Achane didn't reply, the soldier called for a page-adjutant to lead the healer to her quarters, and the young man who responded was Ilaumeleus of the boots that pinched—now, Achane could not help but notice, he wore larger boots that didn't quite disguise that he was growing too tall for his brightly colored trousers. The boy gave her a tired frown as though he were trying to remember who had eyes of that shape, but the freeze of recognition did not come until he had led her into the fortress proper and halfway up the stairs to a guestroom. "You're the witch," he said, one hand on the grey stone of the wall and the other holding a lantern high to illuminate his wide eyes. "At Terichone's shrine—the one who raises zombi."

Achane laughed, but the black veil muffled what little mirth came with it. "I never thought I'd be known as such a person."

Ilaumeleus stared for a moment. His mouth worked as though he were trying to snatch words from the air with it, but then he shook his head and continued up the stairs.

It occurred to Achane then that she had no need to follow him; it occurred to her, too, that she had nowhere to go if she didn't. Even if she could somehow get out of the fortress with the drawbridge raised, there would be only the deep pit hewn into the earth around her. Even if she could escape the pit, she couldn't find her way home again.

There was calm in surrender, for all it was the calm of having every other option barred.

The hall into which Ilaumeleus led her was well-illuminated with oil lamps that, from the lingering sulfur smell of matches, had just been lit; Achane wondered if the oil had been brought from as far away as the stone and timber that made this place, or the people who now lived in it. She followed the adjutant to a room at the end of the hall, which had a heavy wooden door and several bolts driven into the stone on the inside.

Ilaumeleus bowed to her and handed her his lantern when she entered, and Achane could see his shadow under the door even when she shut it and rammed each of the three bolts home. She leaned against the door with the lantern still clutched in her hand and her eyes fixed on those bolts that held her safe.

She knew that she would starve if she remained barricaded in this place, but the idea held a clean appeal—the priests and priestesses of Terìchone had never fasted to purify themselves, because they had never believed in diminishing their ability to help others even if it did bring them closer to the divine, but in legends, other mystics had given up food, shelter, and clothing to spend their time cleansing their bodies and awaiting their reunions with the gods. In scrolls of legends, brave priests had sat between city walls and besieging armies and slowly wasted away, refusing to move or be moved until they had moved the hearts of those who would harm others. Stories had crossed the ocean with the whalers and the coast-men who traded with the rice farmers, and in these stories the most beautiful women in the world had shut themselves in towers so as to die praying to their own gods rather than marry the followers of different gods.

Surely she, neither the most beautiful nor the most mystical woman in the world by any stretch, could nonetheless shut herself in this room and so save herself from the temptation of the king's mad idea?

To learn how to raise a man from the dead—really raise him from the dead, and not merely animate his corpse— to learn to turn time backwards to before death and to save a thousand mothers from the grief of losing children, a thousand sisters from the grief of losing their sisters—if it meant raising an army of the dead, would you not do that so that you could bring them all back to life in the end?

Achane coughed, just as Shabane had coughed every day of her life because her older sister had been unable to heal her, and she breathed in through her nose to steady her nerves.

She could shut herself away in here, and in time the decision would be out of her hands. She had already eaten so little that it would be mere days before she wasted away.

Achane lifted the lantern over her head, and she

turned and surveyed the room for the first time.

The queen knelt in a dark corner with a bowl of water at her knees, and her moss-agate eyes were rolled up so that only the whites showed like milk against her face.

The queen was called Carisica; Achane knew that because it had been shouted up and down the rice paddies when the old king had died and the new one had taken a wife from up the coast. Carisica had been the daughter of the lord who owned the ricelands; she had once, years ago, ridden her horse down the slat-roads and splashed through the rice paddies, laughing with suitors and retinues of maids. She had been beautiful, Achane had been told, and once the witch had fancied that she had heard the caroling laugh of the lady trilling in the alligator palms. The laugh, though, had only been a bird's cry, and slowly even the rice farmers forgot the name Carisica and that their laughing young lady was now the queen.

Achane knew in the hollow of her chest that this woman who knelt unseeing and unmoving was not the same woman who had once been the lady of the ricelands. She knew it in the same place she knew that a storm was coming. Something had broken in Carisica, or else had been made so hard that it couldn't break. Those who prayed to Loukaros were those who had suffered; their prayer was always, "Lift this storm from my life, O lord of storms."

Their prayer was often, "Grant me the power to strike back."

Achane slid each bolt out again as carefully and silently as though the queen could see or hear her, and she hung the lantern on the hook in the center of the room so that there would be no dark corners in which terror could hide.

When Ilaumeleus brought in a basket of bread with bean paste and a plate of fresh-cooked meat, the queen hadn't moved, and Achane took the food in trembling fingers without daring to think of starving herself inside this little room. She had far greater faith in her ability to overcome temptation than in her ability to overcome the queen.

When the mountain people traveled, Gamela soon discovered, they walked. The coast-man from the steamboat and his bird-boned wife led the procession, followed by Erlen, the pale-haired man who spoke for the mountain people. Behind them wound a long line in single file, like a rivulet of grim-faced men and women with cheeks battered by wind; at the very end of the line walked Gamela.

Erlen had asked his friend with the four-fingered hand to help the corpse travel; the tall man had considered for a moment, then nodded and hefted the corpse onto his back. The scent of her decay had made him hold her more carefully, perhaps to keep her flesh intact, but his grip on her legs was firm, and he leaned forward under the weight even now so that the dead woman's weak grip on his shoulders wouldn't be the only force keeping her in place. Gamela had given him a tablet so that the odor of the corpse wouldn't make him ill, but he couldn't speak Erekoi and so had only put it in his pocket as a curiosity.

They toiled uphill many paces behind the last in the line before them, and the four-fingered man offered no complaint at the weight or the smell or even the company. The mountain people didn't travel as the Erekoi did, singing under their breaths and chattering to one another as they went; they were more grave than soldiers walking to battle and bore themselves as silently as hunters in the woodlands.

It was a strange road that they walked, edged with mist as it twisted through columns of trees; not a twig snapped under an incautious foot, and not a bird called against the dimness of morning. Gamela had an eerie feeling that the mist around this path wouldn't lift when the sun rose high in the sky and burned away the vapor in the valleys.

These trees had no flowers, no high air-trumpets clinging to branches and catching water in the fluted white cups of the blossoms, no snakeblossom vines twisted around the limbs of every tree. They had long since left behind the last alligator palm, which made Gamela feel as cold inside as if the goddess Terìchone had forsaken her. The mountains were not a charitable place—everything that the mountain people had, they had carved from an unwilling earth.

The travelers passed across a weather-beaten bridge one by one, their faces lined with trepidation at the quick-rushing waters beneath them; even the man with the four-fingered hand, who had borne death on his back for hours without complaint, grew paler at the sight of the bridge and the thick fog that surrounded it. Points of red stood out at his cheekbones where the wind had scraped them raw.

Gamela faced the thin bridge of planks alone, and walked across it as easily as if it were a paved road. The bridges in Erekos were far worse, and she had walked dozens of them in Terìchone's name.

At last, the tall man who bore the corpse on his back set his feet on the wet wood.

Gamela swallowed the throb of her heart.

Each step was an eternity of testing the solidity of the wood and the slickness of the bark; each step was laid as carefully as a mosaic tile onto the rough framework of split logs and planks. Each step brought the two of them closer to the other side.

Gamela heard a rumble like thunder and peered upriver, straining her eyes against the thick mist.

She froze.

Through the thick fog, a massive boulder was buffeted by the current; the man on the bridge dropped to the planking and Erlen and Gamela leapt forward, as though they could reach the two on the bridge—

—the boulder struck the bridge and surely must have ripped the frail frame out of its foundations, but for that it didn't.

The river rushed onward, and the boulder lay trapped against the triangles of wood that supported the spray-soaked pathway.

As the man with four fingers stood again, the corpse still on his back, Gamela noticed for the first time that the supports of the bridge were made of rough-barked, resilient alligator palm, the tree that weathered storms by bending against the force without breaking. Made of alligator palm—

miles away from where alligator palms grew.

Gamela said a prayer of thanks to Terichone even before the man's feet touched solid earth, and she hurried close when he set down the corpse to examine her for wounds.

The fall had ripped at the dead woman's shins through the fabric of her dress, rending the flesh there and leaving great, dirty splinters embedded in the skin. Through the gashes, Gamela could see a few young maggots beginning to crawl, and she knew that she would have to tease out these insects as well so that the corpse wouldn't lose all movement.

She touched Erlen's wrist and told him carefully about the need for a fire on which to burn stimweed, and he replied in dazed half-Erekoi, "All to need resting *ength* now."

The mountain people helped her to build a fire and tie together a framework of sticks with the lengths of rope that she had salvaged from the steamboats—for a daughter of the fishing villages never loses the instinct to have rope, even when she has been educated and walks far from home—before the tall man who had carried the corpse came to help her slather the frame with mud and lift the woman's body onto it. Some of the mountain people regarded the zombi carefully, as though she were dangerous; others examined the scene with frank fascination, and the man with the four-fingered hand only nodded at the procedure.

Perhaps he was a hunter. Hunters understood how to salvage wormy meat, although surely he had never burned stimweed under a human corpse.

Gamela didn't like to think what was going through the zombi's mind as she lay on a bed of wood and rope over a roaring fire, so instead she tossed a papyrus-wrapped packet of stimweed into the fire and stood to watch the gruesome spectacle of living insects emerging from a dead woman.

"Gamela," she said, touching her chest.

"Jeiger," the man replied, touching his own. "Erlen he say," he began, and then paused to consider the next words before continuing in still-rough Erekoi, "You are an healer."

Gamela nodded at that. "I am a healer," she answered in the mountain dialect, and was glad that Erlen had given her those words this morning.

The exodus made the fire sizzle, and if the corpse's clothing hadn't been dripping wet, Gamela might've worried about a spark catching it. The mud began to harden, though, and the corpse lay as still as—well, as still as the dead. The shawl caught the insects; Gamela used a large stick to lever the body upright and allow the worms and beetles to spill from the black fabric and into the fire.

Jeiger nodded at the same time that Gamela did, after neither had heard the sound of an insect falling away for a long moment, and together they lifted the framework from over the fire and eased it to the ground. As Jeiger began to dismantle the frame, Gamela propped the corpse against a tree and unpinned the black shawl to shake it out so that not one white maggot or shining beetle might remain in its folds to eat away the corpse's flesh.

A large patch of skin from the corpse's temple fell to her lap as she sat where she had been propped, and she picked it up in her burned fingers and laid it aside as though it had never been a part of her. Quite suddenly, Gamela found herself crying.

She didn't dwell on why she was crying, or how she

must appear to the solemn mountain people who gathered around her; she only stood straighter, brushed off the shawl once more, and dried her eyes. It was not for the priestesses of Terichone to dwell on the experience of suffering when they could do something to end it.

Jeiger, though, looked between the two of them as though he understood. He rose to his feet with the rope neatly coiled in one hand and passed it to Gamela without a word, then said something quiet in his own language to the gathered mountain people before going to sit at Erlen's side.

When the camp disbanded, Jeiger took the corpse on his back again, but this time, Erlen walked with them at the end of the line, and although little conversation came between them on the long and misty road, the pale-haired man translated between Erekoi and the mountain speech. It wasn't a friendship, exactly; Gamela didn't know what to say to these strangers who were bent on keeping these mountains for themselves, and they seemed not to know what to say to a woman who loved Erekos despite the flaws of its leadership. Instead, they talked only of safe things—of family, of the strange road they walked, and of the misconceptions of the Erekoi that the Weigers had represented as fact in a book that Erlen had recently lost.

They arrived at a village called a holt late in the evening, when the old woman and the coast-man had to light a dim lantern so that the straggling line of walkers could follow them along the uneven path. By lantern-light, the holt seemed enormous and made entirely of tents, which Gamela thought unbelievably primitive until Erlen commented to her that the rest of the "Wigs" would surely arrive within a day and that the mountainside would bristle with water-proofed wool when the full force was present.

The holt itself, the village around which this army had camped, lay within a cavern that smelled of goats and sawdust. The low entrance forced the line of mountain folk to stoop as they navigated the first narrow stretch; Gamela watched Jeiger walking spread-legged with the corpse on his back and prayed quietly that he would remember her and not stand too quickly. The idea of the woman's brains dashed out in a cave in the mountains after they had come so far almost brought tears to Gamela's eyes again.

Jeiger stood straighter in front of her, and Gamela's heart lurched until he stepped aside and revealed that this narrow tunnel had emptied into an enormous cavern, the whole of it lit by blown-glass lanterns and torches that burned in brackets along every wall, as well as an enormous fire in the very center of the floor. Stone enclosures lined the cavern around the fire, each wall eight feet high but roofless—for those who live together under a great stone roof nonetheless need not see their neighbors every moment. Varnished, elaborately carved wooden panels stretched between stalagmites as thick as Gamela's considerable waist, and behind those panels milled herd upon herd of goats and mountain sheep like the rams of Erekoi heraldry.

It was hardly primitive, for all it was a cave; here, Gamela realized, was a civilization that was equal to the civilization of the average Erekoi fisherman in every way.

Erlen and Jeiger led them and their force of thirty through the cavern to a wide gateway lined with waterfalls of stone; at this place, the mountain people had carved the very rock of the cavern with stylized scenes of horses pulling carts across expanses of flat land, of huddles of men and women leading their flocks, and above all, of joyous people pointing fingers at a line of stalagmites like the mountains themselves.

Beyond those stalagmites, in an alcove with the same images of pilgrimage in bas relief on its walls, sat dozens of old, tough men—and one white-haired woman who hailed Erlen and Jeiger as soon as they appeared in the doorway. Jeiger lowered the corpse carefully from his shoulders and helped her to lean against the illustrated wall, and then the two men went to kneel by the old woman's side and speak with her over the shouting of the men gathered here.

The thirty mountain people dispersed, perhaps to seek their friends among the tents and perhaps to sit by the central fire and cook dinner. Even the coast-man and his wife vanished back into the main cavern, and they were gone when Gamela looked for their faces.

She stood awkwardly beside the corpse, wishing in that moment that she were still wearing her black shawl to hide her foreignness from these people who made war upon her kind.

Erlen looked up over his shoulder then and motioned them over, and Gamela walked with her arm clasped in the corpse's so that neither of them would fall in a heap before these important and angry people; if nothing else, it would only draw their attention.

"This is Eppa—she is our holt matriarch now," Erlen said when the two were seated against the wall, gesturing to the white-haired woman. "I have told her that you are a healer, and she is glad to have you. That," he added, pointing a subtle finger to a tall, broad man who spoke words that she did not understand with a harsh and rasping voice, "is Halgirth. This is his holt."

He smiled a little. "He doesn't know it, but I probably owe him my life."

No explanation came, but only more words that Gamela did not understand; Eppa spoke quickly and got quick answers from the men, until Jeiger looked at Gamela and the corpse again and asked something. Eppa considered for a moment, then pointed out the entryway and spat out a string of syllables that Erlen hastily translated. "She says that you can stay in the healers' tent—Jeiger will show you the way," he said, and then returned to what must have been his report of the theft of the steamboats.

As Jeiger lifted the corpse in his arms like an ailing child and carried her across the threshold, Gamela remembered the last that she had seen of the steamboats. Fishermen had climbed aboard and listened to instructions from an oddly familiar woman, a solid, clear-voiced figure with her grey hair pulled back in a bun and heavy, ruddy arms like Gamela's, and with the first light of morning, the steamboats had been cut free from their tethers and had moved in a slow procession down the river.

Gamela had thought in that moment, as the smoke began to billow from the smokestacks of the first ship, that the clear-voiced woman was the most beautiful woman alive.

She shook her head, closed her eyes to clear them of the memory, and then followed Jeiger through the stone teeth of the cavern.

Erlen is walking the halls of the university with his book in his hands; he is looking for the man to whom he is supposed to give it, but the high walls echo emptily with his footsteps as rain pounds at the stained glass windows. Master Tuefweil is not in his office, although a fire burns in the grate and the papers scattered across his desk say that he is soon to return. Erlen kneels before the fire and warms his hands there; they are caked with white clay.

Part of him knows then that he is dreaming, and that if he looks down, he will be naked and painted with prayers in Old Erekoi. The part that knows he is dreaming opens the book and leafs through to the diagram of the steamboat and the notation of the war council at which the holt-holders determined to wait until the remaining Wigs reached Halsgard and then mount a night assault on the nearest fortress; he leafs past the reports of how many mines have been cleared out throughout the mountains—

—the next pages have been burned away.

Suddenly the flagstones are screaming; he drops the book and it begins to burn as he clutches his ears but he doesn't care that the words are crying out as well; he can only stagger to his feet and run through the empty halls of the university as the vaulted ceilings fill with clouds and the flagstones scream calumnies and the stained glass windows break one by one to let the rain inside as lightning flashes against the falling shards of blood-red glass and a silhouette of a man stands before him with arms spread wide—

—Erlen woke in an instant that drew him to sitting; he checked his book with the horror of a mother who has dreamed of her child murdered, and he only breathed out

when the pages lay whole and unburned before him. With
that fear put to rest, he looked around himself again.

In the dimness of the dying fire, he could only remind
himself that this was the medical tent, larger and more perfectly waterproof than the rest of the tents that Mittler Holt
had brought, and that he was sitting in the darkness with his
blanket over his waist and Jeiger lying asleep beside him. A
few other healers lay curled up in the tent, none of them mag-
ic-workers but all of them skilled at setting bones and ampu-
tation; most of them were snoring gently against the patter of
heavy rain on the woolen tent roof. Again, Erlen was seized
with a desire to go walking in the night, but the memory of
the lightning-struck book and his fall from the mountaintop
made him shake his head and mentally confine himself to the
healers' tent.

He felt around in his pack for the heavy lump of potato bread that he had salvaged from dinner and impaled it on
his knife, then rose to kneel by the fire and warm the bread
there. Gamela had been pleased with the new taste, she had
said, for the Erekoi had yams instead of the Weigenland potatoes. She lay sleeping apart from the other healers, and the
corpse lay unmoving beside her.

Erlen didn't know enough about zombi to know
whether they could sleep, or whether their bodies slept but
their minds did not. He couldn't return to the passages in *The
Wayes and Custommes of the Ereckoy* that had referred to such
creatures; the book lay in its ashes on the top of the mountain
of Mittler Holt. The thought still made a feeling rise in him
that he couldn't name, and so he didn't try to name it.

He brought the bread to his lips and felt the heat rising from it, then took a careful bite.

The nearest fortress, as he knew very well, was the one at which he and Jeiger had been honored guests—if the Erekoi honored their guests with sharp hooks and cunning machines, hot powders and truth serum. If such were the case, then they had been very honored indeed.

In all probability, Halgirth didn't know that he had saved their lives. A lord with olive skin and hair dyed to a ruddy brown had come to the dungeons on the third day, when the afterimages of sigils were still hanging on the air, and announced that the northern holt-holder had lobbied successfully for the release of all borderlander prisoners, which meant that they were free to go as far away as they could manage. In his mind and in his stories, Erlen always called it an escape from that fortress, but it had only been a release.

If they hadn't been released, they would have died in that place underground.

In all probability, the Erekoi lord hadn't known what his dungeonmasters did in the lamp-lit darkness. Such men as he, dressed in silken robes from across the sea and talking offhandedly about the negotiations between local powers, were creatures of the light, and they seldom ventured into the darkness.

Most men were creatures of light. Most men didn't do well in crowding and stench and darkness day after day, and in time jailers became prisoners as well. In time, the darkness crept into even the most decent of people and made them afraid of the shadows that lurked in other men, and so they carved those shadows out with red-hot metal and imprecations.

The Erlen who had attended university could never have killed a man, and yet the Erlen who sat in the dim medical tent and tore at potato bread with his teeth had killed many. It terrified the part of him that still wrote his Great Work; it terrified him most of all because he didn't know how many men he had killed.

The zombi lay facing the tent roof with her ruined face, staring without eyes at the ripples as water washed it.

How had she died? Who had she been in life? Gamela couldn't these questions, for the witch Achane had never spoken of her sister but to discuss her health. Achane had been hard as stone, incapable of surrender, beautiful and brilliant and determined to heal her sister—she had raised a woman from her deathbed, and she had summoned a snake to send a message across the miles. Such a woman had done a dark deed in raising the dead, and yet she had done it for the purity of her love.

Such a woman would never have allowed herself to be broken in the hands of the king's torturers, deep in the bowels of the fortress on the mountain. Such a woman's love for life and desire for accomplishment could never have been shattered when she heard the stones screaming and realized that nothing could be kept whole and pure in the world.

Erlen glanced across the tent to the faint outline of a sparsely bearded face, and he felt a growing cold like the sensation of the book's burning.

He loved this mountain land and its promise; he loved the sunrise over the plains and the way the trees sounded when he stood absolutely still. He loved the people who lived here and the way that they lived, quarreling and yet loving each other like family as they built a new world together.

And yet the war had brought a darkness over this

place, and that darkness was alive inside him.

He finished his bread and put away his knife with a slow, chill understanding of what he had felt on the mountaintop.

Erlen slipped under his blanket again and put a fire-warmed arm around Jeiger, but it was a long time before he returned to sleep.

he papyrus lay before her, and she dipped her reed pen into the bottle of ink at her knee.

Aekos.

Erekos.

Choraa.

"Shonè, give me the strength of the wood."

The incense rose to the stone walls of the castle, seeking herbs that were not there; the circles drawn in Achane's blood were still wet on her scrolls. Letters of power coiled around one another in those circles, and candles burned at their centers and spilled wax onto the papyrus.

Heira.

Orekos.

The light flickered around her as a chill breeze swept in through the arrow-slits, and the heavy shawl made every movement achingly slow as she wrote the name of the minutes-dead soldier who lay beyond the candlelight.

"Aenikus, give me the force of the blacksmith."

Ræta.

"Loukaros, give me the lightning of your storms."
Sweat trickled between her eyebrows; she could feel the flesh
knitted by her anger and her fear. "Take the storm from this
man's life, and give him the power to rise again."

Orekos.

"Terìchone, I am sorry."

Sibar.

"Aechoros."

The soldier Aechoros rose heavily to his feet, and
Achane watched him stand. The wound in his gut still gaped;
he glanced at it with a kind of wonderment and touched the
crusted blood. He took a slow step forward, then stood still
again when the movement drew a gout of blood from the
wound.

"I was dead," he whispered as blood seeped down his
hip. "Am I alive?"

"You're a zombi," answered Achane through the veil
of her shawl. "I wish I could have brought you back to life."

Aechoros stared at his hands, dripping with his own
blood; he looked around the barren, empty room in the castle,
sank to his knees, and screamed to the rafters like the last echo
of every lost thing.

Achane felt the chill of the castle flowing into her
bones, and she had no words to stop the dry, lonely sobs of a
man who had lost everything and had been brought back to
witness that loss.

"Please," Aechoros gasped. "I have a wife. Children.
They wouldn't want to see their father return a zombi. Better

I should've died—better I had died, than live like this."

Achane's face was as stony as the walls.

"Please." The soldier sat with his hands clutching his knees, his shoulders shaking. "Please, witch, let me free of this body. Let me free."

The blood runs from the wound and sinks into the stone of the castle, just as the circles of Achane's blood sink into the scrolls and fill them—

—The horse took a step onto the steep switchback road, and the jolt brought Achane awake.

The fortress stood above her, high at the summit of the mountain. She glanced up the dizzy slope and looked down again immediately to the arms of the soldier who held her. She was as safely encircled as could be, when not even dreams were safe any longer.

$$\Rightarrow\Leftarrow$$

"Your problem, brother, is that you don't understand what gods are *for*."

Lord Adriolaus smiled at the king and cupped his golden goblet as though it were an accessory rather than a vessel, taking a measured sip of wine with his eyes closed in real or feigned enjoyment. He had graciously allowed his drenched brother the seat nearest to the fire in the great hall, but the honor dried Milaus's clothes very little and his pride not at all. The wound in his side ached as though it had just been made, and water trickled slowly down his back as he waited for his chance to leave and interrogate the witch again.

"What are gods for, then?" he snapped. There had

been Weigers in the fortress on the mountain when the king
had arrived; three had been high-ranking officers in dress uniform, one of them a woman, and they had whispered to Milaus's brother with looks of horror as the soaked contingent
of fresh soldiers had spilled into the hall. The king had seen
the Weigers' lady general press her hand against Adriolaus's
shoulder with far too much familiarity for one enemy to show
another, and it had been all he could do not to rip down the
Erekoi banner that hung from the great hall's rafters and rub
it in his brother's face. «What are gods for, atheist, and why is
it my problem?"

 Adriolaus laughed as though it were a good joke, but
his laughter rang hollow against the empty walls. "You've
read the texts. Loukaros creates trouble so that humans will
have to learn to change their ways. Shonè and Aenikus take
care of their children so that we puling humans will eventually bugger off from their sacred hearth and make our own
homes." He raised an eyebrow to see if that blasphemy had
hit particularly hard, but Milaus watched the fire and didn't
particularly care. "Even Terìchone the great philanthropist
doesn't help any man who can't be arsed to help himself.
The gods," he concluded with a toast to thin air, "are here to
see whether we're ever going to become godly. And it's your
problem because you are going to spend the rest of your ad-
mirable and kingly life never striving for godliness."

 "The gods don't sire children by housemaids, nor in-
vite their enemies to dinner, nor lie with the same damned
enemies before a battle," Milaus told the fireplace. His fist was
buried in his jacket again, and in the firelight his face wore the
same hard lines as his father's portrait.

"Only a few of them," said the lord of the Fortress of Storms, but his bravado had vanished into the air with his vainglorious toast to atheism. "I keep the peace here, Milaus, and it's harder than keeping the war. Fewer of our men have died in the Great Bowl since Father died—you have to admit that."

"We've regained fewer fortresses, as well, and held fewer than we've regained. We've given you the cannons you asked for; we'd expected better in return. The queen doesn't care for your laxity, and I don't care for the cost." In the fire's brightest embers, the king saw the heat of Achane's defiance, and yet he had seen it wane and flicker in the tomb of kings, if only briefly. He could still turn her—he could still bring to life the army of the dead that he dreamed of. "Father ran an economical war, for all his failings."

"He did, at that. He killed a damned lot of people, too, and you were nearly one of them. I see the way you still grab at that stick in the gut." Adriolaus stood and undid the cloak-fastenings from Milaus's shoulders, hanging the cloak itself on the back of a chair. "It's too early in your visit for us to be talking about the war. We can't even be besieged here, with the walls and the well; we certainly won't suffer from a full assault even if every Weiger in the Bowl manages to climb that blasted road up the mountain. The latest truce doesn't run out until more than a month from now, so I've diverted a few of our troops to the border fortresses to keep an eye out for Wigs and wandering gods."

"Gods?" Milaus asked, fighting the temptation to strip down to his underclothes and finally get truly dry in the warmth of the fire. Adriolaus would only have laughed, but it would not do for any wandering servants, soldiers, or female

Weiger generals to see the king of Erekos unclothed. "Have the gods been walking these blasted mountains? Are they fraternizing with the enemy, too, or is it only my brother?"

"You may well laugh," snorted Adriolaus. "We had a report from a mining camp that Loukaros himself had walked through one morning, white and blond and mother-naked. He said something that made the miners clear out pretty quickly—something like that he was going to flood the mine and drown the lot of them—but the scout I sent down again couldn't see more than superficial flooding in even the lowest levels. It sounds like a crock of shit, to be honest."

Thunder made their goblets vibrate on the table and set a dog howling somewhere in the fortress. Adriolaus chose not to consider it a comment on the matter. "Who was your prisoner?" he asked instead. "The old healer woman."

"She isn't old—she's starving herself to decrepitude. Ilaumeleus tells me that she's barely been eating." Between them lay the unspoken acknowledgment that Ilaumeleus was the younger brother's son by a chambermaid; Milaus gulped at his wine and tried not to feel either disdainful or jealous. "She's a witch from the swamp, and she can raise zombi, like in our old nursery stories—don't laugh, Adri; I've *seen* her do it." Adriolaus wasn't laughing. "I hope that she'll raise sufficient zombi to take over for our troops in the borderlands; perhaps she can even raise enough of the dead to conduct the war here in the Great Bowl, and then it'll never cost us another human life. Does *that* please you?"

By the shadows in Adriolaus's handsome face as he stood by the fire, it did not. Not a trace of their father lined his brow or drew his nose into a hook; even the fine, dark color of his hair now bore faint reddish streaks that might have been mental patricide and might have been concession to his fair-haired Weiger guests. Not a trace of the war-economy of a brutal king existed in Adriolaus, but perhaps it was fair to say that not a trace of most noble virtues remained, either. The shadows curved across his fine cheekbones, and he held his goblet between his fingers with a carelessness so long affected that it had become real.

"The men won't like the idea of serving with their own dead comrades," Adriolaus said against another sip of wine. It might have been his real belief; it might have been a convenient excuse. Milaus had learned long ago not to try discerning the difference. "I can't say I'd enjoy it much, either."

"And if I died—" Adriolaus heard the unspoken end and turned to his brother with a voice like a hammer and an expression like a blacksmith facing hot metal.

"No. The last thing in the world that I'd want would be my brother's body defiled, and I shall kill anyone who tries it."

When the younger brother led the older to his chambers, they did not speak of the war or of the Weigers who had been lounging at their ease in the great hall. They didn't speak of cost, and they didn't speak of zombi or of the black-shawled woman who had been taken to the dungeons beneath the fortress to face their father's portrait. For the space of time that they walked the halls of the fortress on the mountain, they were only brothers and not king and lord, and they talked of music and stories and tournaments and all of the things that we humans use to distract ourselves from the real concerns of our lives.

When they parted, Milaus watched his brother's back

through a haze of pain from his side and listened to the drip from his clothes to the stone floor as it played counterpoint to the brewing storm outside. The king knew then, as his only surviving kin turned the corner and passed from sight, that he would have risked the horror of a zombi in place of a loved one for the slim chance of once more meeting Adriolaus's politician's eyes and hearing his younger brother make some off-color remark about the gods.

He thought he knew the name of the zombi that he had left behind in the swamp, facedown in the mud, and the knowledge ached like a gut wound long healed over.

Someone had carved at the stone floor of the dungeons—several someones, some of whom had counted the days of their imprisonment in cold tallies, others who had passed the time in the dim cell writing their names or cursing the darkness, and a few who had lamented lost freedom and its handsome women by imprinting such naked beauties across the hard stone floor. But someone who had been a great deal more patient and dedicated had left the strangest marks of all, and those held Achane's attention. Letters that Achane didn't know ran in straight lines across the rock for an armspan, then spun out in loops and whorls as abruptly as though the lines had been tossed down by an angry giant.

They must have been carved years ago, perhaps centuries—the most recent scratches in the stone showed pale against the limestone walls and the floor, and the older etchings had been partially obliterated by the press of dirty feet, but these particular carvings seemed to exist in another time-frame altogether. The grooves of the letters were as thick as a finger, and worn to the same texture as the surrounding stone. It reminded Achane of the flood monument near her home, carved with rushing currents in the same loose coils; like the monument, these broken lines of unreadable text held a feeling of despair at the broken world.

The rain had caught the king's party as it rounded a corner halfway up the mountainside, and Achane was even now grateful for the shawl that the blue-eyed healer had given her. Although it was heavy with water, it had kept her clothing dry, and she had been able to draw shapes of power in the dust to dry the black cotton fabric before wrapping it again around her body.

Perhaps, she thought as she studied her own markings in the dust, the shapes in the stone had been a spell carved by prisoners long ago. She wondered idly if even such a massive undertaking as the carvings in the floor had been able to help them, or if they had only died with dashed hopes and raw fingers on the filthy blue-grey stone. *Could* magic be turned to escape? Could it transport one person or a dozen through solid stone, or bend unyielding iron, or blind a hundred guards and thousands of soldiers?

It could raise the dead, couldn't it? Why shouldn't magic break down physical boundaries, when it shattered spiritual borders so easily?

She had never needed such magic before. Her life had been given over to healing the body, to knowing where the spark of divinity lurked in each leaf and each letter of the old alphabet and to combining these symbols together into a channel through which her prayer could flow to reach the gods.

Achane had always been taught that magic was neither a resource inherent in the world nor a power of her own,
but rather an answered prayer, and she didn't know the forms
of prayer to use to ask Shonè to rend the fortress's stones or
to ask Aenikus to melt the iron of the bars in his forge. It had
taken her three days to find the texts that told her how to raise
Shabane from death, because she had never thought that she
would have to know that particular magic. In the darkness of
a dungeon carved with foreign words, any treatises on escape
were as incomprehensible as though the moon herself had
written them.

She didn't dwell on the memory of open scrolls
marked with blood and papyrus still wet with inky letters, because then she would have had to remember whether these
had been the scrolls of reality or this morning's dream. It was
better not to know.

Two guards passed by the barred door, laughing with
one another; another man stopped them and spoke in a low,
harsh voice, and the laughers stood straight immediately and
glanced over their shoulders. They were young, by their faces, but their eyes were as old as stone. They wore their uniforms with the ease and lack of attention of men who did
not often meet the world's eyes, but now they straightened
buttons and scrubbed at their faces with their sleeves, clasping undone buckles hastily to give the appearance of greater
competence—or at least greater cleanliness.

Someone important was coming, then. Achane
traced the carvings with her eyes again, and although her
stomach gnawed at her with neglect and her very bones felt

exhausted, for the first time in days, she felt real hope with every heartbeat.

Let the king come to talk with her; let him fill her with truth serum or pleas for zombi or any damned thing that came to his mind. Let him bring her corpses to raise or grieving mothers or even the hard-eyed queen with her prayers to the god of storms. Let the king use those sharp knives and metal hooks that she had seen on a rack in the guards' chamber, even if it all but killed her.

Let him do anything to her—any *damned* thing—but if he left her alive, Achane would be out of this dungeon before nightfall.

Footsteps rang from the stairs down which Achane had come hours earlier—two pairs of footsteps, both of the walkers wearing hobnailed boots far sturdier than the leather boots that Achane still wore. They were wealthy, then; it would be the king and the lord of the fortress, which explained the guards' terror of inspection. The king was a temporary power in their world, but the master of this place would remain long after King Milaus had departed to conquer new lands.

The idea that she was making conjectures, putting together thoughts in a logical order and then trying to deduce what information filled in the gaps, made Achane's blood sing as it hadn't since Shabane had died. When the two lords appeared at the bars, it was all she could do not to smirk at having guessed correctly.

A rumble of thunder echoed like a conversation far away, but Achane heard it and climbed to her feet to meet Milaus's eyes.

He studied her in the lantern light as though she were

difficult to see, with her black shawl in the shadows of her cell. She stepped forward into what light there was, to where nude women of stone gestured lewd promises to generations of dead floor-carvers, to where the whorls of unreadable text began in seven neat lines, and made a bow. "King Milaus," she said with the calm neutrality of the just-repossessed. Her voice echoed like a crow's, even to her own ears. "To what do I owe the honor of your visit?"

"Have you decided to aid the war effort?" the king asked her. His companion's eyes flickered in the light of the nearest lamp.

Achane smiled, the expression safe beneath the black fabric of her warm, dry shawl. She couldn't help noticing that the king's hair still glistened as though it hadn't dried well. "I am considering the offer," she told him. "It's no small thing that you ask of me, and I've been very long opposed to it." *And I will be leaving your company tonight, tonight, tonight! I will walk free as the wind and the river back to my sister's arms, and then I'll make all things right with her.*

"Come with me," answered the king as he looked to the lord of the fortress, as though her answer hadn't mattered against his intentions. His hand touched the fabric of his jacket without mangling it, and between his eyes, agony had drawn a furrow to plant still more pain in him. "I would have you see something."

The fortress lord touched the king's shoulder for a ghost of a moment as he unlocked the cell, and Achane followed them from the prison with none of the reluctance of her descent.

No more thoughts of joining the dead. No more

dreaming of such an escape from the king's machinations, because now she had to study the guard placements in this great maze of rooms-on-rooms that was a fortress. She had to follow every passageway with her eyes and mark where it led, because tonight she was going to work such magic as she had never worked before, and she would need every advantage that she could make.

The thunder grew louder as they walked ever higher in the fortress, up broad staircases and winding ones, past arrow-slit windows with rain pouring in through the breach in the defenses, and in time up a tower that must have speared the very sky and made it bleed thunder and lightning.

At the top of the tower, in a little room empty of all but a wooden chair, there was a broad window paneled with glass that let the lightning in as the arrow-slits could not. The king and the lord of the fortress stood at either side of the chair, and Achane sat between them.

Before her, through the rain-washed glass and the flashes of lightning, Achane could see a broad expanse of clear land as smooth and as curved as the inside of a serving vessel. No trees grew there; only a few immense rocks littered the Great Bowl, like crumbs left by a feasting giant. Ringing the valley stood mountains almost indistinguishable from fortresses, and fortresses almost indistinguishable from mountains.

This was the place where so many men and women had died, Erekoi and enemy alike. Those were the fortresses that the farmers in the fields had named so glibly, as though they hadn't existed at all.

In the center of the Great Bowl, miles from the tower

lashed with rain, two armies camped across from each other. Their tents would not protect them from such a storm as this, nor would their weapons. Achane shivered in sympathy as she eyed the snaking line of earth between the camps, and she wondered how thin that no-man's-land was.

Some religious traditions have no concept of Hell, and so Achane had no word for the scene that she watched in silence.

"They have to run or ride for miles after a battle," said the lord of the fortress under his breath. She looked up at the voice, but his eyes were fixed on the king. "When they retreat, I mean. Injured as they are, the exertion takes a good deal of blood out of them and exacerbates the wounds. Most of our casualties don't die on the battlefield or in the healers' hands, but rather, halfway in between." He smiled a bitter little smile like a dried-up melon rind. "I've been telling you for years to garrison all the men, when we're in a state of truce. They die of the coughing sickness far more often than they lay a decent strike against the Weigers."

No decoction or potion, no spell or prayer could do anything to heal one with the coughing sickness. Achane looked at her hands against the rough brown of her skirt, and remembered how utterly alive she had felt when she'd been denying that healer's truism to fight for her sister's life. Her blood had pounded for new ideas, her feet had pounded the earth to heal rice-farmers and fishermen and sailors, and her fists had pounded against the walls of convention with every intention of breaking them down entirely.

She smiled at the thought—that perhaps she only felt free now because she was more surely confined than ever.

"I'll help you," said Achane to the storm and to the men who watched it. They looked down at her, as though surprised to remember that she still sat between them and listened to their bickering about strategy, and the king turned to her with the first truly happy expression that she had ever seen him wear.

"You raised your sister, didn't you? Achane, sister of Shabane?"

The witch watched the patterns of rain on the glass. "I did."

"I'm sorry for her passing," said the lord of the fortress with a queer inflection like warning. "I'm sure that you *miss* your sister."

At that, Achane swallowed her terror of falls, of scavengers, and of terrified villagers with long knives. "My sister still walks, somewhere."

Only the roll of thunder answered for long moments. Achane folded her hands in her lap and looked across the Great Bowl in search of an escape route, but her eyes kept drawing back to the huddle of tents in the center, and her mind kept returning to her sister's burned fingers holding the match to light a candle so that Achane could see. "It's no wonder, then," the lord muttered finally, "that you've got such old eyes."

Achane found a sharpened metal spoon in a corner carved with obscenities, as she had hoped she might, and she cast a forlorn glance at the shadowed curves carved deep into the stone. Some men etched the earth itself to make their spells, but Achane pressed the blade-sharp bowl of the spoon against her palm and spared a moment of regret that she had always worked best with blood.

It was possible to cast a spell without a form that another witch or wizard had discovered; it was possible to explore the realm of magic and to get the desired result, but only for those who were absolutely certain of getting what they wante. For such a person, the cost would always be great; the forms *existed* in their designated circles and words and materials because many men and women had spent long years discovering the easiest and least costly ways to perform useful magics. But for a person who needed magic in a moment, and had a quick mind for the intricacies of spellwork, and who had enough personal energy to meet the cost of a venture into the unknown—

—for such a person, the forms didn't matter.

The spoon's handle dipped easily into the little well of blood staining Achane's lifeline; she traced long, unsteady letters across her forehead, and they curled around each other like the carvings on the floor. So, too, did she draw words on her left arm, on her right leg, on her stomach; they were all but black in the dimness at the edge of the pool of light that stained the floor.

She chanted the words that no longer looked like words, quiet in her cell, and focused entirely on her reflection in that little pool of blood in her upturned hand.

Shonè, mother, force your children's eyes away from this black-cloaked daughter. Loukaros of the lightning and the zephyr, Loukaros who reigns in the tempest tonight, make

me as faint as the breeze to all who would turn their eyes to-
ward me.

She lowered her hand so that she would have more of
nature's own red ink, pumped to her fount by gravity and the
living energy in her veins.

With a trembling hand, Achane began to draw long,
straight lines on the floor, underlining the first precise rows
of carvings in the stone. Beneath each line she painted words
thick and clear: *These are the bars that hold me.*

She followed the lines with her blood-laden spoon as
the text warped and twisted; she didn't dip her prisoner's pen
again in her palm until she had dragged the spoon's handle all
the way from the straight and proper beginning of a line to the
last, desperate coil at its end.

It was making her weak, to crouch like this and walk
on her knees along the hard floor, feeling at the stone for the
indentations that were her only guide; it was making her weak
to hold her hand forever poised so that she would lose not a
drop of her sweet red ink. When at last she had finished tracing the final line, she stood and nearly fell again for dizziness;
her vision doubled and her joints ached, but she only leaned
heavily against the wall and made her way to the bars of the
prison door.

Aenikus, she begged at the floor and the lintel, *bend*
these bars like the words that they follow.

Achane closed her eyes and sank to her knees once
more, feeling the tingle of the blood drying on her forehead
as her hair rose.

It didn't feel like a river of power, as some wizards
claimed; it didn't feel like a slow, deep creature moving

through the dark ocean to the light at the surface, as some of Achane's scrolls suggested.

Magic, when it came, felt only like being very scared and very tired all at once.

Achane opened her eyes on twisted iron, and she bowed her head and thanked the gods for their generosity before she staggered to her feet and through the gap in the bars. She clenched her cut hand in her skirts so that she wouldn't leave a trail of blood.

Up the stairs now. *So damned tired,* but she walked past the guards' chamber without their notice falling on her.

It was difficult to walk invisibly; every text that Achane had ever read had said as much. In the same way, it was costly to force every man and woman's eyes away; control of another's conscious mind was one of the most difficult and least rewarding forms of magic, and it required more energy than Achane readily had.

Better, then, to control the unconscious. To edit the thoughts as she had those of the ratsnake, a few days and forever ago—not to change what was perceived or done, but rather how it was interpreted. The part of the guards' minds that had been prepared to tag a shawled woman walking through the halls as "significant" now saw her and glanced onward, finding nothing at all unusual about the situation.

Achane glanced through the halls that she had so recently traveled, and she tried to remember whether the first or the second passage on the left would eventually lead her to the great hall and the escape that it afforded.

Thunder resounded from her tired bones and rattled her skull, and she chose the second passage. Thunder meant the higher parts of the fortress; thunder meant passages to escape.

Too many rooms. Too many bloody rooms. A house should have only one room, even if it were a house for an army; one room kept the family together.

Damned family had never been together.

Achane clutched the railing of a staircase that she wasn't sure she remembered, looking for a tapestry or an unusual lamp that might point her to freedom. At the head of the staircase, she searched the narrow hallway for a spiral stairway to the next level but only found three locked doors and one that lead down a long hall full of unfamiliar banners.

She retreated back down the staircase and took the other passage, unsure whether she had chosen the wrong staircase at first or merely been one locked door from her path to freedom.

Never again would she work magic without studying the techniques of the masters. Never again, for her feet ached with every step that her joints protested, and her fingers were growing numb where she held them clutched in her rough brown skirt. Her head was buzzing like a nest of bees searching for a new place to make a hive, and the fortress walls were beginning to glisten horrifyingly like the glass that she had seen in the capital. Only the dregs of utter elation drove her onward; only the first feeling of being alive in weeks kept her from falling forward like the dead.

The guards, at least, didn't see her walking like a woman blinded through the corridors, searching for the ones that she had mentally marked as she had walked behind the two lords. She kept to the shadows and scurried from alcove to alcove, and on the tapestries pumas danced merry jigs with rams as heroes hunted alligators to extinction in the days after the great flood.

No one noticed her, but when she heard the sudden pound of running feet and a shout, she nonetheless tucked herself into the space beneath a winding set of stairs and peered between its boards. No one would notice her, no one would notice her, no one would notice her *unless they had magic of their own for seeking the undetected* and she forgot the aches of her body as the shadow crossed the floor.

A man ran backwards past the entry to the stairwell— a guard in uniform, holding off a fur-clad man who was the one shouting, but it was a foreign shout and the words all ran together against the clang of long knife against short sword and the pounding of more feet, more feet against more shouts against more weapons clashing and furs uniforms shouts of pain thunder and the itch of someone working magic not far from where she hid—

—Achane crouched beneath the stairs and willed herself unnoticed.

She was not in the least tired any longer.

he zombi hunched on Gamela's back and watched the Wigs streaming in a tight line through the narrow tunnel bored into the mountainside. The first three had carried a long ladder and longer knives; every other grim-eyed man and woman had worn thick furs over tanned leather and woolen jackets, because the people of the mountains made no armor, and only the holts on the very edge of the border had begun to make shields.

The healers would enter last of all, after this river of men had disappeared into the crack in the earth and emerged to clear the way.

Erlen and Jeiger, the men who'd brought them to this place, had helped to carry the ladder. Shabane had watched them go and remembered the sympathy written in their pale eyes.

At the end of the tunnel, there would be a deep hole.

At the bottom of that deep hole would be over sixty armspans of water; the Wigs didn't know how much water, because their weighted ropes had never touched the bottom. This was the well of the fortress on the mountain, and it made the place impervious to siege even as it had showed one of the mountain lords where the rock was permeable enough to create an invasion tunnel. Just in case.

Shabane could feel the earth waking in the lightning; it reached out unfamiliar branches to greet the sky and drink in the rainwater, and every crack of thunder drew a thousand resounding shouts from the trees that reflected the sound. The wind tore at her shawl as though it sought to rip it away and reveal her flesh to the hungry air, and if Gamela hadn't held her in a steady grip, Shabane might have flung her body down the mountain and let the trees and stones tear it to pieces and reclaim it.

The last fur-clad figure followed his clansmen into the gaping mouth of the ground, and Gamela ducked in next as though she were entering a grave.

Shabane had never had a grave. A stream of rainwater trickled beneath Gamela's feet as twisted roots broke off abruptly over their heads, and Shabane wanted to let those roots reach into her body and draw her back into themselves. The chill earth would close around her skin without the flickering of torches to light it, and burrowing ants would find her bones—

Gamela stood where the tunnel became abruptly larger and looked at the ladder that two Wigs held steady. She put Shabane's body down on its feet and looked it over once, quickly. "Can you climb?" she asked, holding the body's shoulders as carefully as she could. "I don't know if the ladder will take my weight as well as yours."

Shabane looked to the ladder, built of light wood pegged together and tied sturdy with rope, and she nodded once. *Slowly,* she thought as her body stumbled to the wood and placed its hands against it, *but I haven't lost so much yet that I can't climb a ladder.*

The boots on her body's feet gripped the wood and held, leather against the grain. Her body's fingers did not bend on the rungs, but she leaned forward and forced one foot to the next rung. The other foot up as well; she steadied herself with her decaying hands and climbed out of the shadows of the sides of the well, into the light of the torches above.

Her body's fingers slipped.

She fell forward rather than backwards, her body's face pressing the black shawl against the wood, and she only had time to be glad that she couldn't feel pain before she was climbing again. Her sightless eyes peered over the edge of the well, into the light of a kitchen, and she crawled over the wall of stones and onto the flagstone floor.

No one here, living or dead or anywhere in between; yams lay half-chopped on a table and stew bubbled in a cauldron that might have fed a hundred. Shabane held the edge of the table and rotated the stew out of the fire as she had at home, because anyone who survived this attack would need something to eat when the battle had ended, and stew did no one any good when it had burned or boiled over.

The cooks must have run when Erlen and Jeiger had climbed out of the well. Shabane believed it firmly because otherwise she might have had to imagine that the two men who had laughed with Gamela and sent the steamboats down to help the coast-people could kill the innocent as well as protect them.

Gamela hauled herself out of the well, followed soon after by one healer and then another; the strangers talked to one another in quick whispers and spaced themselves out around the room, laying down bandages and herbs and salves in preparation for the wounded.

"Can you walk?" Gamela asked with the same wild look that she had worn when she had asked if Shabane could climb. "I have to heal the wounded—you have to look for Achane, and we can move more quickly if we do both at once."

Shabane nodded again. She felt the gaps in her body's muscles where insects had eaten at her, but still she could move. *Slowly.*

They followed the sound of thunder and screaming through the halls, room-on-room like the buildings of cities in the dry lands where flooding was less of a danger; Shabane clenched her body's unbending fingers around doorknobs, both hands to the metal so that she could get the leverage to turn it, and peered into storage rooms by the dozen—into rooms full of beds narrow and stacked three high—through the keyholes of locked rooms, all of them dark.

They found the first body in the third passageway, an Erekoi guard at the foot of a long flight of stairs, and Gamela sagged against the wall as she saw the pool of blood around him. He had fallen down the staircase and smashed his head hard against stone, and it had been a far more deadly enemy than the Wigs.

The next body was alive, at least. Shabane felt an ache of sympathy at the gaping wounds in the man's shoulder and side, but she was trying doors and Gamela was whispering words of magic as she drew shapes across the Wig man's arm and bared his chest to scrawl invisible letters on the gash beneath his ribs. This door, nothing; that door, locked and dark. Another room, locked and full of terrified soldiers; they shivered as the shadow of Shabane's body paused in front of their hiding place, so she did them the grace of moving on to check a narrow passageway.

Nothing, nothing, nothing. Blood dotted the floors where the Wigs had passed, and Gamela knelt every few steps in some hallways to tend the fallen or to close the eyes of the dead. Overhead, thunder pounded war-drums, and Shabane caught glimpses of the coast-man or his wife sometimes through open doorways—walking, walking, as slowly as if they weren't fighting a battle against their own people.

Perhaps Achane wasn't even here.

A man with streaks of reddish brown in his hair shot past them suddenly, sprinting through the halls with a sword clenched in his fist and a cape flying out behind him; only steps behind ran a man whom Shabane had seen just once, clutching the fabric of his jacket as he ran doubled over and gripping his own sword like life in his free hand—he caught a glimpse of Shabane as he ran, and he stumbled; his mouth worked soundlessly for a long moment as he stared at her, but then he ran onward and around a corner, shouting "Adri!" as he went.

The king. That man had been the king, and if he was here, then Achane was here. Shabane stood straighter, and for the first time she forced herself to think instead of trying doors blindly.

She knew nothing of fortresses or castles. Stories were her only guide, and in every story that she had ever read with Achane when they were young and had braided each other's hair, the king had put the beautiful young woman in a tower.

It was a poor idea, but it was all she had. As Gamela followed the fighting through the fortress, Shabane stopped rattling knobs and instead kept her blind eyes open for stairs.

The place was a maze of stairs. Shabane climbed as fast as her body allowed her, up every spiraling fan of boards to the inevitably unlocked doors at the top; up every broad staircase that led to unfamiliar halls that she and Gamela would surely reach in time; down every flight again to stumble forward with her body's hand on the wall and Gamela grimly sketching healing spells on Wig and Erekoi alike.

Shabane heard the king shouting again, but far away; more voices were shouting in the wood and stone maze, but Shabane only longed for one voice so that she could cry "Achane!" to the thunder-crashing sky.

Ahead of her, at an arched door through which spilled brilliant lamplight, stood a hunched man with a staff in his hand. He seemed a silhouette at first; Shabane took a wavering step toward him, but as her body's foot touched the stone, she knew in her soul that he was as black as the clouds overhead, for lightning crackled at his fingers and cast his body in darkness and white light.

He let out a laugh that drew a clap of thunder from the sky, and he walked away.

Shabane's body did not tremble in fear, nor pause in

its pacing, nor take its hand from the stone. She had already lost her life; what more could even the god of storms do to her?

Gamela came gasping up behind her and leaned heavily against the wall. "Never so many," she whispered, fumbling at her waist for the pouch of dried meat and fruit and shelled nuts that had been her sustenance for days. The priestess chewed at handfuls of the mix, swallowing so that she could move on more quickly. Shabane remembered how Achane had spooned rice and fish into her mouth to regain lost energy after healing the injured crew of a fishing boat that had caught fire; she understood Gamela's haste.

They hadn't yet found the end of the injured or the dead.

The priestess stood still for long moments against the stone, whispering the prayers that she had read on the deck of the steamboat. When at last the woman levered herself away from the stone and continued through the hall, Shabane walked beside her.

If she hadn't been looking for stairs, she would have walked straight past this stairwell. Its wooden planking was just like every other as it spiraled up and up and up; she could see the stones through the gaps in the planking, and she was about to climb it to see whether her sister was imprisoned at the top when she realized that the grey-blue limestone didn't show through the lower planking. Someone crouched there hidden, perhaps hurt, and Gamela would need to—

—a healer dressed in black stood from her crouch under the stairs.

She was old, old, old. The dark skin around her eyes bore wrinkles like the skin of an alligator date, and yet Shabane looked into those eyes without her eyes, looked with the sight that remained to her spirit through the spell sketched in blood on the woman's forehead; she looked into the old woman's eyes and knew those eyes.

You look like my sister, Shabane thought with an eerie rush as the woman raised thin, trembling fingers to unpin Shabane's shawl and draw it away.

"Shabane," she whispered, as though the name were a prayer. "Shabane."

Achane. Shabane raised her stiff hands to the shawl that her sister wore, and she pulled it from her sister's shoulders and let it fall to the floor.

Every plait on Achane's head was cloud-white and twisted like the wrinkles on the old woman's ashy face; Shabane lifted her body's burned fingers to the face of her sister and touched the folded skin even as her sister's bloody palm came up to caress the zombi's cheek.

"Be free," Achane breathed.

In the instant before Shabane's soul departed her body, she saw her sister sink to her knees and topple over, her fine white plaits spilling across the flagstones.

⋟⋞

The first shouts of invasion came as Milaus and his brother made their way to the great hall to take a late dinner; in an instant, both men had drawn their swords and pressed back to back to check both ends of the corridor. "This way," Adriolaus hissed. The courtier had fled from his voice, and only the soldier remained as the lord of the Fortress of Storms took to his heels with the king close behind.

"Where are they *coming* from? There aren't any entry points for a bloody invasion!" Adriolaus called over his shoulder as he ran; a knot of fighting men whirled through the hall and out again along a crossing corridor, belying his words. "Have to mass the soldiers and trap the invaders!"

"Where?" shouted the king, with every step drawing an ache from his side—he clutched the old wound and ran on. "Chapel's only got two doors!"

"There, yes!" agreed Adriolaus, and then the men ran in silence toward the barracks where they had both lived as princes once upon a time.

Agony like drowning in air.

Banners fluttered in the breeze of their passage. They slipped on the blood of battles past; once, the king thought he saw the witch Achane standing in the hallway with her eyes gouged out, but he ran on before he could decide to dash back and make her raise the casualties; he called to his brother as he went.

The cannons mounted on the walls hadn't been enough. The guards hadn't been enough; they had fallen like children before the invaders. Perhaps the soldiers would fare better against the enemy.

Adriolaus skidded into the soldiers' quarters with his sword drawn and his curling hair flying like his cape behind him; murder flashed in his eyes as every man sat up from his dice game or his conversation and then stood at attention.

"Arm yourselves. Full armor, quickly if you please," the fortress lord hissed, hurling himself through the doorway and gripping his brother's arm in his own to keep the king upright. "We are under attack. *Now!*" he shouted to the dumbstruck soldiers; like insects, they scattered under the light of his ire.

One man, though, stood still as stone for a second and pointed to the doorway through which Milaus and Adriolaus had come; the king glanced back, and into the eyes of a dark-cloaked man with a staff of white cedar.

The man's eyes were as black as his face and his staff, and shadows moved across him in the lamplight like shifting clouds. He snapped, "It's no business of yours!" and whirled off down the passage, walking as though he expected pursuit but didn't care whether it caught him.

A few score soldiers assembled before the brothers, only half of them properly armored but all of them at least armed. It was pitifully inadequate; Milaus knew it with a certainty as cold as the ache in his side and as ominous as the lightning that flashed through the arrow-slit windows. And yet it was all that he had.

"Your enemies won't be wearing our uniforms and armor," the king panted. He breathed shallowly against the ache in his side, but his voice did not betray him. «Force them to the chapel of Loukaros. We can trap them inside if we're careful. There are two entrances—I need twenty of you to defend one, and twenty to defend the other. The doorways are narrow there and easily defended. The rest of us must lead all invaders we find to the chapel! Once we lure our enemies into the room, we'll make our way to the doors and slip out to join our comrades in defending the entrances. Loukaros walks tonight," the king proclaimed, "and we'll let him do whatever he damned well likes with the invaders!"

He got no cheer for that speech, but he got swift compliance, and that was better.

There was an army at their backs now. A small army, but Adriolaus's eyes glittered less wildly and Milaus breathed with more ease as they chose forty men to secure the chapel doors. No arguments of strategy or cost passed between the brothers as they clutched their weapons, motioned to their followers, and began the hunt for the enemy.

Instead, in a flurry of wordless screams and meaningless words, the enemy found them.

Milaus took the first leather-clad invader to stumble into his path; he parried the woman's long knife as she thrust it at his stomach and heaved it out of her hands with a twist of his wrist—then decapitated her with a two-handed stroke of his bastard sword. Her head lay blinking at him as her body fell, but he had moved on to face a tall man wielding a sword in each hand. Adriolaus caught the man's wrist with the backswing of a swipe that cut through the fur of another man's vest to disembowel him, but Milaus's enemy hissed and spat a foreign curse at the king as he flung one weapon in an arc meant to see what the king had inside; Milaus blocked the strike and the rough overhand blow that followed from the other hand to thrust his sword neatly between the man's ribs and out the other side.

The tall man fell, still swinging his weapons as his head hit the flagstones.

It wasn't neat; it wasn't beautiful; there was no footwork involved, no style, no graceful bladeplay. There was only terror and force and pain and metal as the king and his brother hacked their way through the invaders and broke into a run for the second time that day. Their army followed in a rush that peeled off into corridor melees and ambushes from the stair-wells; a knot of guards broke into the press of soldiers and was almost massacred before the men recognized their uniforms.

It was Hell, but the Erekoi have no word for Hell, so they called it war instead.

After an eternity of frantic instants, the soldiers broke through the hallways of invaders to the chapel, diminished by the fighting to a ragged-edged group; they threw themselves into a desperate charge with Milaus and Adriolaus at its head as they crossed the grey-and-blue mosaic of Loukaros slicing off the sea-goddess's hair.

Milaus saw blood in the mortar, and his heart sank because the soldiers sent to guard this doorway no longer waited here. The king only had time to scream that it was a trap before the press of warring bodies forced him through the doorway and into the stone chamber.

The doors creaked shut behind the last soldier, and the invaders threw the bolts home.

They had been caught in their own ambush, and the lightning drew blue patterns from the stained-glass windows to the floor.

A man stood silhouetted against the window, his shadow stretching across the floor. "My lords!" he called; Milaus spared a moment of relief that this man was not Loukaros as his voice resounded from the chapel walls. The man paced back and forth across the window ledge, secure on a few inches of stone set four times the height of a man above the ground.

Milaus looked into the shadows of a dozen pillars; a flash of lightning illuminated an old man sitting on a bench with a straw hat on his head, and another white flare showed a woman seated across the chapel, her grey hair plaited back in a braid and her face serene.

Thunder pounded at the torn sky and drowned out the words of the man at the window, but Milaus heard neither man nor thunder because his wife the queen emerged from the darkness by the altar, where she had knelt unnoticed from the very beginning. She held a bowl of water before her; her eyes shone milky white in the darkness.

"Husband," she whispered. "Drink."

Milaus took the bowl from her cold fingers as though in a trance, raising it to his lips while his brother and the soldiers and guards remained staring; they were looking neither at him nor his queen, though, but beyond both of them, to the man who stepped through the altar like a cloud and put his lightning-tipped hands on the queen's own hands. He pressed his body against the queen's own body and sank into her as though she did not exist.

Her moss-agate eyes rolled to face the king, and nothing of Carisica remained there.

One hand shot out like a striking snake to sink fingers into Milaus's side, and as he howled at the pain, the other hand gripped the chain on which he wore his wife's iron ring.

Lightning ripped through his body, stopping his heart as it coursed from the ring to the splinters of iron lodged in his side.

The old man and the old woman bore Milaus to the ground and laid his head on the stone. As the king passed on to death, he lay in the arms of Shonè and Aenikus, and they held their devoted son.

>⊰⊱<

The woman looked up at Erlen with eyes that crackled with lighting as she left the lord's body behind her.

He stood against the window of blued glass, pressing his back only gently against the surface so that he wouldn't break it and tumble down to the rocks far below. Thunder rattled the panes; he remembered the tall woman's hands on the metal at the dead lord's throat, and he pulled his hands and the back of his neck away from the lead of the panes.

This was an avatar, then.

This was an Erekoi god.

Erlen drew his pen from his pocket and felt its smooth, stained surface under his fingers as he unsheathed it from its cap. It was no sword, but a sword hadn't availed the man who lay on the floor with the lightning flashing blue glass flickers across his body; it was no magic wand, but the Weigers had never used wands to write their magic or their history.

He sketched a sigil in the air—*stairway*, said the glittering symbol as it hung in space. He stepped out to balance on nothingness, meeting the blank nothingness in the woman's lightning-flashing eyes.

"You thought you could play me," the woman snarled as over a hundred men looked on and Erlen descended step by invisible step to the safety of stone. "You thought me a myth, to be taken and made as you liked; you filled me with your own language and your own ideas and you *bent* me to your own ends. What think you of gods now?" laughed the woman. The sigil fell to pieces in the air above them, and Erlen's boots touched stone.

He didn't answer, but only stood lightly on his feet so that he could leap away.

"What think you of gods, book-man? What think you of book-burners who destroy lies to reveal the truth to you? What *think* you, human?" She advanced, and all around them the Erekoi soldiers backed against the walls and pounded at the doors to be let free.

No one outside knew. No one would be coming to save him; not Eppa with her sword nor Jeiger with his bow nor Halgirth with his politicking. Erlen drew his weapons and tossed them away, and the woman laughed as though it had been a challenge.

The avatar laughed; the god laughed. Loukaros of the storms laughed inside a woman who had just killed her husband, and thunder beat mercilessly at the air as though it sought to pummel it to death, and so Erlen stood here in the fortress that had drawn a lightning scar across his collarbone and sketched a sigil like lightning in the air.

Weapon, it said. The pen became a staff within his hands, dark and stained and thick as a wrist with ink gathered like blood in the nib.

He dove at her with the staff swinging; she ducked the hard metal nib like a spear's point and struck out with an outstretched hand to snatch at Erlen. One end of the staff came up to bat her hand away, and she caught it and almost wrenched it out of his grip.

Strong as stormclouds, strong as the wind that

tears down the mountainsides; he twisted the staff to dis-lodge her and she sent lightning searing toward him from cheated fingertips.

He planted the staff's butt against the stone and let the metal point take the shock; it jolted down the seam of metal that had been the pen's core and dispersed to the ground.

"What purpose do you think this serves?" Loukaros asked with a woman's beautiful lips; he sneered at Erlen with a woman's face as the scholar stood shaking by the corpse of the king. "You are only human. You can prolong your life, perhaps prolong the lives of others, but in time the peace you enforce will break and this will be *my* country again. War is change, human, and change is war! Change is as inevitable as the tides, as inevitable as the storms!"

If you answer, you're not thinking about keeping your skin intact. Erlen drew a circle around himself and named it *protection,* named it *stone* and *wood* and *shelter.* He backed to its very boundaries as the woman advanced again with her eyes alight and a moss-agate flickering on her brow; she stepped through the pools of light left by the stained glass windows, and she stepped over the edge of his circle and broke the shimmering letters into fragments.

"Wherever there is a fortress, there shall I be," she hissed. "Wherever there is *mine* and *thine,* wherever there is *we* against *they,* I shall not be kept out; wherever *shelter* and *expo-sure* are pitted against each other, I shall reign, and your circles only feed my power." She cast her lightning-ringed hands high and pulled—one by one the stained glass windows shattered—the shards filled the air and scraped at the flesh of soldiers, whose screams throbbed against the darkness and the light and the thunder, throbbed against the crackle of glass shards as they struck still more shards in their haste to tear at Erlen. He threw himself to the floor and covered his head; a blue shard scored across his eye, though, and he flung himself under a bench with his hand pressed to his uncut eye to shield it.

He thought he was screaming. He couldn't hear himself for the thunder and the soldiers' screams like the cries of mountain rocks screeching *heal us, take us home* in the dungeon where he had carved letters with his fingers in the stone.

He looked up and into the rain-struck hall, past the glass shards that spun around the chapel and reflected lightning, past the face of the avatar of Loukaros as she cast aside her finger-rings one by one, to the man who lay between the grey-haired woman and her husband on the floor.

She would never be defeated through battle. He couldn't shield himself against her with a shield, he couldn't destroy her with any force of destruction—he could not could not *could* not defeat her—

—he rolled from beneath the bench as she struck it to splinters.

A man with his dyed hair in disarray and his cape flapping in the gale from the broken windows stood in a corner, marshaling his men into a huddle to protect them as he shouted imprecations at the wind; his eyes met Erlen's one good eye and he nodded even as he and another man began to pile benches into a shelter. "Anything you want!" the Erekoi bellowed; he hacked at glass pieces in the air to bat them away from his men. "Anything to get us out of this!"

"Healer!" shouted a soldier who clutched his fountaining neck; "*Healer!*" Erlen snatched up his pen-staff and ran to the man's side, writing a sigil with haste but with care on the flesh there to heal it. The lord clasped Erlen's shoulder and then Erlen sprinted across the chapel to draw the god's attention away—and the avatar blasted the rock before him as he leapt over the altar and ducked behind the shattered stone.

Healer.

He clenched his hands around the staff and turned it around, and then he sprang back across the altar and into the woman's line of fire.

The avatar pressed her hands together and drew a webwork of lightning from them; Erlen only ran, dragging the nib of his staff behind him. He ducked glass shards as big as his fist and felt smaller ones digging furrows into his face; he threw himself around a pillar and almost collided with the grey-haired man who stood at the edge of the room where he and his wife had dragged the lord's body. Still Erlen ran; still he watched the woman begin to pull her hands apart as the lightning grew thick as yarn between her palms; still he crossed his trail of ink as he wove and dodged across the room.

"You will never defeat war with warring," laughed the avatar, with her arms spread wide and lightning arcing between them like her white, white grin, like the milky whiteness of her upturned eyes as the thunder drove the world mad. "Those who imitate Loukaros only serve him in the end."

Erlen stood still at the edge of the room and planted the butt of his staff against the faint ink traces on the floor, surrounded by flying glass and the world-shattering brightness of lightning. He smiled at her in return, pointing the nib of his pen at the god in the shape of a woman. "I don't have to."

She clapped like thunder, and the lightning between her hands struck the staff in a searing bolt and flowed down the nib, down the nib and through the metal rod in the middle and into the sigil that Erlen had just drawn across the floor—

Healing.

The floor melted together like a mending wound in the center of the room and Erlen stood at the edge of the healing stone as it rejoined the mountain, and he watched the queen sink to her neck in molten rock.

Her eyes were bright with joy even when the godlight left them, and the moss-agate at her brow glistened in the lightning as the floor closed over her head.

Erlen stood leaning on his staff and gasping as the floor grew solid again, staring half-blind across the chapel at a score of Erekoi soldiers who slowly removed their helmets and saluted him.

The lord of the fortress rose, bloodied and wearied, from his barricade of benches. He walked at the very edge of the floor, along the wall; he moved as though he had need of a healer as well. Erlen dipped his finger in the ink still remaining in his nib and drew a healing sigil on his own cheek, his vision blurring and then coming back into focus as the gash across his eye repaired itself.

"I'm Adriolaus," the lord said in a voice hoarse from shouting; he bowed low before Erlen and extended a hand to be shaken in the Wig way. Erlen took it, clasping the Erekoi man's wrist and shaking it with fingers still trembling with adrenaline. "I don't know who you are or what you wanted when you invaded my fortress, but you've won the right to negotiate now with the king."

"Where is the king?" Erlen asked; Adriolaus indicated the lord lying dead against the wall.

"My brother Milaus will remain the king until I've interred him in the family tomb," said Adriolaus quietly. His voice shook more than his hands had; tears glittered in his eyes, but not one of them fell. "When that's—when that is finished," he said, "I would speak with Weigers and Wigs and my own people, as their king. Until then, there must be a truce between us."

"Indeed." Erlen's head hung with exhaustion, and he tapped at the door behind him with one fist. "Let me out, Mittler," he called through the doorway; a low rumble of thunder made him shudder, but the sound was far away now.

The door opened on several hundred borderlanders and one Erekoi priestess who leaned heavily against a wall, but Erlen stumbled past them all. "Need healers inside," he told Gamela as he passed her. "King wants to speak with you," he said to Gaerthe Mittler as the holt patriarch stood strategizing with Eppa and Halgirth.

He passed by his staring companions, the borderlanders of dozens of clans who had fought beside him to take this fortress, and at last he stopped before one man and sank to his knees at Jeiger's feet.

"Wake me up," he whispered to Jeiger as the hunter stood breathing in the first air of victory. "Wake me up just before the sunrise."

he sun didn't rise on the next morning; at the tenth bell of the new day, the muzzy sun drew back the grey and blanketing clouds to blink sleepily at the world, then promptly pulled the covers over his head again and fell back asleep.

No rain fell on Erekos that day—the diminished storm had blown on across the plains to Weigenland, and it drove heavy droplets against the slate of the university roof and the marble arches of noble houses with the same force that it lent to the poor roofs of the shantytowns. The notion pleased Master Tuefweil in a private part of his mind, but because it had struck him in the middle of a lecture, he let the sociopolitical ramifications of rain fall away into the gutters and instead continued to discuss the history of diplomatic failures between Erekos and Weigenland. His students copied frantic notes with goose-quill pens that sometimes snapped under the fervor of their penmanship.

He didn't yet know about the fate that had met his unbreakable pen with the metal core.

In Erekos, in the Fortress of Storms where the dead king's brother reigned, that pen was even now rewriting the diplomatic history of two nations and working to create a third. Erlen sat at the long table in the great hall with the fire at his back, scribbling notes as an unprecedented meeting took place around him: The prince of the Erekoi, three generals of Weigenland, and three holt-holders sat together to set the agenda for a diplomatic summit that would occur when the dead king had been interred and the new king crowned.

It wasn't the end of things—not by any way of reckoning. Although mounted messengers had been dispatched to keep the remainder of both Erekoi and Weiger forces from fighting without orders, their leaders now warred with one another in words. The issues of the mines, of property rights, and of saving military face still remained to make Gaerthe Mittler narrow his light green eyes; the lady Weiger general had whispered cold, harsh words to the prince of the Erekoi when he had talked of retaining the northern farmland that his people had conquered centuries ago. Eppa still stroked her sword's handle as though it were the head of a babe, but no weapons had been drawn in the great hall. It wasn't the end of things and perhaps wouldn't be for many years, but Erlen liked to believe that this was the beginning of the end. Politics had at long last entered the arena to spell that aging gladiator, War.

Erlen had spent his morning tending the wounded with Gamela in the kitchens, both of them half-glazed with weariness and turning again and again to the cauldron of thick, cold stew beside the hearth. She had drawn shapes with her fingers on bruised brows, putting traces of her own personal energy into every spell; it made her tired as Erlen's magic did not, and eventually he'd told her to find a place to sleep and tend to her friend.

She'd told him that she had found the zombi dead, truly dead, lying across her dead sister. With a cup of stew in one hand to fill the void left by her spent energy, Gamela had continued to work.

Erlen wrote down the latest subject of squabble, the southern wall through the hill-country and the fortress that guarded it, and knew that the conclusion would not be a happy one. Only stories ended happily ever after, because only stories ended; *people* went on even after the last page of the book had been turned and the last villain defeated.

He had been thinking again and again about what would come next, when the politicking brought his book to a close.

The borderlands filled him with joy as no other place in the world had ever done; the mountains gave him a freedom that he had never known in the city or even in the university, and the people had taken him in and made him one of them. He felt in his heart that he could not live without the clean air of mornings on the mountaintop, nor without the space to be exactly who he really was.

He felt he could not live without the first place that he had ever felt he belonged.

And yet he knew that he would have to go back and show the world what he had learned in the mountains, or else no one else would ever know what he had seen when he walked to the edge of an impossible line and peered over the edge. He knew that these diplomatic meetings that were being planned as he feverishly wrote down notes—these talks that would put an end to his own story—would change the face of his dear, adopted land forever. Even if it became a nation of its own, mines would burrow through the mountains and cities would come to perch where holts had been; the freedom and emptiness of that threshold-land would slowly fall away as the nobility of both larger countries chipped away at the stretch of mountains between them.

He would have to teach the nobility of both lands to see the borderlands as he saw them, or he might lose them entirely. Far more so than his book, that work would be the Great Work of his life.

Jeiger had already said that he would follow when Erlen went back across the plains.

><

In the mountains, at the holt that she had remained to guard, Marla paced past the empty doors of those who had gone to the north. She didn't know whether her friends and relatives, neighbors and petty enemies would ever return; she didn't know whether they had yet faced a battle, or whether the Erekoi would attack her holt today, or whether the clouds blanketing the sky would ever break. She had knocked on the doors again this morning, forgetting once more to skip over the doors of the missing. She had cooked rutabaga mash for breakfast and sharpened her weapons; she had combed her hair out of its braids and pulled it up in a bun, then braided it again. She had taken an hour up in the watchtower, keeping the watchbell silent company, and then she had returned to the hallway where those young and strong enough to fight lived.

With no attack to plan or execute, she had nothing to do with herself.

Marla opened the door to her room with a kind of slow caution, as though entering her own room for any purpose but sleeping was a kind of betrayal of the cause, and sat down beside her spinning wheel as she hadn't for months.

Between her fingers she felt the woolen fibers, lying untouched in her basket, and she looked to the spindle all twisted with perfect yarn.

Slowly, as tentatively as if she were an invalid rising at last from the bed to take tottering steps across the floor, Marla began to spin again. The yarn that emerged at first wasn't perfect, but her foot on the treadle soon moved with its old easy rhythm. The wheel rasped and whirled as it had before the war had begun, and Marla smiled as she hadn't since she put the wheel away.

Sharp-eyed Kemaeros was the first to see the rider coming from his new post on the walls of a fortress on a crag; the mounted man waved a bright red flag with the ram's head emblazoned on it to advertise the importance of his message, and Kemaeros called down the man's arrival before the other sentries even saw the movement of the horse.

He didn't mind the new stationing; it was closer to

his home in the hills, and he could write letters to the town watch to keep up with his friends and the recovery of his old comrade who had lost an arm. The food was better, too, with less half-rancid goat and more good carrots and potatoes on the menu, and he was given a great deal of respect by his fellow sentries for the uncanny power of his eyes.

It was for this, perhaps, that he was granted permission to go down to the courtyard and listen to the messenger's story as well as the orders to hold tight; it was for this that no man interrupted his thoughts as he stood staring out over the trees to the northern road, long after he had heard the last of how the king had died and a borderlander had defeated the god Loukaros in single combat.

For most men, he thought, it would certainly have seemed as though Loukaros had been defeated. The god of war had sunk in the form of his avatar through the fluid stones of the chapel, and the warlike King Milaus had died in the fray.

But Kemaeros was a man who saw what others did not, and he was a man devoted to Loukaros with his body and soul, and he smiled a little as he peered up at the massed clouds. A change was in the wind, one king supplanted by another, the order to attack replaced by the order to hold.

And Loukaros is the god of war only because war is a means for changing the world.

Kemaeros turned his eagle's eyes to the south and watched the rider disappear down the rutted road.

As he stood by the great mirror of his lighthouse, the

lighthouse-keeper peered out to sea and watched the steamboats coming one by one to what remained of the docks.
Three of them sailed in formation on the waves, riding out
the choppy breakers with their decks crowded with refugees;
the lighthouse-keeper remembered the last flood and turned
his mirror again to advertise his available docking.

It was always a grim thing to go through a flood, but
the way-station of Shonè and Aenikus stood prepared for
the influx with their brothers and sisters from the washed-
away shrine across the sea. The priestesses of Terichone,
too, had felt the storm coming, and had sent a middle-aged
sister with a great mulecart laden with food and blankets
and medicine to help the lighthouse-keeper tend to any
refugees who came his way. She was even now waiting on
the docks to greet the arriving steamboats, calling out in
her coastal accent that there was safety and shelter here
for all who needed immediate attention. Even a traveling
doctor had set up shop in the lower floors, although the
lighthouse-keeper hadn't noticed any difference in his bun-
ions since he'd tried the man's foot cream.

The lighthouse-keeper swung his mirror around and
reflected forth the light to all who might need it to steer by.

➤◄

In a slow, silent procession that moved past acre
upon acre of soaked beans and wheat, Adriolaus rode with
his illegitimate son walking to one side of him and the Weiger general who would be his wife riding on the other. They
moved toward the capital, that old city of Telessa that never

got called by her name any longer, with Milaus's body interred in an oaken coffin that rested in a hearse behind them. An honor guard rode behind the hearse, their dress uniforms bright against the black of their horses and the grey of the sky, and they rode at the same dejected and plodding pace as the nobleman before them. The pace they kept because it made the journey easier for the body in the carriage; the quiet they kept because everything that needed to be said had already been spoken.

Adriolaus would become a king in a mere day and a half, and he would commission a sculptor to carve battles around his brother's funereal dais; he would have the authority to change Erekoi law and policy and to get this damned war over. He would have to marry, of course, so that he could have the requisite heirs, but he and Alise had spoken quietly after their diplomatic meeting and had agreed that both nations would be best served by a marriage between an Erekoi king and a Weiger general to cement their successful negotiations. There was real affection between them, which was a start; perhaps, one day, they would be so in love that his eyes wouldn't wander to the shapely forms of servant girls and unmarried noblewomen.

He highly doubted that such an eventuality should ever come to pass.

As they rode, though, and Ilaumeleus cast his gaze down at the wet earth soaking through his boots, Adriolaus found he couldn't muster the least amusement. The fields moved past with the scent of bean blossoms drowned beneath the smell of wet earth, and the horses' hooves churned the dirt road to thick and clutching muck.

His older brother was dead. His older brother was dead, and that was the price of getting everything that he had wanted.

He looked up at Alise, who turned her keen, grey eyes to meet his at the motion. "He is finally at peace," she said simply, in her thickly accented Erekoi. "You have long wanted him to be at peace."

"I have. Do you really think he is? Father always told us that the next world was a battlefield—"

"You have always told me that your father was full of shit," Alise answered, and her grave expression coupled with the phrase made Adriolaus laugh for the first time since his brother's death.

Ilaumeleus looked up at his new lord, and with the tentativeness of the sun as it darted between cloud banks, he smiled.

It didn't fill the empty place in the lord's heart, but Adriolaus looked back at his brother's coffin and thought that, perhaps, everything was going to be all right.

In the limestone castle of the capital, an adjutant with a bright smile and an easy manner attended to the nobles as they first heard of their king's untimely death. He took the news immediately to the streets, of course, running across the stone pathways as he sought out influential butchers and bakers and costermongers to tell of the king's demise. Flower-girls on the corners passed out the news with their posies, and patrolling guardsmen shook their heads gruffly and told every man they met.

The people had loved Milaus more than they had ever loved his father, and so they would gather in greater numbers to usher him home than they had for Imlaus. But to do so, they would need to know of the procession's arrival; they would need time to purchase or pluck flowers to strew in the streets; they would need to come to terms with the shock before they could truly be asked to appear to pay their respects.

Since the first days of the capital, no king of Erekos has ever had a public funeral. The passing of his body through the streets is the only chance that ordinary men and women have to say goodbye.

The adjutant ran to the stones over the gateway to watch for the coming procession, because the practical work of everything that is beautiful and solemn must be done by those who are level-headed and who barely grieve.

A woman stood there already, her face almost totally concealed by a black shawl and her hands on the moss that had grown into the stone. "Chilly day," the youth offered by way of greeting, and the healer turned to regard him.

"Perhaps it is," she replied. "Do you know anything of the king whose death you've been heralding throughout the streets? Do you know what he accomplished in his life, what he felt in his dark hours, or how he met his end?"

The adjutant stood still for a moment, then shrugged and offered a white-toothed smile. "I only work for him. I don't analyze him. I know that he took a witch captive recently, and I gave her tea. I know that he was killed by a god. His brother will be the next king."

He didn't know how he knew, because the healer's mouth was covered by her shawl; he didn't know how he knew, and yet he knew that she was smiling grimly.

"The crown is a symbol," she said against the fabric "The crown, and the shawl, and the castle, and it passes on from man to man and masks the humanity. Kings aren't witches, but they feel their houses change around them, because their houses are in a way what define them—you don't understand any of this, I know," she whispered with apology in her eyes. "And you don't particularly care."

The adjutant tried to smile, but instead he shook his head and thought of the shawl on the witch as she had stumbled through the castle hallways on his arm. She had been the same kind of certain, and it had been as arresting then as it was now.

"And so you won't understand why I throw moss from the walls instead of flowers when the king passes." In that indefinable way, she smiled again, with echoes of bean fields stretching to the forest's edge in her eyes. "But he will."

><=<

In a waterlogged yam field, Keiros hummed *Hey-oh, mother long gone* and smiled to know that he had once again escaped flooding. His children had just carved their names on the bark of the daughter of the grove at the head of their road, and his wife had told him yesterday that she was pregnant again—an unexpected reward for returning from Palamea with a blacksmith's job that he could reach without moving the family from their home of hundreds of years.

He would be going down to help with Palamea's flooding cleanup that afternoon, taking a boat with a boy who'd also been hired on at the smithy. Palamea was one of the better-built river towns, its streets all cobbled rather than dirt and its houses built on stilts or else fashioned like boats always in dry-dock, and the smithy itself rested far above the river on a great outcropping of rock that had always kept it safe from flooding. He and the lad were mostly going to help sort out livestock that had been brought to the high ground around the smithy, arbitrating between men whose beasts bore similar brands and shoveling shit from the walkway up to the smith's shop.

The young man's name was Aerus, and he was a quiet sort of boy with wide, dark eyes.

><

In Palamea, a family reunion many years overdue was taking place on the cobbled streets.

A grey-haired man and woman embraced one another tightly as the man's wife looked on; the wife's face was lined with worry against the black of her healer's shawl, and yet the grey-haired woman embraced her and kissed her cheeks and called her sister, then kissed the forehead of the little girl who stood shyly behind the folds of her healer mother's skirts.

The woman said softly that the little girl was so pretty, exactly as her own daughter Achane had been at that age.

Too many years of living in a pristine house empty of people had made Achane's mother old and tired, and when she had heard from the priestess that both of her daughters were dead, she had fallen to weeping on the quilt that she had sewn for her oldest daughter's wedding gift. For the first time, she'd taken out the scrolls that Shabane had read as she'd lain in bed, and she'd cried at the stories of beautiful girls languishing for want of True Love.

When her son had told her that he was about to take his boat down to Palamea, she had asked him with a surprising degree of gentleness whether she could come as well.

Achane's mother looked around at the mud that left high-water marks on the stilts and docks of Palamea, and she glanced at the mud staining her shoes, and she didn't care at all that the world was full of mess and disorder because she was standing with her long-lost husband and his family, and they were almost her family, too.

"If you have the chance," she said to her former husband and the woman he now loved, "I'd like for all of us to go down to visit our daughters' graves together. I think—I think they'd like that."

Former husband and former wife embraced again, and the healer remembered when she had told a little girl as old as her own the only truth that mattered.

Your body is a vessel for your soul, and one day you will realize how much stronger is your soul.

The sun broke through the clouds overhead, and it made the wet roads glisten in the light of morning.

>≡<

In a place that was not really a place, in a house beside a road that led to anywhere (for those who knew how to walk it), an old woman with her grey hair in a braid waited for her husband to return from the coast. She walked around the house three times to see whether it needed any repairs, and then she took a few light steps through her garden and scattered life from her skirts.

Her husband arrived, trudging up the road with his straw hat on and the sunlight smiling on his bare, copper shoulders. He sang a soft little song that he had invented himself, and behind him came their sturdy daughter with her hair in a bun and her wide arms crossed over her chest.

Shonè ran to her husband and leapt into his arms, and Aenikus swung her around on the pathway. "Thank you for watching 'n house, love," he laughed as he put her down, and the gods then embraced their daughter.

Terìchone bore it with a little smile that suggested that she had other work to do elsewhere but no pressing need to do it. "I'm glad to be home, even if it is for this," she said. "Our children are unhappy in the floodplains, and I've been doing all in my power to help them."

The birds never called here, on the road that led to anywhere, and the flowers never bloomed on trees forever caught in summer; mist rose through the trees, and yet today the sunlight glanced on the low fingers of fog and burnt them to a shimmering glory. It was a beautiful place, if quiet; it was a place full of ancient trials of the heart, and yet the gods had always known the depths of their own hearts.

Shonè linked arms with her daughter and her husband, and together the three of them walked up the path and to the little cottage in the mountains.

Inside, a man with skin as black as thunderheads at midnight sipped tea from a white china cup that flickered with lightning. "I see you've returned," he said. "You vanquished me, you know. All of the legends will say that you have, when they ever get around to writing legends about this. They'll say that you three helped to defeat me, and then what in the world will happen to the *moral* of the story?"

Shonè and Aenikus laughed to one another at that, and even Terìchone joined in as Loukaros put down his cup on his saucer with a look of great annoyance. Lightning danced across his fingers, but the effect was rather ruined by the brightness streaming in through the windows.

"I fail to see why you are laughing," he hissed. "I would rather maintain my dignity in the house of fellow gods."

Shonè only smiled at him and put a wrinkled hand on his coal-black shoulder. "We laugh, child, because only you of all the gods would ever care to look for a *moral* in a story." She glanced out a window that looked out on all the world from the vantage of a place that was not really a place, her hand still on his shoulder. "Sometimes, Loukaros, things just happen. Sometimes, there is no moral, but only a tally of the cost."

Gamela stood over the graves of two sisters, who lay together in death as they had in life—side by side. There was nothing to be said, really; the dead had been interred in the earth of their homeland, and soon the roots would grow through the all-embracing earth and draw new life where old life had been. The sisters would become a part of the dendrove trees with their long and leafy arms, a part of the daughters of the grove with their white flowers and their thick-hulled nuts, a part of the snakeblossom vines dripping scarlet blossoms, and a part of the alligator palms, sacred to Terichone. Such was the way of death, and such was the way of life.

There was nothing to be said, because there was no one to hear it, but still Gamela whispered over the graves, "Goodbye, Achane. Now you can rest."

She smiled softly, blinking back tears as she twisted her skirt in her hands. "Goodbye, Shabane. I'm glad to finally know your name, because I grew to care about you—at last you can rest, child. Be well."

She turned away from the graves and began walking through the clearing, smiling back at the garden by which she had buried the sisters. She had given away their belongings to the needy, as Achane would have wanted; she should have given away the cottage, too, but witches feel when someone moves their furniture, and a witch's spirit doesn't rest easily with someone else living in her home.

Gamela walked inside with measured steps, glancing at the snake-writing on the floor and the dark patches where the bed or the table had once rested. Even the hearthstone was gone; even the herbs that had once trailed from the rafters now hung in the shrine of Terichone, where they would go to serve the needs of the sick and the displaced and the hungry. The texts of magical instruction, she had locked away safely in the care of the priestesses, and the scrolls that Achane had used to work her magic, Gamela had piled carefully on the floor with the little cottage-shaped censer to Terichone on top.

She lit a long match and fitted it through the slats of the tiny brass cottage, and when the fire caught, she blew the flicker of burning incense to a smolder of red.

With a prayer to Terichone, the goddess of the alligator palm, Gamela tossed her match onto a scroll traced over with bloody circles, and she saw the fire catch.

She stood in the clearing around the cottage and watched it burn.

The Languages of Erekos

Erekoi

Like most languages, Erekoi is a vital, changing language with many regional variations in sound, intonation, and even meaning. What follows here is a general summary of Erekoi as it is spoken in Achane's region—the central part of Erekos, along the great river's floodplain—with important regional variations noted and remarked upon.

In general, Erekoi vowels are sounded thus: *a* as in *ha*, *e* as in *bay*, *i* as in *sea*, *o* as in *rose*, *u* as in *wound*. Erekoi diphthongs glide between these vowels: *ae* and *ai* as in *eye*, *oi* as in *oil*. Some vowels are not considered diphthongs when placed together, and each is sounded separately; this is usually the case with *io*, *eu*, and *au* combinations. For the most part, consonants are hard; *g* is always sounded as in *gate* rather than as in *gender*, and *c* is always sounded as in *castle* rather than as in *cell*.

One consonant deserves special note, though, and this is the *ch* sound combination. Among most Erekoi, *ch* is pronounced as a *k*; thus, *Achane* would be said AH-kah-nay, and *Terichone* would be said tay-REE-ko-nay. However, people with strong coastal accents will often pronounce a *ch* as in *chime*, or even as a *sh* sound. Thus, the high priestess of *Terichone* would say her goddess's name tay-REE-cho-nay, while Queen Carisica would say it tay-REE-sho-nay. People from the motherland will always pronounce *ch* as *sh*. Only in the accents of the motherland is the connection between Terichone and Shonè readily audible, for "Terichone" literally means "daughter of Shonè."

In most human names, the accent falls on the third-to-last syllable; only in rare cases or in two-syllable names does it fall upon the second-to-last. Therefore, *Shabane* would be said SHAH-bah-nay, and *Aenikus* said AY-nee-koos. Milaus and Adriolaus, who were named for ancient heroes in the tradition of the motherland, are outliers; their names are pronounced, respectively, mee-LAH-oos and ah-dree-oh-LAH-oos. However, the names of places and things are frequently accented on the second-to-last syllable; *Telessa* is said tay-LAY-sah, *Palamea* said pah-lah-MAY-ah, the *Tarancha* said tah-RAHN-kah, the *Ithucha* said ee-THOO-kah.

Weigenspeich

Like the Erekoi, the Weigers have a vital and varied language with distinct regional pronunciations. Whereas the strongest distinction in Erekos is the east/west split, the great plains that break Weigenland in half have created a strong cultural, political, economic, and linguistic divide between the north and south. We will mostly be meeting residents and former residents of the urban north, but we must not imagine that their southern cousins will brook slights against their language.

Weiger vowels are rougher and less musical than those of the Erekoi. In both the north and the south, the vowels are sounded thus: *a* as in *ha* or *up*, *e* as in *earl*, *i* as in *light* or *bit*, *o* as in *rose*, *u* as in *wound*. The greater divide comes in the vowel sounds represented as diphthongs. In the north, *ei* rhymes with *pay*, but in the south, it rhymes with *buy*; in the north, *oe* rhymes with *roe*, but in the south, it rhymes with *fee*; in the north, *ae* rhymes with *pay*, but in the south, it rhymes with *fee*. Both northerners and southerners pronounce *j* as a *y*, but the north tends to pronounce *w* as in *water*, whereas in the south *w* is said as in *vie*. Northerners and southerners each regard the other's accent as uncultured.

In Weigenspeich, the second-to-last syllable of a name is usually accented; thus, *Erlen* would be said UR-lun, and *Marla* said MAHR-luh. However, Weigenspeich is full of compound words, and each of these retains its accent. Thus, *Weigengraff* would be said WAY-gun-GRAHF in the north and VAI-gun-GRAHF in the south.

About the Author

A.M. Tuomala grew up in the wilds
of West Virginia, and now cares for
four affectionate and energetic plants,
as well as two cats.

You can follow the author online at:
www.amtuomala.com
Twitter: @amtuomala

CPSIA information can be obtained at www.ICGtesting.com
Printed in the USA
LVOW060355280612

287889LV00001BB/151/P